CONQUER THE FLAMES

ARIEL TACHNA

Dreamspinner Press

Published by
Dreamspinner Press
5032 Capital Circle SW
Suite 2, PMB# 279
Tallahassee, FL 32305-7886
USA
http://www.dreamspinnerpress.com/

Conquer the Flames
© 2013 Ariel Tachna.

Cover Art
© 2013 Anne Cain.
annecain.art@gmail.com
Cover content is for illustrative purposes only and any person depicted on the cover is a model.

ISBN: 978-1-62798-321-1
Digital ISBN: 978-1-62798-322-8

Printed in the United States of America
First Edition
September 2013

ARIEL TACHNA
Contemporary M/M Romance at its Finest

Inherit the Sky

"…a well-crafted, beautiful book that I would recommend to anyone looking for a love story that takes courage." —Guilty Indulgence

"I enjoyed this excellently researched and written book very much and hope there will be additional stories about all of the characters on and near the Lang Downs sheep station." —Mrs. Condit

"This story is beautifully, realistically handled." —Joyfully Jay

Her Two Dads

"…one of the most emotionally rewarding and uplifting love stories that I have read in a long time." —Dark Diva Reviews

"This is one of the best books I have ever read."
—Judging the Book by Its Pages

"…a sweet and stirring novel about the power of love and family."
—Romance Junkies

Seducing C.C.

"…a great comfort read." —Blackraven Reviews

"…a seductively sexy and romantic story." —Night Owl Reviews

Once in a Lifetime

"… a coming-of-age story that introduces heart-pounding firsts and nostalgic lasts." —¡Miraculous!

http://www.dreamspinnerpress.com

To Janelle Taylor, who introduced me to romance when I was twelve and reminded me to write the story that calls to me most when we met in Kansas City this year.

ONE

FIRE licked over his skin, smoke choking him. He tried to flee, but he couldn't make his arms and legs move. He gasped for breath, trying to reach the source of the screams he could hear. He knew those voices, had known them better than his own, but he couldn't find them. He couldn't move, couldn't breathe. It burned. Oh, it burned.

With a muffled scream, Thorne brought himself out of the nightmare. He scrubbed his hands over his face, his short beard catching on his raw palms. Fuck, he hated fire. With everything the army had beaten out of and into him in his twenty years of service, they hadn't been able to drive out his hatred of or fascination with fire.

He pushed open the flap of the tent he slept in, trying to decide if the light on the horizon was the dawn or the glow from the grassfires that had broken out all across the tablelands of New South Wales in the past month. He'd shipped out at the first reports, and he'd be here fighting for every inch of ground until the last fire was out or until the fire had taken him too. It would almost be a relief, but he wouldn't give it the satisfaction.

He snorted at the personification, as if the flames making their way through the outback cared who or what stood in their way. Thorne cared, though, and he'd be damned if he'd let the grassfires win.

CAINE NEIHEISEL stared at the new report detailing acres burned, property damaged, and the reporter's prognosis for the grassfires that raged north of the sheep station. He'd been lucky, he supposed, to have made it seven years at Lang Downs without a serious fire. They were careful every summer, of course, not wanting to risk starting a fire on the station itself, but always before, the winter and spring had been wet enough to carry them through the summer without any serious threat. This season, they weren't so lucky.

"Staring at the telly won't change anything."

"I know." Caine didn't look up at the sound of Macklin's voice. His lover and partner had been on the station for more than thirty years now. He was inured to whatever the outback threw at them. Caine wasn't nearly as sanguine. "I'm tracking the progress, trying to decide if we should be worried."

"We should always be worried when fires get out of control, but watching it on the telly isn't the way to deal with it."

"So what is?"

"We move the sheep down into the valley," Macklin said, "and then we build firebreaks all the way around the rim. We'll lose fences, maybe even the drovers' huts, but we'll protect the livestock and the station proper. Fences and huts can be replaced."

"Okay," Caine said, standing and reaching for his hat. "Let's get busy."

THORNE shoveled dirt on the approaching flames, trying to smother them before they could reach the firebreak behind him, but the wind had picked up that afternoon, whipping the smoldering embers into determined flames that he couldn't fight with dirt alone. He didn't stop trying. He'd never given up a fight in his life; he wasn't going to stop now. He took a step back as the heat became intolerable even with his protective gear. The flames might be winning, but Thorne would make them work for every inch of ground they devoured.

He ignored the shouts around him. Half of them or more were echoes of other battles, a different kind of firefight. They couldn't be allowed to govern his actions in this fight. People were counting on him. He'd seen a building over the crest of the nearest hill as he'd gone out to meet the fires early that morning, and buildings meant people.

"Lachlan, fall back."

Thorne nearly ignored the captain of the fire brigade, but while the army hadn't driven out his visceral reaction to fire, it had driven into him obedience to the chain of command. He withdrew to the firebreak, scattering dirt behind him with a vengeance as he went. "Sir?"

"We'll hold the break," Captain Grant said. "I need you to head south to Lang Downs. If we lose this break, we'll have to fall back onto their land. They need to know what they're facing, and we need to know what kind of support we can count on from them."

"Captain," Thorne protested, "can't someone else go? I'll do far more good here than I will talking to some grazier whose only concern will be saving his own skin."

"That's why I need you to go," the captain insisted. "If that's his only concern, I'll need your expertise to make sure the fire doesn't take the whole place and beyond, and if he is willing to help, there's no one better than you to make sure the station is as ready as it can be and the men there deployed to greatest effect."

"I need to stay here," Thorne said.

The captain shook his head. "You want to stay here, but you're exhausted. You've been out here for weeks without a break. Everyone else has taken at least a day's rest to wash up and get a real meal rather than rations."

"I'm a Commando, sir," Thorne reminded him. "A few weeks is nothing. We're trained to survive months in the harshest conditions imaginable."

"You *were* a Commando," the captain replied. "You're retired now, remember?"

"Once a Commando, always a Commando, sir," Thorne said, hiding the flinch at the reminder of his current status. He hadn't wanted to retire, but his superiors had taken him out of the field, and he couldn't live with that either. Fighting fires wasn't the same as fighting in East Timor, Afghanistan, or Iraq, but it was better than a desk job that would kill his soul no matter how it protected his body.

"Then obey your orders, soldier," the captain said. "With the wind as high as it is, I don't know how long we can hold this firebreak."

"Yes, sir." His superior in the 1st Commandos would have ripped him a new one for the sullenness in his answer, but then his superior in the Commandos would never have ordered him to retreat from a battle they could still win.

Thorne tossed the shovel toward one of the other firefighters and trudged back toward his ute. His GPS pulled up a route to Lang Downs, but it took him all the way west to Cowra before heading south, which seemed klicks out of his way. With a muttered curse for spineless superiors and nonsensical orders, he turned the ute south. He'd drive until he found a fence, follow it to a gate, and then follow the station roads from there. He'd reach Lang Downs eventually.

IT FELT strange to see civilization again after a month of sleeping rough and living in the outback. Thorne followed the gravel road down into the valley, the first place he'd seen in a month that didn't show the ravages of the hot, dry summer. It wasn't as lush as he imagined it would be after a wet spring, but it wasn't the same sere brown or charred black as the parts of the outback he'd been living in. In the center of the valley, a collection of houses and outbuildings nestled together amid a green sward, looking for all the world like the center of its own little universe.

Thorne ignored the pinch in his heart at the sight. This wasn't just a group of buildings. This was a home. Thorne hadn't had a home since his had burned down when he was eighteen, taking the lives of his parents and younger brother, but he could still recognize one when he saw it. More than that, he'd spent twenty years in the Commandos defending home. Not his, never his, not since it had burned to the ground while he spent the night with a friend, but the homes of everyone who would have been the victim of the terrorists they stopped, the insurgents they put down, the guerrillas they contained. The station below might not be his home, but it was *a* home, and Thorne would die before he let the grassfires take it from the men and women who could claim it as their own.

He coasted to a stop and put the ute in park. After climbing out, he took a moment to survey the valley, mentally calculating angles and wind direction and defensibility. The upcoming fight wouldn't involve bullets and other ammunition, but it would be a fight nonetheless, and the better they defended the valley, the easier it would be to win the battle. The valley walls were steeper at the far end than they were where the road entered. It would make choosing the location of the firebreak simpler and possibly easier to defend, since the drop-off would make it harder for the sparks to catch on fresh tinder. Closer to the road and the entrance to the valley, the slope was gentler, but even then, Thorne saw what he considered a clear line of valley versus tablelands. They would set their defenses there and concentrate the manpower along the gentler slopes, where jumping the firebreak would be more of a concern.

Plans in place, he climbed back in the ute and drove the rest of the way onto the station. As he neared the populated area, two men stepped out to greet him, both wearing battered Akubras and well-worn boots. The resemblance ended there, though. Beneath the hats, one was blond, the other brunet, one as craggy as the hills that surrounded them, the other fresh-faced and clean-shaven. Thorne pulled to a stop in front of them and rolled down the window.

"Can we help you?" the brunet asked, surprising Thorne with his American accent.

"I hope so, mate. I'm looking for the grazier. There's a grassfire headed this way, and I'm here to help get things ready."

"We own Lang Downs," the Yank replied. "Caine Neiheisel, and this is my partner, Macklin Armstrong. And you are?"

"Thorne Lachlan," Thorne said. "I'm with the Firies who are at the front north of here. The captain sent me to warn you and to start setting up defenses around the population center of the station."

"How long do we have?" Armstrong asked. Thorne relaxed a little. Armstrong was an Aussie, and one who had the look of a stockman.

"If conditions stay like they are now, maybe forty-eight hours," Thorne replied. "If the wind dies down, we might get a break and stop it where it is, or slow it enough to buy more time here, but we can't count on that. By the time we know for sure, it will be too late to build new firebreaks here."

"We already have our jackaroos bringing the mob down into the valley," Neiheisel said. "As soon as they return, we have fifty men and all the station's equipment we can put at your disposal. Uncle Michael built this place from the ground up. I'm not losing it now."

Thorne let out the breath he hadn't realized he'd been holding. His chances of successfully protecting the station increased with every pair of willing hands and every bit of cooperation from the station owner. He would have fought tooth and nail to stop the fire even if he'd had to do it alone, but this was far better.

"Good. Where can I pitch my tent? I'll get my gear out of the way and we can start marking off the areas for the firebreak."

"You don't need to pitch a tent," Neiheisel said. "There's a perfectly good bed in the guest room in the station house. You can sleep there."

"That won't be enough when the rest of the Firies get here," Thorne warned.

Neiheisel shrugged. "So we'll find couches or double bunk the kids. Nobody will be sleeping on the ground if I can help it."

The thought of kids exposed to the fire froze Thorne's blood in his veins. "Perhaps you should speak to the families with children about evacuating until the fire is under control again. Property damage can be repaired. Children can't be replaced."

"We already gave their parents that option," Armstrong said. "If it comes to it, Carley and Molly will take the kids and head to town, but for now, everyone prefers to stay and help."

It wasn't Thorne's place to argue, but as he parked his ute where Armstrong indicated and grabbed the gear he'd need to begin setting up the valley's protection, his determination to see them through the upcoming inferno increased even more.

By the time he returned to the station owners, another man had joined them, his horse dancing restlessly beneath him.

"Neil, this is Thorne Lachlan from the Rural Fire Service." As Caine spoke, Neil swung off his horse and tossed the reins to a passing jackaroo. "He's been fighting the fires north of here and has come to help us get ready. Thorne, this is Neil Emery, our foreman."

"Cheers, mate," Neil said, offering his hand. Thorne shook it, appreciating the firm grip and the calluses that came from hard work. "You can see the smoke on the horizon already. I've been waiting for someone to come warn us."

"You didn't need the warning," Thorne said, looking around as sheep spilled over the edge of the tablelands and down into the valley.

"Your bosses were already getting ready, but I have some tricks up my sleeve to help keep you safe."

Neil nodded and turned to Caine. "Tell Molly she has to leave now. Please?"

"She's your wife," Caine retorted. "If she won't listen to you, what makes you think she'll listen to me?"

"You're her boss. I'm just her husband."

Thorne shared an amused look with Armstrong. It had been years since Thorne had been around women much, but he still remembered his father trying fruitlessly to convince his mother of something she didn't want to do. The thought brought a familiar pang, the grief no less now than it had been twenty years ago, no matter how people said time healed all wounds.

"If it gets that dangerous, we'll all be leaving," Caine said with a sharp look at Macklin. "Buildings can be rebuilt, livestock can be replaced. That's what we have insurance for, if it comes to that."

"It won't come to that," Thorne swore. "I won't let it."

BY THE time the sun started to set and the bell tolled for dinner, Thorne had developed a healthy respect for the men of Lang Downs. They had taken his suggestions seriously, and Emery had issued orders to ensure those suggestions came to fruition. When the men heard the bell, though, they stopped what they were doing as if someone had given an order and started trooping back down into the valley.

"We'll finish it tomorrow," Emery said before Thorne could protest. "It's getting dark, and Kami's already pushed dinner back for us. Come on. You should eat too."

"I have rations in my ute," Thorne said automatically.

Emery snorted. "Yeah, you try telling the bosses that. Better yet, you try telling Sarah and Kami that. They'd come after you with their ladles, and you'd never win that battle."

Thorne almost argued. He was a Commando. No ladle-wielding cook was going to get the better of him. It wasn't worth the conflict, though. He'd be a fool to refuse a home-cooked meal when he could get it. He'd be back to rations before long. "If you say so."

"I do," Emery said with a grin. Then he sobered. "One other warning. You're new to Lang Downs, so you can't be expected to know about the bosses or anyone else, but we don't tolerate any homophobic bullshit around here. Caine and Macklin have built a safe place here for themselves and anyone else who needs it, and we don't tolerate anything that threatens that."

Thorne looked at Emery without blinking. He wasn't surprised by the foreman's revelation concerning the two graziers, but Emery's defense of his bosses was less expected. Stockmen weren't known for being open-minded. "The only threat around here is the grassfire," he said evenly. "Concentrate on that."

"Good to hear," Emery replied, and the smile he gave Thorne was far more open than any he'd given the rest of the day, leaving Thorne with the feeling of having survived a gauntlet without even realizing one was in front of him.

CAINE collapsed on the couch in the living room of the main station. He'd gotten used to working hard since moving to Lang Downs. The physical labor required here far outstripped the demands of his former life in Philadelphia, but today had gone beyond even the usual exertions of life on Lang Downs. At Thorne's insistence, they had started preparing a firebreak around the entire valley, hoping to protect the buildings and livestock sheltered within from the oncoming fires. By the end of the day, they'd turned up a swath of dirt forty feet wide along the entire north side of the valley. They would spend the next day preparing the southern rim of the valley, and then they would go out to meet the fire head-on.

"Did Thorne say how many firefighters were in his brigade?" Caine asked when Macklin joined him a moment later. "It's one thing to put him in the guest room and tell Kami we have an extra mouth to feed, but if we've got a whole brigade on the way, we need to figure out how we're going to house and feed them."

"He didn't say." Macklin sat down next to Caine and slung his arm around Caine's shoulders. Caine leaned into the touch, taking comfort where he could. Lang Downs was his life, his livelihood, and his salvation. He'd meant it when he said buildings could be rebuilt, and he would rebuild if it came to that, but the thought of losing the house Uncle Michael and Donald had built with their own hands, the place where their love had been safe and sheltered, felt like sacrilege. It wasn't worth losing anyone's life—Uncle Michael would roll in his grave if he thought Caine was endangering the men who worked for him for a house—but if they could keep it from coming to that, Caine would.

The sound of footsteps in the hall drew Caine's attention back to their guest. He didn't move away from Macklin—he wouldn't hide in his own house—but he did brace himself for the possible negative reaction to come. Thorne just nodded at them as he trudged toward the stairs.

"I know you must be exhausted," Caine said before Thorne could reach the bottom of the steps, "but could you spare a minute or two before you go to bed? I have some logistical questions, and I'd rather ask them tonight so we can make plans as soon as possible."

Thorne turned back toward them without comment and came to stand next to the armchair.

"Sit," Caine urged. "You'll be more comfortable."

"If I sit, I might not get back up," Thorne replied ruefully. "I was up at dawn this morning fighting at the fire line and I haven't stopped since then."

"I won't keep you long," Caine promised. "I just need to know how many people to expect when the rest of the RFS gets here. We need to figure out beds and food for everyone."

"You don't need to do that," Thorne insisted. "We all have tents and bedrolls, and we carry field rations with us. We're not going to be a drain on your station."

Next to him, Caine heard Macklin snort, but he ignored his lover's reaction and focused on the firefighter across from him. "I don't recall implying you would be a drain on the station. You and your brigade are coming to protect my station. The least I can do is make sure you're all fed and have a place to sleep. My uncle would come back to haunt me if I did anything less. Now, you didn't answer my question."

"There are thirty men in the brigade I left this morning," Thorne said stiffly. "The captain didn't tell me if he would be sending everyone here and giving up a section of land to the fires or if he intended to fight all the way back, so I don't know if everyone will arrive at once or even if anyone will arrive at all. His orders were to make sure Lang Downs was prepared for whatever happened."

"Then we'll plan on everyone," Caine said. "One more question. Lang Downs is an organically certified station. Does the RFS use fire foam?"

"We do," Thorne said. "We only use class A foam, which is biodegradable. We try not to get it in bodies of water, but it's safe for soil."

Biodegradable was a good start, but it didn't mean it was approved by the organic certification board. It appeared Caine had some research to do. "Could you ask your captain not to use it unless absolutely necessary? Losing the organic certification is preferable to losing the station, but only if there's no other way."

"I can ask," Thorne said, "but I can't guarantee he'll listen. Was there anything else?"

Caine felt Macklin bristle at the shortness of the question, but Caine could see the exhaustion on Thorne's face. "No. Sleep well. We'll see you at breakfast."

Thorne trudged up the stairs. When Caine heard the door to the guest room close, he turned to face Macklin. "What do you think?"

"I think we'll weather this the same way we've weathered everything else that's come our way."

"That's not what I meant," Caine said. "What do you think of our resident firefighter?"

Macklin chuckled. "Still taking in strays?"

Caine flushed. "Maybe. If he needs a home."

TWO

THE sound of gunfire shattered the otherwise perfect spring day. Thorne cursed under his breath. He needed to get back to his squad. Screams followed next, far more damning than the gunfire that accompanied them, and then silence. Thorne tore through the underbrush, his weapon at the ready, determined to cut down anyone in his path. But the jungle had gone silent, and when he reached his comrades, only the bodies of the dead waited for him, their ghostly death masks accusing him silently.

Thorne woke with cold sweat covering his body despite the heat of the room. He stumbled out of bed and across the hall to the bathroom, where he threw up the contents of his stomach. Even after he'd brought everything up, his stomach continue to heave, dry retching that tore at his body while the images of the nightmares tore at his mind.

He thought he'd put this particular nightmare behind him. His commanding officer had ordered him away from the front lines with a wounded comrade on his back to seek medical attention for a soldier who wouldn't have survived long without help. He'd received a fucking commendation for it, but while he'd been carrying Walker to safety, the rest of his squad had been cut down by enemy fire. Everyone told him one more soldier wouldn't have made a difference. They had been so outnumbered nothing could have saved them. The shrinks had diagnosed Thorne with survivor's guilt, which was bullshit, but he'd gone through the required sessions, mouthed all the platitudes, and shipped out the day he was cleared for duty. He, Walker, and their new squad had found the insurgents who had killed Thorne's squad and put an end to them. He'd taken great pride in being able to retrieve his commander's stolen dog tags from the rebel who'd desecrated his corpse. He didn't know if the dog tags would provide any comfort to the grieving widow, but he hoped knowing his killer had faced justice would.

Deciding his stomach was done rebelling, Thorne forced himself to stand up so he could rinse his mouth out and splash cold water on his face. He had dark circles under his eyes, but those never really went away. His beard had filled in enough to need a trim, but he hadn't expected to be able to do that until he had a roof over his head again instead of a tent—something that wouldn't happen while the fires still burned—so he hadn't brought his beard trimmer with him. His black hair had more silver in it than he was used to seeing, but he ignored that. He remembered his father having the same silver strands in his hair and beard by the time he was Thorne's age. His mother had called it distinguished and said it only made him more handsome. Not that Thorne had anyone in his life who would care if his hair was black or gray, short or long. He had ties in his bag to keep it off his neck and out of his eyes while he was working. That was all that mattered.

Fed up with his own weakness, he flipped the light off and went back to bed. It was still dark outside. He would go back to sleep, with no nightmares this time, and everything would look better in the morning.

He lay back down and pulled the covers up, but as soon as he closed his eyes, images from his nightmares flashed before his eyes again. "Fuck," he muttered as he turned over and tried to focus on anything other than his memories.

Neiheisel and Armstrong had been quite the revelation. Thorne had spent half his life ignoring his own sexuality, going out with his squad and fucking anything that moved. Most of the time, it had been girls, who had generally been accommodating enough to let him fuck them in the arse so he could ignore the girly bits. Only when he had been far away from base on leave had he dared to find a guy to mess around with, and those times had been few and far between. Caine and Macklin, though, weren't anything like those furtive fucks or any of the similar hookups he'd had since he'd retired from the military. He'd spent his life in homophobic milieus and hadn't expected to find anything different when he drove onto Lang Downs that afternoon. Instead, he'd found Caine and Macklin, with all their openness and their jackaroos who defended them and a house they shared where they could sit on the couch together and talk about their day like any other couple. He'd never considered such a possibility. It only made him more determined to protect this place. Few enough safe havens existed. Thorne couldn't see one destroyed on his watch.

He'd rolled onto his side, trying to get comfortable enough to sleep again, when he heard a noise from down the hall. He froze, every sense on alert as he tried to place the sound. He knew his battle instincts were out of place here, but they had kept him alive for too long to disregard them now. He stretched his senses, listening for any other sign of trouble, and heard it again—a moan followed by a broken-off curse.

Thorne sat up, automatically taking stock of the weapons at his disposal. He no longer had a gun, but he kept a knife on him at all times. He reached for it now, waiting for a signal to act. Then he heard it again, the voice growing clearer and the words more distinct.

"F-f-fuck, Macklin. D-do that again."

Thorne collapsed back against the mattress, the knife falling from his hand with a clatter. No danger to his hosts, only to his sanity. The noises grew louder, more impassioned and explicit, Macklin's deeper tones reverberating beneath Caine's sighs and groans. The bed frame squeaked then, and then again, setting up a rhythm that left Thorne hard and aching.

How long had it been since he'd fucked a willing arse? He couldn't even remember. He closed his eyes, trying to summon the image of a lover, real or imagined, to pleasure himself, but his mind remained unhelpfully blank. He wrapped his hand around his cock in time to the noises from the next room. When the fires were out, he would go to Melbourne or Sydney to find a club. He'd find a willing arse and take out all the tension he couldn't release any other way. He spurted as the noise from the next room crescendoed and then fell silent, but the release felt hollow. He wasn't hard anymore, but he could hardly call it satisfied.

He'd need a shower before breakfast, so he dragged himself out of bed to dig through his bag for clean shorts and his toiletries. He'd shower and then go see what time the day started on the station.

THORNE walked into the canteen to find the room already half full of men and an unfamiliar woman behind the buffet serving the men as they came in.

"Ma'am," he said politely as he reached her.

"You must be Thorne," she said. "Kami told me about you last night." She looked at him critically and put a second scoop of scrambled eggs on his plate. "You look like you've missed a few meals, son, but don't worry. We'll feed you up in no time."

"Thank you, Mrs…."

"Lang," she said, "but everyone calls me Sarah." She handed him a plate.

"Lang like Lang Downs? I thought Neiheisel owned the place."

"He and Macklin do," Mrs. Lang said, "but Caine's great-uncle took my husband in when he had nowhere else to go." She glanced back toward the kitchen, where Thorne could see Kami washing dishes. "He changed his name to Lang years ago in tribute to the man who saved so many lives by never turning anyone away, even an aboriginal boy with only the clothes on his back to call his own. Fortunately for all of us, his nephew has followed his example. Coffee's against the wall, or there's tea if you prefer that. Anything else you need, you just let me know."

"Ma'am," he said again as he took his food and looked around for a table. Her revelation only made him more determined to protect this place and the people who lived on it. It was obviously too special to lose. Emery waved him over, so he joined the foreman, his wife, and several other jackaroos.

"Do you know everyone?" Emery asked when Thorne took his seat with his back to the wall. "I can't remember who I introduced you to yesterday."

"Mrs. Emery," Thorne said with a smile, "and I met…. Simms, was it?" The young man nodded. "But I don't know the others. Thorne Lachlan, RFS."

"Jesse Harris, Kyle Jones, and Patrick Thompson," Emery said. "Patrick's our head mechanic. Kyle has been here almost as long as I have, and Jesse and Chris showed up at the same time about six years ago. We haven't been able to get rid of them yet."

"And you won't, either," Emery's wife scolded. "So stop with the ribbing."

"Molly's protective of her 'brood'," Emery said. "She won't let me have any fun."

"I don't trust you not to say something stupid in the guise of a joke," Molly said. "Some things aren't funny."

"She lost her sense of humor where certain things were concerned about the same time she found out she was pregnant," Jesse confided.

That explained Emery's insistence the day before that his wife leave the station. "What things? I wouldn't want to end up on her bad side." He'd watched her bop her husband on the head more than once the night before.

"Anything that might make Chris or me uncomfortable," Jesse replied. That didn't help Thorne at all, but before he could ask for clarification, Neil lifted a hand and waved another jackaroo over to them.

"Look what the cat dragged in," Neil teased.

Thorne froze in his seat. He was sure the man coming toward them hadn't been at dinner the night before. Thorne would have noticed him for sure. Like the other jackaroos, he was lean and weathered, his skin wind-burned and covered in freckles, but something about this man called to Thorne in a way he could not explain. He grabbed his coffee and took a sip to cover his reaction.

"I'm not the last one here," the newcomer retorted. "I don't see Sam and Jeremy anywhere."

Neil moaned at that and clapped his hands over his ears. "Not listening."

"I'm sure there's a perfectly innocent reason why they're late," the man continued. "I'm sure the noises I heard when I walked past their house weren't anything like *that*."

"Not listening," Neil repeated. "Not listening, not listening, not listening."

"I thought you said you wouldn't put up with comments like that," Thorne said.

"I won't," Neil replied, "but that doesn't mean I want to think about my brother having sex. That's not homophobic. That's self-preservation. Just… no."

"How many couples are there on Lang Downs?" Thorne asked before he could stop himself.

"Eight," Neil replied. "Caine and Macklin, Patrick and Carley, Chris and Jesse, Sam and Jeremy, Sarah and Kami, Kyle and Linda, Andrew and Elizabeth, and Molly and me."

"And you all have houses of your own?"

"Yes," Neil said, "and so does Ian. Ian, did you meet Thorne last night?"

"No," the man Thorne was trying not to stare at answered.

"Thorne Lachlan, this is Ian Duncan. Ian, Thorne's one of the Firies. He's here to help us prepare for the fires."

"Cheers, mate," Ian said, holding out his hand. Thorne took it, ignoring the way the contact sent tingles up his arm. Ian snatched his hand back as if burned, though, so Thorne pushed his interest aside. "So what's the plan for today?"

"Get the firebreak built on the south side of the valley," Thorne said.

"Patrick's going to start outfitting the utes with the water tanks," Neil added. "Jesse will probably stay and help him. You can work here in the station or you can help with the firebreaks. Did you get the last of the mob brought in last night?"

"I'm not convinced I got all of them," Ian said, "but I'm not sure it's the best use of manpower to search for the strays. Not until the valley is secure, anyway. The fires will drive them this way as it is."

"So what'll it be, then?" Neil asked. "Firebreaks or prepping the utes?"

"You'll never let me hear the end of it if I stay and work on the utes," Ian said, "so firebreaks it is."

Thorne didn't pretend to understand the undercurrents between the two men, but all the banter was clearly in good fun. No one else seemed bothered by it, so Thorne resisted the urge to jump to Ian's defense. He didn't have the right, not really, and the defense wouldn't be appreciated.

"Did you boys get enough to eat?"

Thorne started at the sound of Mrs. Lang's voice. He was halfway out of his seat before he realized he'd begun to react, but he forced himself back into the seat. Mrs. Lang didn't deserve his anger.

"I'll take another piece of bacon, if you've got any, Sarah," Ian said. She served him and patted his shoulder as she moved on down the table. She stopped again where Caine and Macklin were sitting.

"Does she mother everyone?" Thorne asked.

"Pretty much," Neil said. "She didn't see Macklin for thirty years. She's been making up for it ever since she got here, and none of us escape it completely."

"As long as she doesn't walk up behind me, I'll live with the mothering," Thorne said.

BY THE time they broke for lunch, they had completed half the southern firebreak, and Thorne had spent the morning trying not to stare at Ian. When all the other jackaroos had stripped off their outer shirts, leaving them only in T-shirts, Ian had left his long-sleeved work shirt on.

"Aren't you hot?" Thorne asked Ian as they all found a place to sit for lunch.

"Better hot than sunburned," Ian replied with a shrug. He mopped at his skin with a kerchief he kept around his neck for that very purpose. "I have yet to find a sunblock that can keep me from turning the color of a lobster. It's long sleeves and a hat or skin cancer." Ian had a shock of red hair and very pale, freckled skin. Thorne could see how the sun was a serious problem.

"Why stay, then?" Thorne asked. "Why not go somewhere you could work inside?"

"Because Lang Downs is home," Ian replied simply, and the smile that graced his face as he said it was the most beautiful thing Thorne had seen in years. "I've been here since I was twenty, and I'll stay here until I can't work any longer."

"Is that typical?" Thorne asked, since he couldn't ask the questions he really wanted to. "I had the impression sheep stations were more transient than that."

"For the seasonal workers, it is," Ian said, "but every station needs a skeleton crew that stays year-round, and Lang Downs has a very loyal one. Macklin has been here for more than thirty years, Kami for even longer

ARIEL TACHNA

than that. Neil, Kyle, and I all arrived about fifteen years ago. Jesse and Chris have been here for six years, and Sam and Jeremy for five."

"And Caine?" Thorne asked. "He wasn't born here."

"Seven years," Ian replied. "He came after his uncle died. Caine's great-uncle founded the station in the 1940s and ran it until he died. It passed to Caine after that."

Ian mopped at his neck again, and as he donned his hat, Thorne caught sight of a small cut oozing blood. "Did you cut yourself?"

Ian looked at his hand and then wiped it on his jeans. "A couple of days ago. I was working on a chair for Sam and Jeremy's veranda and the chisel slipped. I must have knocked it while we were working today and not realized it with my gloves on."

"You should wash it and put some Savlon on it," Thorne said. "You don't want it to get infected."

"It'll be fine until tonight," Ian said.

"Emery!" Thorne called. "You got a first-aid kit with you?"

"Yeah, are you hurt?"

"Ian is."

Neil came over and joined them with the first-aid kit in one hand. "What did you do to yourself, mate?"

"I nicked it in my shop a couple of days ago," Ian said. "I must have knocked it on a shovel or something today. It's fine, really."

"Don't be a drongo," Neil said as he pulled out a bandage and antibiotic cream. "Give it here and let's have a look."

Ian rolled his eyes but held out his hand without further protest. Thorne grabbed it before Neil could, examining the cut carefully. "It looks shallow and clean. An alcohol swab to make sure and a bandage to keep it that way."

Neil surrendered the first-aid kit. Thorne ignored the expression on his face. Whatever background Neil had, it didn't compare to what Thorne had learned from the field medics over the years. He wiped the area clean and patched it up. "Be careful with it for a few days and it'll be fine."

"Mate, there's no such thing on a station like this," Ian said. "I don't know what you think we do, but a cut like this is nothing. I don't need to take it easy," Ian said, "so back off."

Thorne let the matter drop when Ian stalked off with Neil not far behind, but he resolved to keep an eye on the cut. The worst scar he had— and he had plenty—was from a minor injury that shouldn't have been anything… until it got infected and nearly cost him his leg. Even the bullet wound to his shoulder hadn't required as much recovery time as that infected scratch on his calf.

He ate his sandwich in silence until a kid came and flopped on the ground next to him. "Why are you eating by yourself?"

"Because I don't know anyone," he replied honestly. "They're all friends. I'm just here to help with the firebreaks."

"Caine always says strangers are just friends you haven't met yet," the kid said. With the braces and the short hair beneath the baseball cap, Thorne couldn't decide if the kid was a boy or a girl, but either way, the openness of the statement took him aback. He didn't think he'd ever been that at ease with himself, much less when he still had a mouthful of braces. "I'm Laura. What's your name?"

"Thorne," he said. "Do you live here on the station?"

"Yeah, my mom came a couple of years ago. I like it here. Everyone's really nice."

"You don't miss having other kids around?"

"Nah," Laura said. "Teenagers are a pain. I like hanging out with the jackaroos better. They don't look down on me because I'm a girl who'd rather work outside than do girly things."

"I can see how that would be frustrating."

"So what's your story?" she asked.

"My story?"

"Yeah, everyone who comes to Lang Downs has a story. Neil was a hothead who couldn't keep a job anywhere else. Chris was bashed and Caine and Macklin took him in. Jeremy beat his brother up for being an arsehole and his brother kicked him off the station. So what's your story?"

"I don't have a story. The fire brigade captain sent me to help protect the station. That's all," Thorne insisted.

Laura looked at him like he was full of shit, but she was too kind to call him on it. "If you say so. Why do you keep staring at Ian?"

"I'm just checking on him," Thorne said. "He has a cut on his hand, and I don't want it to get worse."

"Ian always has cuts on his hands," Laura said. "He's always making something in his workshop. He made the furniture on our veranda and now he's making us a new coffee table for our living room. It's going to be beautiful. He lets me watch sometimes."

"That sounds really interesting," Thorne said. He looked down at his hands. They bore their share of scars, but always from destruction, never from creation. He wondered what it would be like to create something out of nothing, to pour himself into something good for once rather than into death, even death for a cause.

"Hey, are you all right?" Laura asked, poking at his arm. Thorne didn't think. He couldn't. His body reacted without his brain's permission, the grassy tablelands blurring until he was back in the jungles of East Timor, the pressure against his arm a machete, not a child's finger. His hand shot out and encircled her wrist, twisting her arm until she cried out in pain.

The sound broke the trance and his vision cleared as he dropped her hand, horror filling him when he realized what he'd done.

"I'm sorry," he said, scrambling to his feet. "I didn't mean to...." Nausea rose up in his throat, and he stumbled away behind one of the tractors they were using to build the firebreak. He leaned against the huge tire and lost his lunch. That girl, that sweet, fresh-faced child, was no threat to him. She hadn't deserved to be attacked that way.

"What the hell, Lachlan?" Neil demanded as he rounded the back of the tractor. He stopped when he saw Thorne bent over, but Thorne could sense him standing there still, waiting for an explanation. When he finally trusted his stomach not to betray him again, he straightened and faced the foreman.

"I was in the Commandos for twenty years," he said. "I was trained to react instinctively to any threat without even having to think about it. I've been out for three months. That training hasn't worn off. When Laura poked my arm, I had a flashback. I'm sorry. She didn't deserve what I did. I'll stay away from her."

"What sets them off?"

"What?"

"You're going to be here for a few more days, anyway," Neil said. "You stopped this time, but if you don't next time, someone could be seriously hurt. If we know what sets you off, we can avoid it."

"Don't walk up behind me and don't touch me unexpectedly," Thorne said. "As long as I see things coming, I can assess the threat and deal with it rationally. It's the things I don't see coming that set me off."

"I'll tell the others, but you owe Laura an explanation yourself."

Thorne felt bile rise in his throat again at the thought of the sweet girl who had tried to befriend him only to fall victim to his instability. He would apologize and explain because Neil was right that she deserved to hear that from him, but then he would keep his distance. He wouldn't put her at risk again. His time in East Timor had eliminated age as a mitigating factor in his automatic risk assessment. He'd faced too many child soldiers for Laura's age to protect her now. He found a canteen and rinsed his mouth out and then went to find Laura.

His stomach rolled again when he saw she was sitting with Ian. They both tensed when he approached, but he stopped well outside touching distance, hoping to reduce the stress on them. "I... don't do well with unexpected touches," he said, knowing it was a lame excuse. "When you poked my arm, I had a flashback, and I reacted the way the military trained me to react to threats. That training saved my life more times than I can count, but you didn't deserve it. I'll stay away from you from now on. I don't want you to feel unsafe in your own home."

Laura looked at him with tear-stained cheeks, but her expression seemed less haunted than when he'd first approached. "What about expected touches?"

Thorne blinked a couple of times. "What?"

"If you know someone is going to touch you, do you still get flashbacks?"

"Not usually," Thorne replied. "As long as there isn't a threat, anyway."

"So if I gave you a hug right now, you'd be okay with that?"

Thorne felt the world tilt on its axis. He'd attacked the child and now she wanted to hug him? "I guess so."

"Laura, this isn't a good idea," Ian said. Thorne didn't even bristle. He'd already proven how dangerous he could be.

"Look at him, Ian," Laura said. "He's more upset about this than I am. He didn't mean to hurt me, just like I didn't mean to startle him. It'll be fine."

Thorne stood perfectly still when she stood up and closed the distance between them. He kept every muscle under rigid control as she put her arms around his waist and rested her head against his chest for a moment and just squeezed. Awkwardly he patted her back a couple of times, not trusting himself to do more, but that seemed to be all she needed. She gave him a bright smile, released him, and bounded off, calling for one of the other jackaroos.

"You don't deserve her forgiveness." Ian's glare cut Thorne as deeply as any knife.

"You think I don't know that?" Thorne spat. "I'm a cold-blooded killer. That's what the army trained me to be. And then three months ago, they dumped me back into civilian life. Why do you think I'm out here in the outback? Fewer people to hurt and more of a chance to protect someone, for once. I'll never get all the blood off my hands, but maybe if I save a few lives now, it'll erase some of the debt I owe the universe."

He'd only eaten half his sandwich before Laura had triggered the flashback, but Thorne knew he wouldn't be able to swallow the rest of it even if he tried. "I'm going back to work. Tell the others to join me when they're done with lunch."

THREE

"LACHLAN has flashbacks," Neil said without preamble when he next saw Caine and Macklin. "He says they're triggered by someone coming up behind him or touching him expectedly. He attacked Laura."

"Is she hurt?" Caine asked immediately.

"She'll have a bruise on her wrist, but he stopped before it went beyond that," Neil said. "He made himself sick when he realized what he'd done."

"He was a soldier, wasn't he?" Macklin asked.

"Twenty years with the Commandos, he said."

"I'll talk to him," Caine said. "Maybe we can do something to help."

"No," Macklin interrupted. "I'll talk to him."

"I don't need protecting," Caine protested.

"And he doesn't need smothering," Macklin insisted. "He's already feeling weak and vulnerable. If you go to him with all your kindness and sympathy, he'll either break completely or lash out at everything and leave. Neither of those helps us. We need his experience with the fires, which means we need him here and functional. I'll talk to him. You talk to Laura."

Caine muttered some more, but Macklin ignored him. He grabbed his hat and pulled on his boots. "Bring me a plate of dinner if I don't make it back to the canteen. I have to find the man before I can talk to him."

Thorne wasn't in the canteen or the bunkhouse, which didn't surprise Macklin at all. The man's ute was still with all the others, so he hadn't left the station. Macklin took that as a good sign. The pack that had remained in the back of the ute was gone, though. Thorne had gone to ground to lick his wounds. Macklin turned his gaze away from the buildings, searching for a tent.

He found it after a moment, about a mile up the road that led out of the valley, off to the side, so it didn't block the road, but close enough to hear any traffic. Whistling tunelessly but loudly enough to be heard prior to his approach, Macklin hiked up the road, making sure his boots crunched on the gravel. Any other time, he'd have walked in the grass on either side, but he wanted Thorne to hear him coming. He wanted to talk, not fight.

Thorne was standing outside the tent waiting for him by the time he reached the little campsite.

"Was the bed in the guest room that uncomfortable?" Macklin asked. "We could have tried another house, you know."

"That's not why I'm out here and don't pretend otherwise," Thorne said, his face contorted with more emotions than Macklin could name. "The firebreaks are done. I'll leave in the morning."

"The fires aren't out. The threat still exists," Macklin said. "Are you only going to do half your job?"

"Look, Armstrong, I like you and I like what you've built here, but I'm a danger to everyone. I proved that this afternoon."

"Neil said Laura was more scared than anything else, and her parents haven't come to complain," Macklin replied. "So unless you're planning on attacking someone else, I don't see the problem."

"Because I never plan it," Thorne shouted. "It's not something I can control. Something triggers it and I react like a mindless killer."

"And then make yourself sick when it's over."

"Like that's going to matter if I hurt someone," Thorne said scornfully. "I'm a trained killer. I don't need weapons. Everything I touch is a weapon."

"Did you tell Neil the truth about your triggers?" Macklin asked. "Because we can work with that if that's all there are. You're only going to be here for a few days. The men are intelligent enough to remember not to walk up behind you or to touch you without warning. If those are really the only ones, you're welcome to stay."

"The only ones I know about," Thorne said. "I don't like loud, unexpected noises, but they startle me more than set off a flashback. It's the flashbacks that are the worst."

"Then pack up and come get dinner. You can eat with your back to the wall so no one surprises you, and I'll tell Mum to keep her hands to herself. She's of the opinion that no one is too old for a hug, but in your case, that might not be true."

"If I see it coming and have a way out if it's not a good time, I don't mind a hug," Thorne said. "It's only when I'm tense or when it's unexpected. I can't take feeling trapped."

"Is that why you're out here instead of at the house?" Macklin asked.

"No, I didn't feel trapped there. I didn't think I'd still be welcome after what I did."

"Don't make a habit of it," Macklin warned, "but you're still welcome. We need all the hands we can get to protect the station. I don't want the children to lose their homes."

It was a gamble, but it seemed to work. Thorne's face lost the haunted, conflicted look, determination taking its place again in the set of his jaw. "No, we don't want that. Give me a minute to pack up."

Macklin waited as Thorne broke camp with an economy of movement that spoke of years of experience. He shouldered his pack, and they hiked back toward the station. "Why didn't you just tell me to get the hell off your land?"

"I told you. We need your help."

"I've done what I was sent to do," Thorne said. "The firebreaks are ready. There's no reason for me to stay until the fire gets here."

Macklin hesitated a moment. He had told Caine that Thorne wouldn't appreciate coddling, but Macklin recognized a broken soul when he saw one, just as Caine did. "How much do you know about Lang Downs?"

"Not much," Thorne said. "I'd never heard of it before the captain sent me here. I've been out of the country for twenty years, and I didn't grow up in this area."

"I didn't know if any of the others had said anything," Macklin said. "Lang Downs is named for Caine's great-uncle, Michael Lang, who founded the station in his twenties. Michael never married, but the jackaroos who came and stayed were his children in all the ways that mattered. He spent his life taking in down-on-their-luck men with no hope of a future and giving them a home. Kami, Neil, Ian, Kyle, me… we were the latest in a long line of men who got their lives together in these hills. Then Michael died and Caine came. And Caine kept right on in his uncle's footsteps. Chris, Jesse, Sam, Jeremy, Seth, who you haven't met because he's off in trade school because of this place, Kyle's wife Linda and her daughter…. The only people we've ever kicked off the station are a drug user and a man who stole from us. Not everyone stays, of course. Some people stay for a season or two. Some people come to work here and don't need anything from us, but we've never turned away anyone who needs a safe haven, and I don't plan on starting now."

"I don't need anything," Thorne insisted. "I'm just here to fight fires."

That was a lie if ever Macklin heard one, but he didn't argue. It wouldn't do any good. "Then stay to protect the people who do need it," Macklin said. "They deserve a place to call home."

THORNE found a seat in the canteen with his back to the wall at an unoccupied table. He didn't know how long he'd be allowed to sit alone, but at least he would see anyone coming well before they got to him. He expected Neil to have told the others, and after what he'd done to Laura, he wouldn't be surprised if no one approached him or if her parents approached him in anger, but it was better to be prepared for any eventuality.

Any eventuality except a small child toddling up to him and pulling on his trouser leg. "Hello, sweetheart." He looked around frantically for the girl's parents, but no one seemed to have noticed her absence. "What's your name?"

"Dani. Why you sitting alone?"

Thorne hadn't the slightest idea how to answer that. He didn't want to scare the kid, so he couldn't exactly explain that he'd attacked Laura earlier and so nobody wanted to sit with him now. "I'm not alone," he said instead. "You're here with me."

That seemed to satisfy the child because she held her arms up to be lifted. He slid his hands under her arms, watching as they dwarfed her sturdy little chest. This was insane. If he squeezed wrong, he could break a rib!

"Eat," Dani ordered as she settled on the bench next to him and gestured imperiously to his still full plate.

Not knowing what else to do, Thorne took a bite of the curry on his plate and nearly moaned in delight. After years of field rations, both in the army and in the months in the outback fighting grassfires, any home-cooked food was a treat, but Lang Downs had a treasure in their cook. The meat, of unknown origin but Thorne had learned not to ask years ago, was tender. The sauce was spicy without being so hot it burned his mouth, and the rice was fluffy and cooked to perfection.

"You want naan?" Dani asked. "I like naan with curry."

"You're just an expert, aren't you?" Thorne asked. "I like my curry with rice, though, so no naan for me."

Dani shrugged and then grinned. "More for me!"

"You can have my naan," Thorne agreed. "Maybe you should ask Kami for it now."

"I eated already," Dani said. "You was late to dinner."

"I was," Thorne replied. "I had to talk to Mr. Armstrong before I could come eat."

"Dani, there you are," Molly said, coming up to the table. "She's not bothering you, is she?"

"She's no bother, ma'am," Thorne assured her. "She's been keeping me company."

"He was lonely," Dani said with great authority. "We is friends now."

"We are friends," Molly corrected automatically. "And I'm glad you made a new friend, but you mustn't bother him when he's not paying attention, okay, Dani? Always come up to his face, not his back."

"Why?" Dani asked.

"Because I want to see your pretty smile," Thorne said. "I don't like it when people sneak up on me. It scares me."

"I cry when I get scared," Dani said. "Do you cry too, mister?"

No, he just attacked people. "Sometimes," he said instead. "And sometimes I get angry and yell at the person who scared me. And you can call me Thorne."

"Mr. Thorne," Molly amended. "Do you mind if I sit down? My feet are killing me."

Thorne stood up swiftly and came around the table to pull the bench opposite his out so Molly could sit. "I'm sorry. My mum would have my head if she could see me. She taught me better than that."

"I'm sure your mum is incredibly proud of your service," Molly said as she took her seat.

"My mother died before I joined the military," Thorne said shortly. "She never knew."

"Oh, I'm sorry," Molly said. "I didn't mean to bring up bad memories."

Thorne nodded, unable to speak as the grief welled up in him again. He choked back the emotions as he had always done, unwilling to expose his soft underbelly even to the kind woman sitting across from him. Vulnerability was weakness, and weakness got you killed. He'd had that lesson drummed into him from the moment he joined the army. "It's fine, ma'am. You didn't know."

He nearly jumped out of his skin when he felt pudgy little arms slide around his waist, but for once the unexpected contact didn't trigger a flashback. He swallowed around the lump in his throat and gave Dani a gentle squeeze in return.

"Mummy, Mr. Thorne needs a hug."

"Then give him another one," Molly said. "I'm too big to hug anyone these days."

Thorne didn't think she looked particularly big yet, but his experience with pregnant women was about as vast as his experience with children hugging him, so maybe he wasn't a good judge. He pulled Dani onto his lap to give her another hug. She threw her arms around his neck and squeezed hard. He buried his face in her brown curls and inhaled the scent of talcum powder and baby shampoo and let himself be soothed.

"Your face is sharp." Dani released her hold on his neck as she spoke and rubbed her little hands over his cheeks.

"It'll get softer when it grows out a little more," Thorne said. "I bet it's not as sharp as your dad's face when he hasn't shaved in the morning. The longer it gets, the softer it gets."

"Daddy's face is very sharp in the morning," Molly agreed. "That's why Mummy makes him shave every day."

Dani rubbed her hand over his beard a couple more times before turning and plopping on his lap. "Eat," she scolded again.

"Darling, you're going to make that difficult, sitting on his lap. Why don't you come sit next to me instead?"

Dani shook her head even as Thorne tightened his arms around her instinctively. "She's fine where she is," he said. "I don't mind."

"If you're sure," Molly said with a smile. "She can be a handful."

"She's a blessing," Thorne said as he looked down at her dark head. He couldn't remember the last time he'd felt this settled, and all it had taken was a hug from a child and her mother's acceptance.

"That she is. This one, on the other hand"—Molly rubbed her stomach—"is going to be a little hellion. He hasn't stopped kicking me in weeks."

Footsteps caught Thorne's attention, and he looked up to see Neil coming toward them with a smile on his face. Thorne didn't know him well enough to guess if it was a real one. "Everything okay?"

"We're fine," Molly said. "I needed to sit down for a minute, and Thorne has been helping me keep Dani occupied. She ran me off my feet today."

"Carley told you to send Dani to their house if you couldn't handle her by yourself," Neil said.

"Yes, and Carley spent today dealing with a valley full of sheep because all of you were up building firebreaks," Molly said. "Sarah watched her for a little bit this afternoon after her nap, but I'm still worn out."

"I'll take care of her tonight," Neil promised. "Come on, princess. It's time to go."

From her spot on Thorne's lap, Dani shook her head emphatically. "Wanna stay with Mr. Thorne."

Thorne took a deep breath as she hugged him tight again before prying her arms from around his neck. "I'll still be here tomorrow," he promised. "You can sit with me then, but tonight you need to go with your daddy so you aren't too tired to play tomorrow."

Dani pouted prettily enough that Thorne wanted to give in to her demands, but her parents wouldn't appreciate that, so he rose from his seat and passed her across the table to her father's waiting arms. "Sleep well, Dani."

"Night night, Mr. Thorne."

He watched as Neil carried her out of the canteen, her head already drooping onto his shoulder. "Thank you," he said to Molly. "Not everyone would trust me with their child."

"Not everyone would take the time to help a station with bosses like ours," Molly replied with a shrug. "Jeremy's spent the past hour on the phone with his brother, trying to convince the idiot that it's in his best interest to keep the grassfires from burning Lang Downs, and Taylor still won't agree to send men to help."

Thorne's confusion must have shown on his face because Molly laughed. "Sorry, you don't know that story, do you?"

Thorne shook his head.

"Taylor Peak is the station to the southwest of us, owned and run by Devlin Taylor. You'll never meet a more disagreeable man. Anyway, about five years ago, Taylor and his brother Jeremy had a falling-out, and Jeremy ended up here on the station. Jeremy's completely loyal to Lang Downs now, but he hoped he could call on any remaining brotherly sentiment to get Taylor to help us out. So far, he hasn't been successful."

Thorne grinned, though there was no humor in the expression. "I could go talk to him."

Molly threw her head back as peals of laughter escaped. "Oh, I would pay money to be a fly on the wall during that conversation. You'd have him pissing his pants in no time."

Thorne laughed at that. "Am I that scary?"

"Not when you're snuggling my daughter," Molly said, her eyes still sparking with mirth, "but I think under the right circumstances you could be very scary."

"If you think it will help, I'm happy to be the heavy," Thorne offered, "but I don't want to make matters worse between the two stations."

"You can't," Molly said. "Taylor is a homophobic bigot who will never see Caine as anything more than a Yank usurper and both him and Macklin as pillow-biters despite the fact that they run a more successful station than he does. The fact that his brother is gay too, not to mention 'shacked up' with our foreman's brother, only makes it worse. He's convinced we're a den of iniquity and that the only good would be if we all burned in hell. He probably thinks the grassfire is judgment on us for our sinful ways."

"Sometimes when a fire is too strong to put out, we try to channel it toward uninhabited areas where it will do less damage. It sounds like maybe we should channel it toward his spread."

Molly grinned sharply. "I had no idea you were so vindictive."

"Lang Downs might not be my home, but a blind man could see what it means to all of you," Thorne said. "If Taylor is that stupid and that vindictive, he deserves whatever he gets."

"Lang Downs is home for anyone who needs it," Molly said. "And I've taken enough of your time. I'm going to rescue Neil from Dani and make sure she actually gets in bed on time. If he's left to his own devices, he ends up playing with her for hours instead of making her go to sleep."

"Good luck," Thorne said as she levered herself to her feet. She gave him one last smile and then waddled toward the canteen door. When she was gone, Thorne slumped back against the wall behind him.

He reached for his fork to take another bite of his dinner, but his hands were shaking so hard he couldn't get the food to his mouth without dropping it. He braced his elbows on the table and buried his face in his hands, trying to control his breathing. If he could get that back to normal, the tremors would stop. He breathed in to the count of eight and out just as slowly, forcing his body into submission. He was a well-oiled machine, a perfectly maintained piece of equipment that did what it needed to do when it needed to do it. He didn't have time for weakness or loss of control. He had to—

"Thorne?"

FOUR

THE sound of his name shattered Thorne's concentration. His vision narrowed to a field of gray penetrated only by a shock of red. *Ian's hair,* he chanted silently. *It's not blood. It's Ian's hair. Not blood. No threat. No threat. Just Ian. No threat.*

"Thorne?"

Ian sounded distressed. That was wrong. Thorne couldn't do that. Couldn't let anyone close. He forced his vision to clear enough to focus on Ian's face. "Get me out of here." He hardly recognized his own voice but for the fact that he needed to say those words. "Get me somewhere safe."

"Come on," Ian said. He offered his hand but waited for Thorne to take it, a small mercy in the sea of chaos his senses had become. Thorne took it and clung to it like a lifeline. Ian led him toward the door, fending off questions and ordering people out of the way, but Thorne focused on the touch of warm skin against his. He couldn't think about anything else or he'd lose it.

They made it outside, but there were still people milling around, minding their own business or seeing to their jobs on the station. Ian didn't stop, though, or let go of Thorne's hand, pulling him past the other jackaroos and away from the bunkhouse and the big house. They reached the edge of the line of houses and passed outside it to the veranda of one of the small houses on the periphery.

"Everyone else wanted their doors facing the rest of the station," Ian said conversationally, "but I always preferred looking out toward the tablelands."

His matter-of-fact tone of voice helped settled Thorne's senses. He grabbed the veranda railing to steady himself, his gaze landing on the fine carvings that decorated it. "This is nice work," he said hoarsely. He'd learned by trial and error to cling to any normalcy he could find when his nightmares overwhelmed his waking mind. "Did you do it?"

"Yes," Ian said. "It was my project my second winter on the station."

"What was your first project?" Thorne asked. He didn't let go of the railing yet. He wasn't that steady, but talking helped. So did the lack of noise beyond their voices and the calm stillness of the view behind them. *No threat,* he reminded himself. *Just Ian. It's safe here.*

Ian grinned. "My kitchen. Do you want to see it?"

Thorne shook his head. "Not yet. I need a minute first."

Ian nodded. "The chairs are pretty comfortable, if I do say so myself."

Thorne let go of the railing long enough to move onto the veranda and look at the chairs. "You made these too, didn't you?"

"I did. I like having something to do with my spare time."

Thorne ran his hand over the armrest. The wood was smooth, not a splinter anywhere along its varnished surface. He tried to remember the last time he'd had spare time to do something so constructive, but he couldn't come up with anything. The army had regimented his days completely except when he was on leave, and most of those hours had been spent getting somewhere he could have a quick anonymous fuck and then getting back again. Since he left the army, he'd been fighting fires and trying to get his feet back under him. Neither had been conducive to any kind of hobby. "You're very talented."

"You're very kind," Ian countered. "These were some of my first efforts. They don't rock, like the newer ones, but they haven't fallen apart yet."

"I'm not kind," Thorne said with a shake of his head. He focused out on the valley and the colors of sunset streaking across the sky from his left. "I forgot what kindness was a long time ago."

Thorne heard Ian's sound of disbelief, but he ignored it. He still knew how to pretend, but that was all it was. The bone-deep generosity that led someone like Ian to make furniture for anyone who asked was completely foreign to Thorne. He hadn't known that sort of goodness since his mother died.

Ian didn't say anything else, so Thorne let the silence stretch between them. Ian was an undemanding presence at his side, a silent companion in the storm of emotion still churning inside him, witness to his struggles without judgment or empty offers of assistance.

The sky darkened as they sat there, blue fading to shades of red and orange and then to gray and black. The stars winked into existence overhead, and Thorne let the stillness of the night settle into his soul. It was a welcome respite after the tumult of the day, and as his mind calmed finally, Thorne wondered what it was about Ian that let him relax so fully in the other man's presence. Usually he had to be alone to find any peace, even Walker's presence more than he could cope with, but he had spent some uncounted number of minutes or perhaps even hours sitting quietly next to Ian without that adding anything to his stress.

"Thank you," he said finally.

"You're welcome on my veranda anytime," Ian said. "The station gets kind of crazy in the summer, even without all the sheep in the valley and grassfires threatening. It's nice to have a bit of quiet at the end of the day."

Another time, Thorne might have asked if the invitation onto the veranda included an invitation to other places as well, but he'd just found a refuge. He wasn't going to ruin that by asking for more. They'd have a few more days before the fire threat grew critical. Thorne could bide his time and see what transpired. Tonight, he needed sleep, not sex. He only hoped he'd make it through without nightmares.

"I should get back," Thorne said. "I don't want Caine and Macklin wondering where I am. Macklin's already had to come find me once today."

"They saw us leave together," Ian said. "They know where you are. If they're ready for bed, they'll leave a light on for you."

Thorne remembered the noises that had filtered into his bedroom that morning. "Maybe I should wait a little longer," he said.

"Oh, did they give you a show last night?" Ian asked with a chuckle. "I remember Chris complaining about it when he first got here and was sleeping in their guest room."

"I had a nightmare and couldn't fall back asleep this morning," Thorne admitted. "I'm sure they thought I was still asleep."

"Doesn't make listening to them any easier, I'm sure," Ian said. "It doesn't bother you, knowing they're together?"

"It's none of my business," Thorne said. "If anyone has a right to be bothered by it, it's you and the others who were here before Caine came."

"It's none of our business either," Ian said, "but it doesn't bother me, if that's what you're asking. Macklin's finally happy. It's hard to begrudge them that."

"And the other couples?"

"Same thing," Ian said. "I stood with Macklin when he stopped those thugs from beating Chris to death, and I stood by Sam and Jeremy when Jeremy's brother came storming onto the station a year after they got together demanding Jeremy come home. They're good men. What they do in the privacy of their own homes and who they do it with is their business."

"The world would be a better place if more people shared that attitude," Thorne said finally. He'd hoped for some kind of sign from Ian, whether he might be amenable to Thorne's interest. He knew better than to assume every man on the station was gay just because the bosses were. Certainly Neil and Patrick were both happily married, as were Sarah and Kami and Laura's parents, and even if Caine and Macklin attracted a higher percentage than average of gay jackaroos because of their openness, Ian had been on the station since long before Caine's arrival. Staying didn't make him gay, just open-minded enough to accept his bosses leaning that way.

"If we're getting into cultural psychology, I need something to drink," Ian said. "Come on. I'll make us some tea. You can spike it or not."

"My flashbacks don't need any help getting the better of my control," Thorne said, but he stood and followed Ian inside the house. Ian wandered off toward the kitchen, but Thorne was arrested by the sight of the living room. Every piece of furniture was a masterpiece, all done in the same honey-toned wood. The pillows were a mishmash of different colors and fabrics, but the wood was polished to a high shine over the intricate carvings. He ran his hand over the back of one of the chairs. He'd seen

Ian's talents outside on the veranda, but the pieces out there didn't begin to compare to this. When he'd picked his jaw up off the ground, he followed Ian into the kitchen.

It was decorated with the same golden wood, the cabinets beautifully carved to match the kitchen table and chairs. "You're incredibly talented. Why are you here working on a sheep station instead of somewhere selling your creations? People would pay a lot of money for work like this."

"It means more when I give it to them as a gift," Ian said as he set a pot of tea on the table. "Besides, I like it here. It's safe."

Ian's choice of words set off warning bells in Thorne's mind. Not comfortable, not fun, not any of a thousand good reasons to stay somewhere. Safe. If Ian stayed because it was safe, he had reason to believe the rest of the world, or part of the world, wasn't, and that triggered every protective instinct Thorne had. Ian had offered Thorne an oasis of tranquility when he needed it. Thorne would be damned if he let anything come and hurt Ian now.

He forced himself through the motions of adding milk and sugar to the cup of tea Ian poured for him. Ian added milk, no sugar, and Thorne stored that away for future reference. Maybe it wouldn't ever be useful, but he'd spent too many years in the field cataloguing every detail because anything he missed had the potential to be deadly.

The tea was hot and strong even with the milk, just the way Thorne liked it.

"So what brought you to the station?" Thorne asked casually. At least he hoped it came across as casual.

"The usual," Ian said. "It was a way to earn some money without a lot of prerequisite skills or experience. Mr. Lang hired me on the spot without checking my references or anything else, and when the season ended, he told me I could have this house. I'd have to finish it myself since it was little more than a shell at the time, but it would be mine and no one would ever come in without my invitation. It was everything I'd ever wanted."

That left Thorne with the burning desire to track down whoever had come into Ian's home without invitation and visit the fires of the damned on them. He knew how. The army frowned on torture, but they turned a blind eye as long as the Commandos got the results they wanted. He'd even learned not to leave marks most of the time. If someone had hurt Ian, though, Thorne thought he might like to see marks left behind.

"How long have you been on the station?" he asked.

"Fifteen years," Ian said. "I was twenty. I've never regretted it."

"Do you get to see your family often?"

Ian's face twisted with such a mix of emotions that Thorne nearly recoiled. The pure revulsion in Ian's expression was not what Thorne had expected when he mentioned family.

"No," Ian said, "and we're all happier that way. Neil, Kyle, Jesse, and the others... they're my family now."

"They're lucky to have you," Thorne said.

Ian smiled at that, his expression clearing. "I'd say we're all lucky to have had Mr. Lang, or Caine in Chris and Jesse's case." His face grew serious again. "We have to stop the grassfire from destroying the valley. The rest of the station is just fences and drovers' huts. It would be a pain to have to rebuild them, but it wouldn't be a huge loss. But the valley itself...."

Ian didn't finish his sentence, but Thorne didn't need him to. In the day and a half he'd been on the station, he'd already seen what a special place it was. Learning about the station's legacy of taking in people who needed a new chance at life and now seeing that played out in the beauty of Ian's home only increased Thorne's determination. He'd fought many a battle in his life, but he wasn't sure any of them had been as important as this one. Maybe on some grand international scale, they had been, but this wasn't about politics. This was personal. He *would* protect the valley if it was the last thing he did.

"We'll stop it," he promised. "I'll head out tomorrow and figure out where the fire line is and then follow it back. Even if we can't get it out, we might be able to divert it away from the valley. I won't let you lose your home."

"Thank you," Ian said. "I know I was harsh earlier today with Laura, but I really appreciate everything you're doing for us."

"I deserved it," Thorne said. "I hurt her when she hadn't done anything to me. You probably shouldn't forgive me so easily."

"You apologized, and it obviously wasn't intentional," Ian said. "I don't know a lot about PTSD, but I've seen you nearly lose control twice now, and it's clearly something you're struggling with. Everyone here has fought their battles. Maybe they didn't involve guns and other weapons, but none of us are unscarred. We wouldn't be here if we were."

"Mr. Lang wouldn't have let you stay?" Thorne asked.

"We wouldn't have needed to," Ian corrected. "That's what sets the year-rounders apart from the seasonal jackaroos, and it's what sets Lang Downs apart from the other stations in the area. For everyone else, being a jackaroo is a job. They do it for a few seasons and then move on to other things. They might like working here, but they don't need it. Those of us who stay didn't have anything else."

"And now that you're here?"

"Now we have everything we could possibly hope for," Ian replied. "Macklin has Caine and his mother. Kami has a kitchen all to himself and Sarah. Neil has Molly and their family. Chris and Jesse have each other, and Chris had a safe place for his brother until Seth was old enough to head off to uni by himself."

"And you?" Thorne asked. "What do you have?"

"A home."

A home. Thorne ached at the words, the longing for a place of his own so great it nearly choked him.

"If Mr. Lang were still alive, he'd already have offered you a place here," Ian said softly. "And if I know Caine, he's just waiting for the right moment."

Thorne stood up hurriedly, nearly knocking the chair over in the process. "I don't know what you're talking about."

"Don't you?" Ian said. "Like recognizes like, Thorne. I know a troubled soul when I see one."

"That doesn't mean I need your pity," Thorne ground out through clenched teeth. He couldn't show weakness. Weakness led to death.

"It's not pity," Ian said. "It's sympathy. Maybe I wasn't a soldier, but I know what it feels like to be dealt a bad hand and to reach a point where you wonder if there's any reason to go on living, and maybe you're right. Maybe Lang Downs isn't the answer for you like it was for me, but I know one thing, and that's this: it *is* worth it to go on living."

He rose as well, more gracefully than Thorne had done, and put his cup in the sink. "Morning comes early. You're welcome to my couch if you don't want to listen to Caine and Macklin again. There's pillows and blankets in the closet there. I'm going to sleep."

Thorne stood in silence as Ian left the kitchen and disappeared down a short hallway. He turned back on the sill of a partially closed door. "The loo is right there," he added, pointing to the door across from his bedroom. "Towels are under the sink if you decide to stay."

And then he went into the room and shut the door, leaving Thorne to his own devices with absolutely no clue what to do now.

It was pitch dark, but the moon was out and the station wasn't complicated. Thorne could find his way back to the big house if he wanted to. Or he could make a nest for himself on Ian's couch. If he went back to the big house, he ran the risk of another frustrating round of listening to Caine and Macklin together, but sleeping in their guest room was station hospitality, a simple courtesy extended to someone who was helping them out. He would probably have a more restful night on Ian's couch, but if he had another nightmare, he wouldn't have the luxury of a private room to hide the evidence. His underbelly would be exposed for Ian to see.

Then again, Ian seemed to have discovered it already without any help from Thorne. He'd zeroed in on Thorne's greatest desire without so much as a hint from Thorne. Maybe like really did recognize like. Thorne didn't know how Ian had been hurt in the past, but it was clear he had been. He'd left it behind him when he came to Lang Downs, but now that too was threatened by the grassfires burning to the north. Thorne couldn't do anything about the past, but he could protect Ian's future.

Making up his mind, he grabbed a pillow and blanket from the closet Ian had indicated. He stripped off his shirt and boots but left his undershirt and jeans in place. He'd slept fully clothed often enough not to even notice anymore, and he didn't want to make Ian uncomfortable in the morning by undressing more than that. He went into the loo and washed out his mouth with the mouthwash he found there. He'd have to get his pack from his ute in the morning to brush his teeth and change clothes, but at least this way he could sleep relatively comfortably. With a final glance at Ian's closed door, he went back to the couch to get settled for the night.

FIVE

THORNE woke with a gasp the next morning, feeling incredibly unsettled but without any memory of his dreams. He counted that a small blessing after the turmoil of the day before. His subconscious could have had a field day with everything that had happened or almost happened, so he was glad not to remember. The house was still dark, but he thought he saw the slightest hint of light through the windows, so he tossed off the covers and pulled his shirt back on. It stank of yesterday's sweat, but he'd lived with worse in the jungle, where a change of clothes was less of a necessity than another day's worth of rations. If he had time, he'd shower and change before breakfast. If not, he'd deal with it that night.

He left his boots by the couch so his heavy tread wouldn't wake Ian and went out onto the veranda, only to find Ian already sitting in one of the chairs with a cup of tea in his hand.

"There's tea in the pot if you want a cup," Ian said. "If you want coffee, you have to wait for the canteen to open."

"I'm fine," Thorne said automatically. He took the empty seat and tried to decide what it meant that Ian had walked through the living room and made tea in the kitchen without waking him. "Have you been up long?"

"Twenty minutes, maybe," Ian said. "I woke up early, and you were sleeping so peacefully. I didn't want to disturb you."

Thorne frowned. Had he really been sleeping peacefully? Maybe the unsettled feeling came from having heard Ian moving around in the kitchen, or even from having heard him and then having the sound stop. If he'd really managed to convince his subconscious that Ian wasn't a threat and was indeed someone under his protection, hearing him and then not hearing him could have been enough to wake him up.

"Thanks, mate. I haven't slept through the night in months."

"Nightmares are a bitch," Ian agreed. "If sleeping on my couch helps with that, you're welcome to stay, although I don't know how much good it does your back."

"I'm used to sleeping on the ground," Thorne reminded him. "Anything that isn't hard dirt or rocks poking me in the bloody back is an improvement."

"Then my couch should feel like heaven," Ian said with a laugh. "No hard dirt or rocks anywhere in sight."

Thorne smiled and turned his attention toward the horizon again. The sun hadn't peeked above the hills yet, but the sky was definitely lighter than it had been a few minutes ago. It would be another scorcher, he was sure, but for now, the temperature was surprisingly cool with what even felt like a hint of humidity in the air. He hoped that was the case, because it would help dampen the fires. A good dew could buy them hours in the morning.

He looked north automatically, searching for the haze of smoke that had lingered there for weeks now. He hadn't looked the morning before to see how dark it appeared from Lang Downs, but he'd been judging that smoke for months. He ought to be able to calculate the distance

"Don't tell me," Ian said.

"What?"

"Whatever you're figuring out by looking at the smoke on the horizon, don't tell me. You can tell us all after breakfast, but let me enjoy the peace and quiet for a few more minutes before I have to think about the fire getting closer or worse."

"What if it's good news?" Thorne asked.

"Is it?" Ian countered.

"I haven't decided yet," Thorne replied honestly. "It's still not full light yet, which makes it hard to judge."

"Then let me pretend until breakfast," Ian requested. "I hate bad news on an empty stomach."

Thorne nodded and returned to his contemplation, but he kept tabs on Ian out of the corner of his eye. The jackaroo kept his gaze focused to the east on the spot where the sun would eventually peek over the horizon.

He sipped his tea in silence and seemed content to let the world wake up around him. Thorne suspected it was a hard-won peace, and he envied Ian for it. What would it be like to have a place of his own, to be able to greet the day on his own terms and choose the battles he fought instead of going where the whims of the government or the needs of the RFS sent him? What would it be like to have a home again?

He'd been so young when he'd lost the only home he'd ever known, younger really than even his years suggested. He hadn't known to appreciate what he had. What teenager really did? Certainly not one of relative privilege, like he'd been. He hadn't seen it until it was gone and he couldn't get it back.

Nothing could bring his family back, but Ian had lost just as much from the sound of it, maybe even more, and he'd found a new home, a new family. Maybe....

Thorne shook the thoughts away. He had a job to do here, and while that job included protecting Lang Downs, it didn't include staying. Lang Downs wasn't the only station threatened by the fires.

The sound of voices calling out greetings shattered the silence between them, and Thorne took that as his cue to rise and gather his things. He went back into the house and folded the blanket, but left it on the couch in case Ian wanted to wash it before putting it away. "I'll see you at breakfast," he said when he came back out. "Thanks for letting me crash on your couch."

"Anytime," Ian said without looking away from the imminent sunrise. Thorne tried not to feel slighted as he walked around Ian's house and toward the canteen. He pushed the thought away and focused on what he would need to do, including calling his captain to check in since he had not done so last night.

Caine and Macklin waved him over as soon as he entered the building.

"G'morning, mate," Macklin said. "I wasn't sure you were still here. You didn't come in last night."

"I crashed on Ian's couch," Thorne said. "We got to talking and it got late and it was just easier to stay."

"No worries," Macklin said. "Where you sleep is your business. Have you met Sam and Jeremy?"

Thorne nodded to the other two men at the table. "No, we haven't met yet."

"Sam is our office manager and Jeremy is one of our crew bosses," Caine said. "They've been on the station for the past five years."

"Nice to meet you," Thorne said.

"I'm going to Taylor Peak today," Jeremy said when the introductions were finished. "Devlin won't budge, but I'm hoping his jackaroos have enough sense to ignore him for once."

"Are you sure that's a good idea?" Sam asked. "The last time you saw him, he tried to beat you up. Again."

"And he left with more bruises than he put on me," Jeremy replied. "I'll be fine."

"I could come with you," Thorne offered impulsively. "They might listen to me since I'm with the Firies. And if they don't, I've been told I'm pretty handy in a fight."

"It's worth a shot," Macklin said. "Obviously we'd prefer it not come to a fight. Tensions are high enough between the stations as it is, but we need every hand we can get."

"I have a better idea," Caine said. "We already know what's going to happen if Jeremy goes. We can give Thorne directions and he can go by himself, because I do think they'll listen to him, and they'll do so more easily if Jeremy isn't there. It's also much less likely to come to a fight if Jeremy stays here. Taylor has never hit anyone but Jeremy because of us as far as I know."

"He's welcome to try," Thorne said with grim delight. After the past three months of having no target but the grassfires for his aggression, he'd almost welcome a fight.

"The foreman's name is Williams," Jeremy said. "If you can talk to him, you'll have better luck than talking to Devlin. I wouldn't go so far as to say he's a fan of Lang Downs, but at least he doesn't have Devlin's blind spot, and he handles most of the day-to-day running of the station, much more than Devlin does. If you can convince him, he's perfectly capable of helping without Devlin knowing what he's doing."

"I'll keep that in mind," Thorne said. "While I'm gone, gather all the rakes and shovels you have and get the containers filled with water."

"This isn't our first grassfire," Macklin said. "We'll be at the fire line when you get back."

Thorne wanted to tell them to wait for him, but they were all capable of taking care of themselves, and the sooner they added their numbers to the people already out there fighting the fires, the better the chances of keeping the damage to a minimum on the station. His own fears had no place in their decisions.

"Macklin," Mrs. Lang scolded, coming up to the table with a plate of food, "you've talked that boy's ear off and haven't let him get breakfast yet. Really! I'm ashamed of you."

"Sorry, Mum," Macklin said as she handed the plate to Thorne.

Thorne smothered a laugh. Macklin wouldn't appreciate it, and Thorne had no desire to forfeit the rapport he seemed to be building with the men on the station, the kind of camaraderie he hadn't known with anyone other than Walker in years. It might not lead to anything, but for the first time in twenty years, Thorne had found a place where he could consider staying.

With a shake of his head at his own dreams, he dug into the plate of eggs and bacon. It was delicious, as every meal had been on the station, and he took the time to say so to Mrs. Lang on his way out of the canteen.

"Oh, please, call me Sarah," she said. "Everyone else does."

He ran into Ian right outside the canteen. "I heard you're going to Taylor Peak."

"Jeremy didn't have any luck getting through to them, so I thought I'd try my hand," Thorne said. "It's a lot harder to dismiss someone from the RFS than it is to dismiss an estranged brother out of spite."

"Be careful," Ian warned. "I know you can take care of yourself, but there's a lot more to the history between the stations than just Jeremy choosing to live here instead of there. Taylor has a lot of hatred built up and no outlet for it."

"I'll be careful," Thorne promised, "but you have to do the same if you get to the fire line before I'm back. Pay attention to the way the wind is blowing. That's your best indicator of where the fire will move next, and whatever you do, don't let it get behind you."

Ian smiled, the expression so soft it transformed his careworn face into something sweet and innocent again. Thorne almost leaned down to kiss him, the need for it an ache in his chest, but he had no indication Ian would welcome his attentions, and he didn't want to lose the friendship they were developing.

He spent another couple of seconds getting lost in the kelly green of Ian's eyes before he took a step back and made himself head toward his ute. He debated calling the captain now, but he would have more information after he talked to Williams and could still alert the captain before the Lang Downs crew reached the front.

TAYLOR PEAK was everything Lang Downs was not: sprawling, almost industrialized, built up to the point of obscuring the land the station proper sat on. It was also unkempt, with roads full of potholes and none of the signs of an established community that Thorne had seen the moment he arrived at Lang Downs. No one had flowers growing outside the houses that dotted the area. No children played in the grassy areas between buildings. Taylor Peak might be a successful station, but it wasn't a home. Thorne didn't blame Jeremy for preferring Lang Downs to the station where he grew up.

"Can I help you?"

"I'm looking for Williams," Thorne said to the man who approached his ute. "I was told he's the foreman here."

"He's over there," the man said. "The one without the hat."

Thorne scanned the men near one of the large outbuildings until he found the one he was looking for. "Thank you. I'll go talk to him."

Thorne pocketed his keys and headed toward the group of men, well aware of the stares that followed him. He kept his stride even and deliberate, projecting an aura of strength and authority. It had got him out of fixes in the past. Hopefully it would help him now. These men weren't hostile, just distrustful of strangers. Thorne could work with that. He had a reason to be here and no reason to pick a fight. He was a neutral party.

Except, of course, that he wasn't. He'd thrown his lot in with the men of Lang Downs from the moment he'd first shook Caine's and Macklin's hands. The jackaroos in front of him didn't know that, though, and he didn't plan on telling them.

"Mr. Williams?" he asked politely when he neared the man who'd been pointed out.

"I'm Williams. And you are?"

"Thorne Lachlan from the RFS. I'm with the company that's fighting the grassfires north and east of here," he said, offering his hand. Williams shook it with the same solid grip Thorne had appreciated from Caine and Macklin. "The captain sent me to apprise the stations in the line of the fires, to warn them and see what assistance we could count on from them."

"You'll have already been to Lang Downs, then," Williams said.

"I just came from there," Thorne replied. "They're gathering men and supplies now. I expect to find them at the front by the time I make it back there."

Williams humphed. "Don't tell the boss that," he said. "Don't mention them at all. I'll send everyone we can spare because the fire's too close already, but if the boss hears any mention of them, he'll order me not to send help, and that's just plain stupid."

"I don't see any reason to mention anything to the boss if silence will get the help we need," Thorne replied. "How long do you need to get things ready?"

"I can have men with shovels and rakes in half an hour. Loading the jugs onto the utes takes longer, but we can go in two waves," Williams said. "I can't send everyone. We have to run the station too, but I can send twenty men at least."

"Any help is appreciated," Thorne replied diplomatically even as he compared the reaction here to the one he'd received at Lang Downs. Caine and Macklin had ordered all but a skeleton crew to the front lines. Molly, Carley, Kami, Sarah, and four jackaroos would stay behind on the station. Everyone else was already on the way to the fire line.

"I know what you're thinking," Williams said, "and I don't blame you, but until the fires are threatening our land, I can't do any more. I value my job too much to lose it."

"Any help is better than none," Thorne repeated. "I'll lead the first group when they're ready, and the second group can join us as soon as they get the utes outfitted."

Williams nodded and turned to the gathered men, issuing orders right and left. The men scattered at his command, and Thorne stepped back to let them work.

It had taken him a good two hours to get to Taylor Peak, and it would take another two to get to the fire line. From here, they could go faster by the main roads rather than going through the tablelands, but even so, Ian and the others would reach the front before he did. He itched to get on the road, to minimize the amount of time Ian spent fighting without Thorne there to watch his back.

He thought back to the tense moment right before he left. Ian's smile had been different. Thorne had seen quite a few expressions on Ian's face last night, and this morning as they watched the sunrise, but Ian hadn't smiled like that before. Soft and intimate and almost inviting. If Thorne didn't know better, he'd take that smile as permission. He couldn't do that, though. However much he liked Ian—and the more time they spent together, the more he liked him—he couldn't offer anything, and Ian deserved better than a night of meaningless sex. Thorne was too fucked up to even think of anything more than that, even if he were in a position to stay beyond the duration of the fire threat. Even so, he wanted to see that look on Ian's face again. More than that, he wanted to know if he really had read invitation in those green eyes, and if he had, he wanted to know what Ian smelled like, what he tasted like, what noises he would make as Thorne made love to him. God, he could imagine it already, and the thought made his body react

He shifted uncomfortably, trying to redirect his thoughts. He couldn't spring a boner in the middle of Taylor Peak while he was waiting for them to pack up equipment to help fight the fires, and he certainly couldn't afford to have those thoughts in his head when he reached the fire line, where a moment's distraction could mean the difference between putting out the fire and getting burned alive.

He focused instead on everything Ian had said and not said about his past. He'd hoarded every scrap of information like a dragon hoards its gold. Thorne didn't know what had happened to Ian's family, but they were clearly estranged and probably by Ian's choice, if the scorn in his voice when speaking about them was any indication. The question was when the estrangement had occurred and why, and Ian hadn't said anything to answer those questions. He also had noticeably not mentioned any of the women on the station when he described them as family. Thorne hoped that meant no sweetheart tucked away somewhere. The omission didn't make Ian gay, although the almost-kiss was a strong indicator in his favor, but it did mean his heart wasn't already spoken for.

Thorne hoped it meant that, anyway. Perhaps Ian was just incredibly private.

"Fuck," he muttered under his breath as he stalked back toward his ute. He was going in circles, and it wasn't getting him anywhere except closer to a headache. He needed to be thinking about the grassfires, not about Ian and whether or not he had a girlfriend stashed away somewhere, and if he didn't, if he might be interested in Thorne instead.

He climbed in the cab of the ute and resisted the urge to beat his head against the steering wheel. It wouldn't solve anything and would just add to his brewing headache. Instead he grabbed the satellite phone and called the captain to give him an update.

"Grant."

"Captain, it's Lachlan," Thorne said. "I have a report for you."

"Let's have it," the captain said.

"Lang Downs is as ready as I can make it. We finished the rest of the firebreak yesterday, as expected. There are about fifty men with equipment, including makeshift fire trucks, on their way to you. They should be there any time. I'm at Taylor Peak now, the adjacent station. They've committed another twenty men including a few more modified utes," Thorne reported.

"Good work," Grant said. "What's the ETA for the Taylor Peak crew?"

"We should be leaving here in the next fifteen to thirty minutes," Thorne said. "Then two hours to get there. It'll take longer for them to outfit the utes, so the first wave won't be the full complement of troops. I'll report back with the first group from Taylor Peak. I've been gone too long as it is."

"You weren't sitting around with your thumb up your arse," Grant said. "You were getting assistance we desperately need."

"It'll still be good to be back in the action, sir," Thorne said.

"See you in two," Grant said.

"Yes, sir," Thorne replied before ending the call.

SIX

IAN sat next to Neil in one of the station's utes as they bounced north across the outback toward the property line and beyond that to a section of unused land where the fires burned. It wasn't the first time fire had threatened Lang Downs in the time he'd been there and it wouldn't be the last, he was sure, but that didn't make it any easier. He worked with wood. Fire was his natural enemy, and as they continued on, he couldn't help but think of all the hours he'd spent working with wood for the station. Every house had some touch of his hand, either in the furniture or in building the house itself. Almost every room in the bunkhouse was the same. He'd spent fifteen years pouring his friendship and affection into those pieces, and all it would take was for the flames to jump the firebreak and it would all be gone in an instant.

"Williams isn't a fool, no matter what I think of Taylor," Neil said beside him. "He'll send anyone he can spare."

"I'm not worried about Williams," Ian said.

"Worried about Thorne, then?" Neil asked in surprise. "He's carved from stone, that one, hard as a rock and immovable as the mountains. Nobody's going to take a swing at him and get away with it."

"He was a Commando," Ian said. "The most highly trained special forces we have in Australia, and now he's fighting fires with a volunteer corps. Does anything about that strike you as odd?"

"Maybe he just needed a break," Neil said. "People get tired sometimes."

"He slept on my couch last night," Ian said slowly. "He almost had another breakdown in the canteen. Too many people, too much noise, I don't know what, but he asked me to get him out of there, so I took him back to my place. No kids, no dog, no wife to disturb the peace. Just him and me and the view. We got to talking eventually. Sort of."

"He's not the talkative type?"

"No, definitely the strong, silent type."

"Not bad-looking, either, if you like that sort of thing," Neil observed.

"Should I warn Molly?" Ian teased, hoping to throw Neil off the scent.

"No, I like my women with… well, I like women. I was thinking about you."

"Me?" Ian said. "Why me?"

"Because you've shown more interest in this guy in one day than I've ever seen you show anyone, mate," Neil said. "I'm your friend. You know it makes no difference to me. Caine and Macklin taught me that, and Sam finished the job. Hell, he made me accept a bloody Taylor in my family. After that, it's all a piece of cake."

"I know," Ian said. "If I were interested in someone that way, I wouldn't be afraid to tell you because it was a guy. I'm just not interested in anyone."

"Why not?" Neil asked. "I mean, I understand if you've never met someone on the station who catches your eye, but you never seem to go looking anywhere else either."

Ian shrugged, willing down the memory of searing pain. "It's just never seemed worth it."

"So you're just going to spend your life alone?"

"I'm hardly alone. The station is full of people," Ian protested.

"Most of whom will either be gone in a few months or are happily married—or shacked up, anyway—with the man or woman of their dreams," Neil reminded him. "It's not the same."

No, it wasn't the same at all, but Ian had accepted a long time ago that he wasn't relationship material.

Realizing Neil was waiting for an answer, Ian shrugged again. "What do you want me to say? We picked this life, knowing it was isolated. You met Molly, Kyle met Linda and convinced her and Laura to move here, and I couldn't be happier for either of you. You and Molly are made for each other. A blind man could see it. I haven't met my Molly, and I don't know that I ever will."

"How will you meet your Molly if you don't go looking for her, or him, as the case may be?" Neil pressed.

He wouldn't. That was the whole point, but he couldn't exactly tell Neil that. Neil might accept it, but he'd want to understand it, and that would require explanations Ian had avoided giving anyone but Mr. Lang for seventeen years. He'd hidden it from his foster mother, his teachers and classmates, the social worker who checked on him once a month. He'd hidden it from the men at the first two stations he'd worked on before finding Lang Downs. It had taken Michael all of an hour to get the whole story out of him, but Ian had never spoken of it since, and if he had his way, he never would. Some things were best left unsaid and unremembered.

"Did it ever occur to you that maybe I don't want to meet anyone?" Ian snapped. "Maybe I like my peace and quiet and don't want someone putting demands on my time. Maybe I want to eat in the canteen and not have to remember birthdays or anniversaries or any of the other shit that goes along with a relationship. Just leave it alone, Neil."

Neil looked taken aback by the vehemence of Ian's response. He opened his mouth to say something else but shut it when Ian glared at him.

"I'm sorry I brought it up," Neil said after a moment. "I won't mention it again."

Ian sighed in frustration and ran his hand over his short red hair. He hadn't meant to snap at Neil, but Neil just couldn't leave well enough alone. His tenacity was a boon when it came to working on the station, but once Neil latched onto an idea, he didn't know when to quit.

"No, I'm sorry I snapped," Ian said. "It's a sore spot, with everyone meeting someone. It was one thing when it was Chris and Jesse, both of whom were outsiders when they came, and I love Molly like a sister, but then Kyle met Linda, and even Kami met Sarah, and suddenly I'm the third wheel all the time. Nobody means to make me feel that way, but it doesn't change the fact that everyone else has someone and I don't."

"So do something to change that," Neil said. "I was joking about Thorne, but if you like him, maybe I could sound him out for you. He didn't seem bothered by Caine and Macklin, and when you gave me shit about Sam and Jeremy yesterday, he called me on what he thought was a homophobic comment. You could get lucky."

"Maybe I could," Ian said, "but he's not here to stay. He's not even here for the summer. He's here for a few days to fight the fires and then it's on to the next fire or the next adventure."

"You said yourself something didn't add up," Neil reminded him. "The same way it didn't add up for us when we got here until Michael made it add up. Maybe he's already one of us and doesn't even know it yet."

"Another of Old Man Lang's Lost Boys?" Ian said with a muted smile. "That's what they called us, you know. If Michael were still alive, maybe he could work that magic one more time, but he's not here and I'm not him."

"No, and Caine isn't either, but he's done a bloody fine job of filling his uncle's shoes," Neil said. "He took in Chris and Seth. He hired Sam and made Jeremy a crew boss. He went looking for Sarah when Macklin didn't even dare try."

"Chris and Seth were fifteen years younger than him, Sam and Jeremy asked for help, and Sarah would have given anything to see her son again," Ian said. "Thorne isn't like that."

"So have Kami talk to him," Neil said.

Ian nearly choked on his laughter. "Kami? He's about as nurturing as your average rock."

"He's got better since he married Sarah," Neil said.

"Okay, then he's about as nurturing as your average soft rock," Ian replied.

"If the problem is that Caine's too young or too kind, then you either have to get someone older and less kind to talk to him, or you have to do it," Neil said.

"You're still assuming I want him to stay."

Neil shot him an incredulous look before turning his attention back to the field they were crossing. "I'm not stupid, Duncan. If you didn't want him to stay, you never would have brought up Michael. So quit lying to me, and to yourself if that's what you're doing, and figure out how the bloody hell you're going to get what you want, because I don't want to live with you moping if you don't."

Ian spluttered out another denial, but Neil clearly wasn't interested in hearing it, so Ian subsided into the seat and grabbed the thermos to hide behind drinking his coffee.

He had enjoyed having Thorne on his veranda last night. The conversation hadn't been the most natural one he'd ever had, but they both had secrets, sore spots they weren't ready to share. Seeing Thorne on his couch that morning had been an almost perfect start to his day. The man was insanely good-looking. Ian could admit that even if he couldn't admit anything else. He'd always had a thing for beards, probably because he couldn't grow a decent one to save his life, and Thorne's was thick and dark for all that it was relatively short. His hair, on the other hand, was on the long side, almost brushing his shoulders when it wasn't pulled back in a short queue. And his eyes…. Ian thought he could get lost in them, they were so deep and blue. He'd caught himself staring more than once last night, although he didn't think Thorne had noticed. Add all of that to a solidly muscular body that probably didn't have even a hint of fat on it, and Ian could easily fall in lust.

If only he had any hope of following through on the desire looking at Thorne churned up in him. He knew better, though. He'd tried, in those disastrous months after he finally could leave his last foster placement. He'd been able to look, to find guys he found attractive. He'd even been able to kiss a few of them, mostly the younger ones, close to his age. He hadn't worked up the nerve to approach any of the slightly older ones, the ones who really got his heart pumping. As soon as it went beyond kissing, though, he'd freaked out. Some of the guys had been understanding, but most of them had been less patient. "Tease" was the nicest of the insults they heaped on his head when he got them worked up and then couldn't follow through.

Somehow he didn't think Thorne would even be that kind. He didn't seem like the kind of man one led on, however unintentionally. At sixteen, Ian hadn't been able to do anything about it, but he wasn't a kid anymore. He wouldn't live in fear in his own home, and that meant not doing anything to make Thorne or anyone else think he was available. He wasn't. End of discussion.

That hadn't stopped him from dreaming last night, though. It hadn't stopped him from wishing he could know the joy of another's company. His dreams hadn't turned into nightmares for once, and he'd sought

Thorne's touch in his mind as he slept, reveling in the intimate contact instead of fleeing from it. He'd awoken earlier than normal with an unusually insistent morning erection. He'd taken care of that silently, but it hadn't brought any real pleasure. It only served to remind him of everything he'd never have.

And then there had been that moment after breakfast before Thorne left for Taylor Peak. Thorne had been so earnest, giving him advice and insisting he be careful if he made it to the fire line without Thorne as backup. Ian wasn't worried about that. He had Neil, Kyle, and the others to watch out for him, as he would watch out for them, and that didn't even count the other Firies of Thorne's company who were already there. He wouldn't be fighting the fire alone. No, it was the look on Thorne's face, the intent way he'd studied Ian's features as if committing them to memory. Thorne had pulled away before it could become anything more than a fraught look, but Ian could almost believe Thorne had considered kissing him.

It was probably just as well he hadn't tried it. Ian didn't know how he would have reacted, and if he ever did get a chance to kiss Thorne, he didn't want it ruined because he couldn't handle it.

Bloody hell, Neil was right.

"I don't even know where to start."

Neil crowed in triumph, giving Ian no choice but to sock him in the shoulder.

"Ow! What the fuck, Ian?"

"You don't have to sound so pleased with yourself," Ian said grumpily. "Maybe I'll ask Jeremy for help. He's been single most recently."

"I can help," Neil protested.

"Really?" Ian said. "When was the last time you set out to seduce a guy?"

Neil's mouth opened and closed again, reminding Ian of a fish, but after a moment, he shook his head. "If all you wanted was to seduce him, you'd have done it last night. Instead you sat and talked to him and let him sleep on your couch. Come to think of it, that's probably exactly what you need to keep doing. Well, other than maybe the couch part. He could sleep with you instead."

Ian ignored the last part of Neil's comment. He wasn't ready for Thorne to come anywhere near his bed, even if all they did was sleep. "Just talk to him?"

"How else are you going to figure out if he's really the one you want?" Neil countered. "I mean, what's dating but doing things together so you can get to know each other and see if you like the same things and want the same things out of life, and if you want to try to get those things together? It's hard to 'date' in the sense of going out places when you're on the station, but the rest of it still applies."

"I never dated," Ian admitted. "Not even before I got here. I wouldn't know where to start."

"Never?" Neil said. "Wow, that's...."

"Pathetic," Ian said. "I know, but my life wasn't good before I got here. You knew that already even if you didn't know the details. I'm probably going to fuck this up completely."

"Focus on getting to know him," Neil said. "If you like what you learn, you can figure the rest out as you go."

"Thanks, mate," Ian said. "I really appreciate it."

"Just, you know, don't give me details, okay?" Neil said. "I don't need to know about your sex life."

Choking, gasping, retching up bile and bitter fluid.

"No details," Ian promised. Neil didn't need to know there wouldn't be any details to share.

"Get the gate?" Neil asked as they reached the edge of Lang Downs. Grateful for the respite, Ian jumped down and opened the gate for the ute to drive through. He shut it behind them and hopped back in, content to sit in silence as they headed toward the clouds of smoke, much closer now than they'd been an hour ago.

"That doesn't look good," Neil said as they drove. "There wasn't that much smoke last night."

"Nor this morning," Ian said. "Thorne didn't sound pessimistic when we talked about it this morning, but things must have changed since we got up."

"I don't know what caused it to get worse, but I know what's going to cause it to go out," Neil said direly. "That bitch of a fire isn't getting anywhere near my family."

"Just don't get hurt. Molly wouldn't forgive either one of us if you did," Ian said.

Neil scowled at him but didn't argue as they drew nearer the fire line. Ian could see tracks left by heavy equipment. Neil steered the ute along the trails they had left behind, and in a matter of minutes, they had reached the RFS brigade.

"Did Thorne mention the captain's name?" Neil asked as he parked the ute.

"Not to me," Ian said, "but Caine and Macklin are already here. I'm sure the captain knows we're coming."

They climbed out of the ute and joined Caine, Macklin, and the other Lang Downs jackaroos to see what their orders were.

"The heart of the fire is on the other side of this ridge," the captain was saying as they walked up. "The ridge itself is rocky, so hopefully that'll stop that portion, but there's the risk of it splitting into two fires and closing us in. I've got my men spread out, watching for it, but it's a waiting game. Unfortunately, there was a huge deadfall at the base of the ridge. All those fallen branches and trees in one place has made the fire hotter and stronger now than it's been in weeks, which makes the risk of it working around the ridge greater."

"Tell us where you want us," Macklin said. "Most of my crew bosses have experience with grassfires, and the rest of the jackaroos are levelheaded enough to do as they're told."

"We've got the foam utes out trying to spray the areas where the fire is most likely to spread," the captain said, "but that's guesswork until we see how it develops from here. I'll assign a crew of your men to each group of my Firies. That way we have men in place no matter what happens."

"Neil, get the crews divided, at least one experienced man per crew. Make it very clear they take orders from the RFS and aren't to do anything without orders. We're here to help, not to get in the way."

"Yes, boss," Neil said. "Ian, get your crew."

SEVEN

THE roaring of the fire was deafening, and the smoke so thick Ian couldn't see the other men in his crew. They were supposed to be watching out for one another as well as doing their best to combat the fire, but Ian could only hope they were safe because he had his hands full with the fire. They'd given the deadfall up as lost and had backed along the base of the ridge to a break in the trees where they had a hope of containing the revitalized fire, but Ian wasn't sure how long they'd be able to hold it. He had cleared the ground as well as he could, but he was limited to a rake and shovel. They couldn't get the heavy equipment to this location, so it was up to the men on the ground. Ian could see bare dirt in places, but there was still far too much dry grass there for his peace of mind. He wished he could see or hear the others so he had some idea of how they were faring, but short of abandoning his assigned spot, he was on his own.

The roaring got louder as the edge of the fire approached, licking greedily at the makeshift firebreak. Ian gripped his shovel more firmly and went back to building a wall of dirt to stop the advance. He coughed through the wet kerchief that covered his nose and mouth. The smoke was getting worse too. His eyes and lungs burned from exposure, but this was his home at stake. He had to keep fighting.

"WHERE'S Ian?" Thorne demanded as the crew came stumbling back into the staging area. "He was supposed to be with you."

"We had to get out of there, Lachlan. There wasn't anywhere viable to make a stand. I wasn't throwing our lives away for nothing."

"Where's Ian?" he repeated.

"I don't know."

"Emery, are you up to a rescue mission?" Thorne said, giving up on getting anything else from the sorry excuse of a firefighter. You didn't leave men behind.

"Who are we rescuing?" Neil asked. His face was covered in soot, but otherwise he looked much as he had for the past two days, cocky grin and all.

"Ian."

Neil's expression sobered. "Tell me what to do."

"I need rope," Thorne said. "I don't know where he is, but his crew was at the base of the ridge. If he's still there, I can climb down to him, but if he's hurt, you might have to help pull us back up."

"Let me get the others," Neil said. "I don't know if I can pull you both up if it comes to that."

"Meet me at the ridge. I'm going to start searching."

Neil nodded and took off at a run. Thorne ran in the opposite direction, to the edge of the ridge and Ian's last known position. The smoke was so thick he couldn't see a thing.

"Any luck?" Neil asked. He handed Thorne a coil of rope.

"I can't see a thing." He tied the rope around his waist. "I'm going down. If I pull twice, pull me up."

Neil didn't look happy but he nodded. "Bring him back."

"I've never left a man behind. I'm not planning on starting now." Thorne didn't admit that sometimes he'd brought back bodies of men he couldn't save. Neil didn't need to hear that part, although the look on his face suggested he'd guessed.

Thorne climbed down the ridge as fast as he could with the limited equipment. If he'd had his Commando team with him, they'd have jerry-rigged a harness and carabiner in the time it took him to blink and his descent would have been both faster and safer, but they were all back in Afghanistan last he'd heard from Walker. He was on his own.

The temperature spiked as he neared the ground. He peered through the smoke, searching for Ian. To his right the fire formed a flickering wall. If Ian was that way, he was too late. Praying with all his might, he moved to the left and continued his search.

IAN coughed again, the force of it bending him double. He had to get out of there. He wasn't doing any good anymore, but he couldn't see a way out with the smoke so thick around him. Away from the fire was the best he could hope for. If he could move faster than the approaching flames, he would win free of the smoke eventually. He just had to keep his head and his feet until then. He took a moment to get his bearings and set out toward safety.

Ten minutes later, he was ready to admit defeat. Either his sense of direction had deserted him in the smoke, or the fire had him surrounded. He collapsed to the ground as another coughing fit took him. Self-preservation dictated he stand up and keep searching for a way out, but he couldn't catch his breath to make his legs support him. He was going to die here, and he'd do so without ever having a chance to see if Neil was right and if Thorne really could be the right one for him. He had no real hope of escaping this alive, but if he did, he swore he'd stop letting fear hold him back. Maybe Thorne wasn't the one, but Ian had nothing to lose by finding that out. If he made it out, he'd make the most of his second chance.

He doubled over again, the coughing almost constant now. He wouldn't have to worry about the fire getting him. The smoke would kill him before the flames could reach him.

His vision grayed from lack of oxygen, and he dropped to his side, hoping the smoke wouldn't be as thick and he could hold on long enough to crawl away. He thought he heard someone calling his name, but he no longer trusted his own senses. He rolled toward where the voice seemed to be coming from, hoping to find some sign that it was real, not a smoke-induced hallucination.

Thorne burst into the clearing where he lay, and Ian knew it was a hallucination.

"IAN!"

Thorne fell to his knees next to Ian and checked his pulse rapidly. Okay, good, he was still alive. He lifted the kerchief covering Ian's mouth and checked for breathing. Shallow but present, which meant he needed to get Ian out of there as swiftly as possible. The smoke stung his eyes as he pulled Ian to his feet.

"Can you walk?" he asked as he supported Ian's weight with his shoulder.

"Try," Ian said hoarsely. That was enough for Thorne. He followed the rope back the way he'd come, aiming for the ridge and from there up to safety. The fires were getting closer. They'd have to hurry or even that escape route would be cut off.

"Thought—" Ian's words were cut off by a hacking cough. Thorne didn't like the sound of that at all, but he couldn't do anything about it until they were safe from the flames.

"Don't try to talk," Thorne said. "Save your energy for walking."

The smoke thinned slightly as they made their way toward the ridge, and as it did, Ian seemed to shake free of some of the lethargy that had weakened him. He still coughed far more than Thorne was comfortable with, but he wasn't leaning as heavily on Thorne's shoulder, nor was Thorne having to drag him along to get him to walk.

"We're almost to the ridge," Thorne said. "When we get there, Neil and the others will pull us up. You just have to hold on a little longer."

"You came for me," Ian gasped as he pulled the kerchief away from his face. "I thought I was going to die."

Thorne tightened his grip. He wouldn't have hesitated to plunge back into the smoke for any of the men he'd met at Lang Downs or for any of the other Firies, but saving Ian had been even more than the imperative of his training. Something had started building between them last night and this morning, and Thorne wanted to see what it could be. He could argue with himself later about how they hadn't known each other long enough for it to be anything more than curiosity, but right now, facing the fact that Ian had been down when he found him, that a few minutes later and he'd have lost him, Thorne gave up being logical.

"I'll always come for you."

Ian stumbled, and when Thorne pulled him to his feet again, Ian was in front of him, completely encircled by Thorne's arms. He told himself they were still in danger, that this was neither the time nor the place, but Ian was reaching for him, and Thorne gave in and lowered his head so he could close his lips over Ian's mouth. Ian tasted of soot and smelled of smoke, but Thorne didn't care. Ian was kissing him back, and nothing else mattered. He deepened the kiss frantically, loving the way Ian practically climbed into his arms, tangling his hands in Thorne's hair and pulling it free of the band that held it out of his face. He felt Ian tense as he supported his weight with his hands on Ian's arse, but Ian didn't stop kissing him to protest, so Thorne didn't move his hands.

Another coughing fit forced them to separate. "Come on," Thorne said. "We've got to get you to a doctor."

Ian nodded and stumbled forward again at Thorne's urging until they reached the base of the ridge.

"This is where it gets interesting," he warned Ian. "We only have one rope and not enough time to pull us up separately." He looped the rope around Ian's chest and knotted it as best he could. "Neil and the others are going to pull us up, but you have to hold onto me while I guide our climb. Whatever happens, don't let go."

"I won't," Ian said.

Thorne pulled hard on the rope twice and braced for the answering tug. The rope bit into his back as it pulled taut and they began their ascent. He'd have bruises, if not rope burn, by the time they reached the top, but he'd had worse injuries, and Ian was depending on him. He braced Ian between his chest and the steep slope, angling his body in the reverse of a rappeler's seat so his feet were at a ninety-degree angle to his hips, creating a cradle for Ian to sit in.

The muscles in his legs protested the extra weight, but he ignored them. His body was a tool for him to use, not the arbiter of his actions. This had to be done, so he would do it, no matter the cost.

Inch by inch, they climbed out of the valley, leaving the flames behind them, but the smoke followed them and Ian's cough returned with a vengeance. "Just a little longer," Thorne said. He wished his hands were free to pull the kerchief back over Ian's nose and mouth, but he needed them to stabilize Ian and hold his position. "There's an oxygen mask in the medic's tent, and we'll get you to Cowra and a doctor in no time at all. Just keep breathing, slow and shallow so it doesn't irritate your lungs any worse than it already has."

Ian nodded through the coughing. Thorne wanted to reassure him, but he had to focus on keeping his feet beneath him or they'd both end up crashing into the ridge. They were bruised and battered enough; they didn't need any more proof of having survived this battle. Another coughing fit, even worse this time, racked Ian's body, and he convulsed against Thorne, throwing him off balance. He tipped sideways, crashing into the rocky slope. The pressure on the rope didn't abate, though, dragging them inexorably upward. He cursed under his breath as the rough surface tore at his skin. He hadn't bothered with full gear when he'd gone searching for Ian, so he had only a thin T-shirt to protect his arms and shoulders, and it would be shredded in a matter of moments. He twisted his shoulders, trying to keep Ian away from the rocks. They were nearly at the top now. A few more minutes and they'd be to safety and it wouldn't matter. He winced as a particularly sharp stone tore through his T-shirt and scored his back, but with Ian's weight against him and with the jackaroos above still pulling them up, Thorne couldn't do anything but hang on. He ran too great a risk of hurting Ian if he tried to get his feet back under him now.

Finally they reached the top of the ridge and hands reached over the edge to grab them. Thorne pushed Ian up ahead of him before grabbing another set of hands and pulling himself the rest of the way up.

"He needs oxygen," Thorne ordered as soon as he saw the Lang Downs jackaroos crowded around Ian's prone form. "Give him space to breathe."

One of the Firies ran toward the supply tent and came back a minute later, pushing his way through the crowd of men to give Thorne the oxygen mask. It was a small container, but it would hopefully be enough to stabilize Ian for the drive to Cowra. Thorne thought he could make it in about thirty minutes if he pushed the ute's limits on the rough outback terrain, forty-five at the most.

"He needs to see a doctor," Thorne said. "The hospital in Cowra is the closest."

"I'll take—" Thorne glared at Neil with such ferocity that he could see Neil swallow hard and change his mind—"your place on the squad so you can drive him to town. Carley can bring a change of clothes for you both, but it'll take her longer to get there than it will you."

"I'm fine," Thorne said automatically.

"No, you're bloody well not," Neil snapped. "Your arms and back are bleeding. You look like somebody dragged you over rocks."

Thorne managed a sardonic smile. "Somebody did. Thanks for that, mate. You saved both our lives getting us out of there. A few scrapes are worth his life."

Thorne wasn't quite sure what to make of the look Neil gave him, but he had other things to worry about, like getting Ian to the hospital. "Do you think you can walk to my ute?" he asked Ian.

Ian started to pull the mask away to answer, but Thorne caught his hand. "Don't talk. Just nod."

Ian nodded, so Thorne helped him to his feet. Ian managed a couple of steps before he stumbled again. Out of patience, Thorne scooped Ian into his arms, ignoring the annoyed squawk, and carried him the rest of the way to the ute. He would tell himself later that he hadn't relished the surprised but touched expression on Ian's face or how good Ian felt in his arms, but for the moment, he took gleeful advantage of the situation. He'd nearly lost Ian to the grassfires, but Ian was safe now, and even better, he'd reciprocated when Thorne kissed him.

When they had time and privacy, he fully intended to see what else Ian would be interested in reciprocating.

The drive to Cowra was harrowing as Thorne pushed the limits of his ute's off-road capabilities, skidding and fishtailing over the dirt and gravel paths the heavy equipment had dug out. Beside him, Ian held on to the door handle with one hand and the oxygen mask with the other, looking pale and maybe a little carsick, but Thorne didn't slow down. Better carsick than choking from the smoke.

When they hit the main roads, Thorne tossed the fireman's light on the console and gunned the engine. He wasn't racing to a fire, but he had a legitimate medical emergency if anyone challenged his use of the emergency light. He ignored the signs that said Emergency Vehicles Only and pulled right up to the hospital doors. "I need a gurney," he shouted as he jumped out of the cab and went around to help Ian out.

Ian stumbled into his arms. Thorne held him close for a minute as he waited to see if the hospital staff had heard him. "It'll be all right," he promised, moving his lips over Ian's short-cropped hair as he spoke. "They'll get you patched up in no time, and I'll be waiting when they do."

"What happened?" an ER attendant asked from behind them.

Thorne turned and helped Ian onto the gurney. "Smoke inhalation," he said, forcing himself to take a mental step back and relate the situation in a way that would be useful for the doctors. "He was helping out at the grassfires east of here. I don't know exactly how long he was out there, but when I found him, he was down. He hadn't lost consciousness, but he wasn't moving on his own. I evacuated him and provided oxygen. A cursory inspection indicated no burns of note."

"He's not the only one hurt," the attendant commented as he wheeled Ian inside.

"The evacuation required being lifted out of a ravine without proper equipment for a climb," Thorne reported.

"They tied a rope around your waists and tugged?"

"Pretty much, but I'll take a few scrapes over dying," Thorne said.

"You did the right thing," the attendant said. "We'll check him out, give him something for the inflammation, and make sure he's not suffering from anything else. I'll have someone come clean out your back and arms. You're caked in dirt."

Thorne scowled, but he could hardly argue when he'd scolded Ian the day before for leaving a nick on his palm untended. "Is there somewhere I could shower?" he asked. "I'll let them treat the scrapes, but it would be more effective if I was clean first."

"Wait here. Let me get him to the docs and I'll show you where to go."

Thorne waited with feigned patience while the attendant pushed Ian's gurney into an exam room. He watched through the glass as a doctor came in and began examining Ian. When the attendant helped Ian sit up and began unbuttoning his shirt, Thorne turned away.

He wanted to know what Ian looked like beneath his work shirts, but not like this. He wanted Ian to show him, to peel the clothes away in an inviting strip tease or else to let Thorne unwrap him like the gift he was.

"Dr. Johnson is with him," the attendant from before said, startling Thorne. For a moment, he struggled with himself, but concern for Ian gave him the control he needed to push back his memories.

"How is he?"

"He's got a pretty bad case of smoke inhalation, which you already knew," the attendant said, "but he's conscious and coherent, and his blood oxygen levels are approaching normal, so carbon monoxide poisoning isn't a concern. We'll keep him here for observation until the swelling in his lungs goes down. Heparin will help with that. He'll probably have a cough for a while, but it should fade. Smoke will always be a potential trigger for asthma after this. We'll give him a rescue inhaler to be on the safe side. He might never need it, but better safe than sorry."

"Thanks," Thorne said. "He had me worried there for a bit. He never lost consciousness, but there was a point when I wasn't sure how coherent he was."

"He answered all the doctor's questions with no problem," the attendant said, "so that's a very good sign. Let me show you where the shower is, and I'll see if I can find a pair of scrubs that'll fit you. Your shirt isn't fit for the rag bag at this point."

The attendant led Thorne to what was clearly the staff showers, but he figured maybe he'd won emergency responder status in their eyes. He hadn't introduced himself or given any explanation for his presence. Then he remembered his ute. He grabbed his keys.

"I didn't bother parking when I drove in," he said. "I was too concerned with getting Ian the help he needed."

"I'll have someone take care of it," the attendant promised. "Do you need anything brought inside?"

"No, I have my wallet in my pocket. Everything else is fire gear. It can stay in the ute."

"Get cleaned up. I'll be back with the scrubs and to take a look at those cuts," the attendant said.

Thorne stripped out of his ruined shirt. His dungarees had held up a little better, but even they were stained with soot and dirt. He tossed those aside as well. He'd wash them and see if they could be salvaged. Fortunately his shorts seemed in decent shape, so he'd have something to wear under the scrubs until Carley got there with a change of clothes for him and Ian.

The hot water stung the cuts, making him realize how many more there were than he'd realized. Ignoring the pain, he grabbed a bar of soap and scrubbed at his dirt-caked skin. He knew the hospital staff would come after him with antiseptic wash later, and he'd let them, no matter how much it hurt, because he couldn't risk another infection and not being able to take care of Ian, but the cleaner he got now, the less they'd have to dig and scrub at him later. He didn't see any shampoo, but he had to get his hair clean so he lathered it with the bar as well. He'd pay for that with tangles, but he had to get the smell of smoke off him before he went to see Ian. Even if the odor wasn't enough to affect his breathing, it would affect his mental state. Thorne knew that much from experience.

The firefighters hadn't even let him all that close to the burned-out remnant of his house and the smell still haunted him. For Ian, who had nearly died because of the smoke, Thorne was sure it would be even worse.

Finally satisfied that he was clean enough not to set off Ian's coughing, he shut off the water and grabbed a towel from the stack the hospital apparently provided for its employees. As promised, the attendant had left a set of scrubs in a pile outside the shower area too, so Thorne dressed and pulled his boots back on before going in search of someone to take a look at his back.

"Feeling better?"

Thorne summoned a smile for the attendant. "Cleaner, at least. How's Ian?"

"The same as when you went to take your shower," the attendant said.

"I guess you want to take a look at my back."

"Since you mentioned it…." The attendant grinned and led Thorne to an exam room.

EIGHT

IAN lay in the hospital bed as still as he could make himself. Even the slightest movement would trigger another coughing fit. At least the oxygen and the medicine the doctor had given him had stopped him from coughing when he didn't move. He didn't know how long that would last since the drugs would wear off eventually, but he'd take what he could get.

He took advantage of the quiet to try to make sense of his memories and to fill in the gaps where he couldn't entirely remember. He remembered feeling his body giving out even though he didn't want to die. Then Thorne had appeared out of the smoke like some sort of modern-day knight in shining armor, swooping down on him and carrying him off to safety. A lot of things had blurred in his memory, but Ian could recall that moment with perfect clarity: the way Thorne had looked, the almost frightening determination on his face as he'd run to Ian's side to check his pulse and breathing, the way his hair had fallen out of its usual queue to brush his jaw, a curtain of black and silver that framed his handsome face, contorted with worry. Ian had tried to reassure him, but the bloody cough kept him from speaking. For a minute, Ian thought Thorne was going to pick him up and carry him, and he had later, but Ian's legs had held him then, with Thorne's help, anyway. He could still feel those huge hands on his chest and neck to check his pulse and around his waist as Thorne helped him toward the ridge, could feel Thorne's whole body cradling him as his friends pulled them to safety. He knew Thorne had borne the brunt of the injuries from the cliff so he didn't have to. He only hoped Thorne was getting medical attention now.

Those memories were surprising enough, but it was the thought of Thorne kissing him that lingered in the forefront of his thoughts. He'd never been kissed like that. Even with the threat of the fire behind him, it hadn't felt rushed or furtive, like so many of the kisses he'd known before deciding he couldn't keep leading on the men he met. Even Thorne's hands on his arse hadn't freaked him out, and he'd never willingly let anyone touch him that way. With Thorne, though, it had just been another part of the adrenaline-fueled kiss. When he thought about it now, he felt the familiar discomfort that had haunted him every time he'd tried to go beyond kissing, but in the moment, he hadn't felt that way. If his cough hadn't interfered, and if they hadn't had the fire to worry about, he'd still happily be there kissing Thorne.

He'd love to believe that meant he was past his hang-ups, but he'd never been one to delude himself. He might make it a little farther with Thorne, but before long, the clothes would start coming off or hands would start burrowing inside them, and it would be the same as all the rest. Ian would pull back and ask for more time. Thorne would call him a tease and either storm off or demand more. If he stormed off, it would be over, and Ian would be left to nurse a bruised ego and probably a tender heart. If he demanded more, Ian would be left trying to fend him off. It hadn't worked with his foster father when he was sixteen, and he had no doubt it wouldn't work with Thorne. Thorne had picked him up and carried him like he weighed nothing. If he decided to take Ian against his will, there wouldn't be a thing Ian could do to stop him.

He wouldn't do that, Ian argued firmly. *He's too honorable for that.*

The hurting teenager inside him shot back that no one had believed his foster father capable of it either, but that hadn't stopped him.

Ian could feel his agitation increasing and with it, the tension in his lungs. He tried to take a deep breath to calm down, but that only triggered the tickle in his throat. He swallowed, hoping to soothe it, but it had taken full hold now. He bent forward, coughing hard into the oxygen mask that covered his face. When the coughing continued despite his efforts to breathe normally, he fumbled for the panic button on the edge of his bed and pressed it hard, summoning a nurse.

The nurse came in seconds later. "I need you to breathe deeply," she said. "I'm going to add a dose of albuterol to your oxygen flow, but you have to get it into your lungs for it to work. The faster you get it into you, the sooner the coughing will stop."

Ian nodded to show he understood and did his best to draw air into his lungs despite their instinctive need to expel the irritants. The metallic taste of the drug hit his tongue, making him scrunch his face in disgust, but his coughing eased almost immediately.

"Feeling better?" the nurse asked with a sympathetic smile.

Ian nodded again since he couldn't talk around the air mask and lay back against his pillows. It was going to be a long few days with nothing to do and no one to talk to, not that he could talk at the moment. He vaguely remembered Neil saying something about asking Carley to bring him a change of clothes. Maybe he could ask her to bring him a book. It didn't even matter which one. He'd read all the books on his shelves and hadn't had a chance to order any new ones, but he loved them all, so he'd gladly read them again. He reached for his cell phone on the table near the bed. Carley was probably already halfway to the hospital, but he texted her anyway, on the off chance she hadn't left yet.

His phone buzzed a moment later. *Any requests?*

He really didn't care, but since she'd asked…. *Dragon Prince. It's on the third shelf on the right.*

Found it. I'll be there as soon as I can.

Ian knew "as soon as I can" was still at least four hours from now, but that was better than not having a book until tomorrow or later. He shifted on the bed, trying to get comfortable on his back since he'd already figured out lying on his side made his cough worse. He closed his eyes, mostly because he didn't know what else to do, and tried not to think.

He heard the door open, but he figured it was just a nurse come to check his vitals or whatever they needed to do, so he didn't bother opening his eyes, but no one came to poke at him. After a moment, he levered his eyelids open to find Thorne sitting in the chair by his bed.

"I'm sorry. I didn't mean to wake you," Thorne said immediately. "I just wanted to check on you."

Ian shook his head to say he wasn't sleeping, but Thorne just looked confused, so Ian raised his shoulders in a shrug and held out his hand. Thorne seemed surprised but took Ian's hand in his larger one. Ian squeezed to say thank you and then held on. It felt too good to have that contact after nearly dying. Tomorrow he'd be strong again, but today he was allowed to be needy.

Thorne didn't try to pull away, which reassured Ian. He would have understood if Thorne was eager to get back to fighting the grassfires. It was his job, after all, not babysitting an injured jackaroo, but Ian was glad of the company, even silent company.

"You seem to be doing a little better," Thorne said after a moment. "You aren't coughing, at least."

Thorne hadn't been there ten minutes earlier to see his last coughing fit, but Ian just smiled beneath the oxygen mask and left it at that. He was doing a little better. He wasn't actively coughing at the moment, and he couldn't say that the last time Thorne saw him. He still had a funny taste in his mouth from the drugs they'd mixed in with the oxygen, and he'd have given anything for a drink of water to clear it away, but he didn't know if that was allowed. He'd ask the next time the nurse came in. For now, though, he'd settle for Thorne sitting by his bed, holding his hand.

"Did you not see when the rest of your crew pulled back?" Thorne asked. "Don't try to talk, just nod."

Ian shook his head. He hadn't been able to see much of anything beyond the trees right in front of him. He shuddered as he remembered how thick the smoke had been, how choking. His throat tightened up at the memory, and he coughed slightly.

"Easy." Thorne dropped Ian's hand as he stood up and helped Ian lean forward. "Slow, deep breaths," he urged, rubbing Ian's back encouragingly. "Just relax and let the oxygen in. There's no smoke now. I shouldn't have brought it up."

The coughing subsided, but Thorne gave no indication of wanting to move away, so Ian let himself rest in the strong arms, cradled against the rock that was Thorne's chest. Ian wasn't a bodybuilder, but life on the station kept him reasonably fit. Thorne, though, felt like he didn't have an ounce of softness anywhere on his body.

Except his hair, Ian's traitorous libido pointed out. Thorne's hair, when Ian had tangled his fingers in it while they kissed, had been soft as silk.

Ian thought he felt Thorne's lips brush against his hair, but he didn't turn to look. It felt too good to simply sit there. A moment later, he felt the slight prickle of Thorne's beard against his scalp, and this time he did glance up to see that Thorne had rested his cheek against the top of Ian's head as he held him.

Ian had no idea what was going on between them, but when Thorne lifted his head at Ian's movement, the expression on Thorne's face assured him of one thing. Whatever this was, he wasn't alone in feeling it.

"Do you want to lie back down?" Thorne asked.

Ian shook his head. He felt bad about making Thorne perch on the edge of the bed instead of sitting in the chair, but he didn't want Thorne to move. In the hours since he'd collapsed from the smoke, Thorne's arms had come to represent safety, and while Ian knew he wasn't in any danger in his hospital bed, he was still shaken up enough to crave that comfort.

"What did they give you?" Thorne asked with a chuckle. "You're positively cuddly."

Ian shrugged again. The doctors had told him what they were giving him to make sure he wasn't allergic to anything, but the chemical names went right over his head. He wasn't allergic to anything, anyway, so he had no real reason to retain all the names. Later, when he went home and had to manage any remaining medication on his own, he'd worry about it. For now, it was their problem.

There was no mistaking the kiss to the top of his head this time. "Close your eyes and rest," Thorne said. "I'll stay until someone from the station gets here."

Ian didn't just want him to stay. He wanted Thorne to keep holding him, to keep talking to him, but apparently Thorne's presence was what his mind and body needed to finally relax, because before he could figure out how to make that clear to Thorne, he fell asleep in Thorne's arms.

THORNE didn't know quite how to react when Ian fell asleep so trustingly in his arms. He was gratified that Ian could relax so completely around him even after seeing him lose control twice the day before. He couldn't decide if that meant he had been less out of control than he thought or if it just made Ian naïve. Either way, he could certainly live with the results.

He shifted on the bed a bit so Ian rested more comfortably against him. He should lay Ian back against the pillows so he could sleep in peace, but he was loath to release him.

Ian's color was better, his skin not as pallid beneath the layer of soot that hadn't been wiped completely away. When he could do without the oxygen for a few minutes, he'd need a shower. Neil had said he'd call Carley to have her bring a change of clothes, but Thorne didn't know how long it would take her to get to the hospital. He supposed Ian could wear a hospital gown until then, if necessary. He had a bed and sheets to preserve his modesty if it came to that.

Remembering his own hospitalizations and how quickly he'd become bored, he cast around for something to give Ian to help pass the time. Thorne could justify staying until he was sure Ian was stable and until someone else got here to sit with him, but Captain Grant would expect him back eventually, and if nothing else, Neil and the others would want to know Ian's prognosis. He was somewhat surprised they hadn't called Ian's phone yet to check on him, but maybe they couldn't get a signal, although that didn't bode well for Carley coming with a change of clothes, or maybe they were too busy with the fires. That thought wasn't particularly reassuring either. In the three days he'd worked with the men and women of Lang Downs, he'd come to appreciate their determination, their friendliness, and their sense of community. A blow to any of them would be a blow to all of them.

He wished he knew more about Ian and what he did with his free time besides work with wood. The hospital staff wouldn't appreciate Thorne bringing Ian a carving knife and a block of wood, but Ian hadn't mentioned any other pastime. Maybe he could ask Carley when she got there. He didn't know how close they were, but she had a better chance of knowing what he liked than Thorne did.

He wished he had his Kindle, but it was with the rest of his nonessential gear at a buddy's house in Wagga Wagga. He never brought anything he couldn't stand to lose to a fire site. He'd lost too much to fire already.

Ian shifted in his sleep, turning his head toward Thorne's chest. The oxygen mask dug into Thorne's sternum, but he didn't move away. If Ian needed to nuzzle closer to feel safe, Thorne would bear it and be grateful he could give Ian the comfort he needed. He wasn't sure Ian realized yet how close he'd come to dying, but at some point he would, and when he did, he'd need all the support he could get to cope with it. Even battle-hardened as he had become in the Commandos, Thorne still had moments of terror when a situation forced him to stare his own mortality in the face. For Ian, who had no training and no expectation of finding himself in such a situation, it would be a hundred times worse.

He'd seen his team seek comfort in a bottle, in the arms of a loved one, in the willing body of a stranger, and he'd seen one of them seek it in drugs. The ones who had a loved one to turn to coped the best, but Thorne already knew Ian had no one special. He refused to hope he could be that someone special, but he'd be the willing stranger if it made a difference. And if that wasn't what Ian needed, Thorne would figure out what he did and he'd move heaven and earth to get it for him, because Thorne hadn't been there to watch Ian's back and he'd nearly died because of it. The twenty men Williams had sent from Taylor Peak weren't worth Ian's life. He should have left well enough alone.

He could feel his hands starting to tremble as the rage that never fully left him built toward a boiling point. He couldn't lose it here with Ian relying on him. He had to keep it under control for a little longer. When Carley got here, he could go take his frustration out on the fire front where it belonged.

He focused on slowing his breathing, on dropping into the battle-ready mindset that gave him complete control over his body and settled his mind. When he attained that plane, nothing could sneak up on him, nothing could ruffle him. He became a machine, capable of anything required of him, from complete stillness for hours on end to lethal motion designed to put an end to an enemy as quickly and cleanly as possible. He had no enemy to fight here, but he had an innocent to protect, and that required complete stillness. It took longer than he would have liked, but he settled into the zone finally, his body coming back under his command so he could sit motionless and hold Ian while he slept.

In his hyperaware state, he heard every footstep in the hallway outside Ian's room, the beeping of monitors, and the sound of voices in soft discussion, but none of them posed a threat to his charge and so none of them disturbed his stillness. As time passed, he separated one set of footsteps from another—the short crisp steps of someone wearing heels, the slightly shuffling tread of someone in gym shoes, the heavy clomp of boots, another set of heels, but this one slower, as if the wearer had all the time in the world to get where she was going. He'd identified fifteen different people by their footsteps by the time a new set of footsteps paused outside Ian's door.

Every muscle in his body tensed in preparation so he could protect Ian if necessary, but he held himself still until he could assess the threat. The door opened and a familiar face peeked around the jamb. "Can I come in?"

Thorne nodded, trying to diffuse the adrenaline that had swamped him at the fight-or-flight reaction. "He's asleep," he said, as if Carley couldn't see that for herself.

"Good, I'm glad he can rest." She carried a small duffel bag in and set it on the chair Thorne had occupied earlier. "There's a change of clothes for him, and one for you, as well as the book he asked for. I'm going to find something to eat before I relieve you. I skipped lunch to get here. Do you need anything else while I'm out?"

"No," Thorne said. "We'll be fine."

She looked like she wanted to offer again, so Thorne turned his attention back to Ian, dismissing her silently. He couldn't deal with her right now, even knowing she was friend, not foe. Everything felt like a threat in his current state. He had to let it go, but he didn't know how. When he was still in the Commandos, this kind of situation either ended with a fight or with his entire team needing the same release, which they got by beating the hell out of each other in the guise of hand-to-hand combat training. He heard the door close behind her and let out a shuddering breath. He had to find a punching bag or a treadmill or a set of weights so he could release some of the tension before Ian woke up and expected him to be normal.

Carefully, so he wouldn't disturb Ian's rest, he laid him back onto the pillows. His boots weren't ideal for a run, but it wouldn't be the first time he'd worn them. He'd do laps around the hospital grounds until he could think straight again, and then he'd come back and keep Ian company.

NINE

IAN looked up from his book when the door opened. Carley had come and gone with the promise of someone coming to visit again tomorrow. She'd also told him Thorne was still around, although she wasn't sure where. Ian had nodded at that and tried to ignore the implication in her smile. He'd sought refuge in his all-time favorite fantasy novel instead, and as always, he'd got lost in the story of Sioned and Rohan and their struggle to protect their lands from the forces aligned against them. He'd only read about fifty pages, not that he needed to finish it when he could practically retell the story scene by scene, but when he saw it was Thorne, he put the book aside and smiled behind the oxygen mask.

"Have a good nap?" Thorne asked.

Ian nodded and gestured to the chair where the bag Carley brought still sat.

"Yes, she told me she'd brought me clean clothes," Thorne said. "I thought I'd wait to put them on until after I showered. I worked up a bit of a sweat."

Ian raised an eyebrow in question. It seemed an odd time to go for a run, or whatever Thorne did for exercise, but he was clearly sweaty and slightly out of breath, so he'd obviously done some kind of exercise while Ian slept.

"I went for a bit of a jog," Thorne said. "Post-mission stress. I have to burn it off somehow, and running is a safe way for everyone involved."

Ian pointed to the door into the en-suite bathroom.

"Thanks. I will rinse off, if you're sure you don't mind."

Ian shook his head and shooed Thorne toward the bathroom. Thorne grinned and grabbed the bag, so Ian settled back into his book. He was so caught up in the story he didn't hear Thorne come back out until he spoke. "*Dragon Prince*. I haven't read that one. Is it good?"

Ian nodded enthusiastically and handed the book to Thorne. He really wished he could talk at the moment. All the wonderful things he could tell Thorne about the book and the series, all the questions he wanted to ask about what books Thorne had read, since his choice of words implied he was a fantasy reader, piled up behind the oxygen mask. He looked around in frustration for something to write on, but he didn't see paper or a pen.

"This looks pretty interesting," Thorne said. "Maybe I'll borrow it when you're done."

Ian gestured for Thorne to take it now.

"Then what will you read?" Thorne asked. Ian glared at him. "Sorry, I shouldn't ask questions you can't answer with a shake of your head. Maybe the nurse has some paper so you can write what you want to say. Want me to ask?"

Ian nodded emphatically and watched as Thorne set the book carefully on the chair before leaving the room. Ian appreciated the thoughtfulness. Some people weren't as careful with their books as Ian was. He'd watched other jackaroos on the station toss a book on a table or a chair like it was nothing special, and maybe that particular book wasn't special to that particular jackaroo, but as far as Ian was concerned, all books were special and deserved to be treated that way. Thorne seemed to agree, or at least he was careful enough to treat other people's books with respect.

Thorne returned a moment later with a pad of paper and a pen. "Here we go. Now we can talk to each other."

Ian took the items from Thorne and started writing.

Do you like fantasy? he wrote.

"I love fantasy," Thorne said. "My Kindle is full of it. I just never picked this one up. I've seen it a couple of times, but I'd never talked to anyone who read it to get an opinion. So you say it's good."

It's my favorite. I've probably read it a hundred times.

"Wow, that good? Maybe I will borrow it when you're done," Thorne said.

Take it now. I'll ask someone to bring me another one tomorrow.

"I shouldn't take it with me," Thorne said. "I'm going back to the fire front. If something happened to it, I'd never forgive myself. I'll read it in the evenings when I come check on you."

Ian smiled, charmed despite himself. He'd expected Thorne to make sure he was okay and then make do with updates from whoever from the station came to visit. He hadn't expected him to come back every day.

How long do I have to stay in the hospital? he wrote.

"I don't know," Thorne replied. "The only information anyone has given me was that you were on oxygen, had been given something for your cough, and were doing better."

Ian knew that much himself. *Ask someone when they come back in?*

"Yes, I'll ask for you," Thorne promised. "Have you read *Memory, Sorrow, and Thorn*? That's one of my favorite series."

Ian nodded. *I liked it, but not as much as* Dragon Prince.

"Then I really will have to read this one."

You're welcome to read anything on my bookshelves at home, Ian offered. *Just put them back where you found them when you're done. Everything's organized.*

"Author, series, and then the order within the series?" Thorne asked with a grin.

And publication date for the series, Ian wrote back. He could feel himself flushing at how picky he was, but Thorne just nodded.

"Makes sense to me. If I borrow a book, I'll be sure to get it back in the right spot. I'd offer to leave you my Kindle so you'd have more choice, but I left it at a friend's house in Wagga Wagga. I didn't want to bring it with me to fight the fires. It's one thing to have it on a base somewhere, even somewhere remote, because bases come under fire far less than individual patrols do, but out fighting a fire, there's no base, really. I mean, we have a base camp, but it's not protected except by distance, and if the fire moves in an unexpected way, the camp could be overrun. I don't have a lot I wouldn't want to lose, but my Kindle is one of those things."

Ian nodded. His thoughts tumbled over themselves at the implications behind Thorne's words, but with only a pad of paper at his disposal for communication, sorting them out seemed a monumental task. The thing that struck him most, though, was that Thorne left the Kindle with a friend, not at his own home. Did he even have a place to call home? It didn't sound like it, and that made Ian incredibly sad.

Where do you live when you aren't fighting fires? he wrote.

"Until a couple of months ago, I lived on whatever army base I was assigned to," Thorne said. "It was cheaper and more convenient than off-base housing, and it's not like I have a family to worry about. Since I left the army, I've been fighting fires, so I've been living out of a tent wherever the fires are."

And when the fires are out?

"I guess I'll have to find somewhere to live," Thorne said. "I don't have any strong attachment to anywhere, so I suppose it'll be a matter of where I can find a job."

What about your family?

"I don't have any family left," Thorne said. "They died in an accident a long time ago."

I'm sorry, Ian wrote, feeling like a dick for bringing up what were obviously still painful memories, no matter how old they were.

"You didn't know," Thorne said. "It's a logical assumption. Maybe I'll get lucky and build a family the way you have."

Ian wanted desperately to suggest Thorne stay on the station, but it wasn't his place to do so without talking to Caine and Macklin first, and even that was presumptuous. He didn't know if Thorne had any interest in working on a sheep station. Ian loved it, but he'd talked to plenty of people who gave it a try for a summer and decided it wasn't for them.

Before he could figure out what to say, the door to his room opened again, and Neil, Caine, and Macklin came in. Ian waved in greeting since he couldn't say hello and listened as they peppered Thorne with questions regarding his status. Thorne answered the ones he could and promised to get someone to answer the ones he couldn't. The doctor came in a few minutes later, and it wasn't until the doctor had left and Caine had sent Neil off to fetch dinner that Ian realized Thorne hadn't come back in after he went to find the doctor.

Where's Thorne? he wrote on his pad. He passed it to Caine.

"I don't know," Caine said. "Do you want me to go look for him?"

Ian shook his head. Thorne was an adult. He could take care of himself, and Ian needed to grow up and stop feeling neglected because Thorne had left without saying good-bye.

"Maybe he went to get something to eat. I'm pretty sure he hadn't eaten since breakfast," Caine said. "I bet he'll be back before long."

Ian wasn't as sure, but he didn't argue. Instead he wrote, *Are the fires contained?*

"Mostly, for the moment, anyway," Caine said. "They're not out, but they're contained again, so as long as they don't jump the firebreaks, they should burn out in a few days. Of course they're forecasting storms again tonight, so we'll have to contend with the possibility of new fires from lightning strikes, especially if we get the lighting but no rain, like we've gotten the last few times we've had storms roll through."

Ian nodded. Storms in this season always brought the risk of fires, especially when they'd had such a dry winter and spring. Nobody expected a wet summer, but the lack of rain over the winter had definitely added to the problems they were facing now.

"Did you get everything you needed from home?" Macklin asked. "We're heading back to the station tonight. We can have someone bring you anything else you need.

Ian nodded. *More books?*

Macklin laughed. "Tell me which ones."

It really didn't matter as far as Ian was concerned. He'd read everything on his shelves. Thorne was interested in *Dragon Prince*, though, so he'd have Macklin send the rest of that series. Ian certainly didn't mind rereading them, and that way Thorne could continue with the series in the evenings if he was interested. And if he wasn't, well, Ian could forgive him his slip in taste since he obviously enjoyed fantasy in general. He wrote the titles down and gave them to Macklin.

VISITING hours were almost over by the time Thorne made it back to the hospital. Things had got a little intense when Ian brought up his future, and he'd needed an escape, but he felt bad for leaving Ian with no explanation. He didn't know what he could have said, but he still felt like he should have said something. He'd driven around a bit until he'd found a small bookstore, and that had given him an idea. Of course, going into a bookstore was always more time-consuming than he anticipated, but he'd walked out with Tad Williams's latest in the hopes it hadn't been out long enough for Ian to have picked it up yet. If Ian already had it, Thorne would keep it for himself. He rarely bought books in paperback since he'd bought his Kindle, but he could keep one book. It wouldn't take up that much more space in the corner of Walker's apartment.

"Hi," he said when he walked into Ian's room to find him alone again. "I got you something."

Ian looked up from his book and lifted that elegant eyebrow at him again. Thorne had the insane desire to plant a kiss right there, but he wasn't sure how Ian would feel about it. He settled for handing Ian the bag with the book in it.

"I'm hoping it's new enough that you haven't read it yet," Thorne said as Ian pulled the book out of the bag and looked at it. He shook his head after a minute, and Thorne finally relaxed. He wasn't sure his apology had worked, but at least he'd bought a book Ian hadn't read.

"Did Caine and Macklin head back to Lang Downs?" Thorne asked.

Ian nodded.

"Did the doctor answer some of your questions?"

Ian nodded again and reached for the pad of paper by his bed. He scribbled for a moment and handed the pad to Thorne. *5 to 7 days depending on how I do*, he read, *but they'll start taking the mask off for short periods of time tomorrow.*

"Good," Thorne said. "This is better than nothing, but talking to you will be much easier."

Faster too, Ian wrote down.

"Yes, faster too," Thorne agreed. "I should probably head back soon. I don't want to try to drive those dirt tracks in the dark. If I knew the area a little better, it wouldn't be so bad, but I don't want to get lost or stuck somewhere. I'll come see you tomorrow evening, though, okay?"

Ian nodded. *Stay safe.*

Thorne smiled when he read the short note. Taking a chance, he leaned forward and kissed Ian's cheek. "I will," he promised. "I have a reason to now."

He watched Ian's eyes go wide for a second and hoped he hadn't overstepped his bounds, but then Ian smiled and reached for his hand. Thorne returned the tight squeeze and the smile. He didn't want to go. He wanted to curl up on the bed next to Ian and keep watch over him for the night. Not that anything bad was going to happen in the hospital, and even if Ian did take a turn for the worse, he was in the right place to get help, but the idea of leaving Ian alone sat wrong with Thorne. He doubted the hospital would let him stay. His status with the RFS had earned him some leniency today, but in his experience, hospitals were pretty strict about visiting hours unless the patient was in critical condition, which Ian wasn't. He'd spend a miserable night on a cramped bed that wasn't made for two people, and he'd pay for it with a sore back all day, and yet he couldn't make himself stand up and leave.

Finally Ian pulled his hand free to pick up the pen again. *I wish I could kiss you again.*

Thorne's breath caught in his throat. "If you weren't stuck in that hospital bed, I'd do a whole lot more than just kiss you," he promised. "Maybe tomorrow they'll take the mask off while I'm here and I can kiss you properly."

Ian nodded and started coughing at the same time.

"Shit, I'm sorry," Thorne said. "I didn't mean to set off another fit."

Ian shook his head, but Thorne couldn't help feeling responsible. Ian's breathing hadn't been at all perturbed until Thorne had brought up the possibility of sex. He pressed another gentle kiss to Ian's forehead. "I'll leave you alone now. I'm sorry I upset you, but I promise I'll keep Lang Downs safe for you. I'll see you tomorrow night, okay?"

Ian frowned and grabbed Thorne's hand to stop him from leaving, but Thorne slipped free of his grip. "I'll see you tomorrow night," he repeated. He didn't know what Ian wanted to say, but he couldn't deal with it tonight. He'd do his job tomorrow, and tomorrow night, when Ian could talk, they'd sort things out. "Enjoy your book."

He heard Ian's noise of protest or frustration or both, but he didn't let it stop him from leaving. He couldn't. He tainted everything he touched these days, and he wouldn't do that to Ian.

He made it back to his ute and rested his forehead against the steering wheel. Fuck, he needed a drink. Actually he needed to get rip-roaring drunk and fuck the first willing trick to come along, but that wasn't going to happen. He'd made a promise to Ian, and he wasn't going to break it, which meant driving back out to the fire line tonight so he could make sure it didn't threaten Lang Downs tomorrow.

IAN stared down at the book in his hand because he couldn't stand to look at the empty hospital room. He'd mostly been okay with his solitude after Caine and Macklin left because he told himself Thorne had gone to get dinner and would be back later, but now Thorne was gone for the night, and that was a very different kettle of fish. It shouldn't have bothered him. He spent far more evenings alone than with company, and he'd only spent one evening with Thorne. Certainly not enough to justify feeling this nagging sense of his absence.

It was the way Thorne had left that unsettled Ian so much. He'd come back in almost shyly with his gift in hand. He'd pressed it into Ian's hands with an endearing awkwardness that made the gift even more precious. Thorne clearly wasn't used to giving gifts and hadn't been sure what kind of reception he'd get, but he'd taken the time to pick something Ian would enjoy. Then he'd kissed Ian's cheek so tenderly, and Ian had ached for another kiss, a real one, and he'd said so. Even now, he could hardly believe his own temerity. He didn't say things like that. He didn't *feel* things like that, except apparently he did, and Thorne had reacted exactly as Ian had expected, wanting more than just a kiss. Ian told himself that wasn't a bad thing. It was normal to want a kiss to become more. They were grown men. They were free to engage in kisses that led to sex. Thorne had no reason to suspect Ian wasn't normal in that regard, that the mere thought of sex scared him witless, although maybe his coughing fit had given Thorne a clue if the way he'd taken off right after was any indication.

Ian frowned at the book again. Had he ruined everything before it had a chance to start? The thought made him feel vaguely ill, but the thought of what a relationship between them would logically entail was even worse. Not to mention that this whole train of thought was predicated on Thorne staying, which didn't seem particularly likely. He didn't have anywhere else he had to be, but that didn't mean he'd want to stay on the station. Nor did it mean Caine and Macklin could afford to hire another jackaroo year-round, especially someone they'd have to train. They'd taken Chris and Seth in, but originally that had been for the summer, and by the time they'd asked them to stay, Chris knew his way around the station. They'd taken Sam in, but his skills in managing the station's finances had proven a huge boon to Caine and Macklin. Sam wasn't a jackaroo, but he had useful skills in other aspects of the business. Ian had no clue what skills Thorne had outside of fighting fires and wars. He was sure Thorne had learned other things in the military, but he didn't know if any of them would transfer to the station.

You're getting ahead of yourself, he scolded silently. *None of this will matter if he wants more than you can give him.*

With a miserable sigh, he set Thorne's gift aside and went back to reading *Dragon Prince*. It didn't require any concentration, not like a new book would. Instead he could relax into the mindlessness of it and forget for a few hours that he was too broken for anyone to put up with him for long.

TEN

THORNE fought his way through the burning forest, slowed down by the dead weight slung across his shoulder. He had to get free of the trees, but every way he turned, something blocked his path: a wall of flames, a pile of dead bodies, insurgents with machine guns and machetes pointed at him and the precious cargo he carried. He spun to the left only to come face-to-face with a suspended body. From the look of it, it had been hanging there for a few days. The fire hadn't got to it yet, but the carrion crows had. Bile rose in his throat, but he made himself check the face in case it was recognizable.

Ian's green eyes stared blankly out of their swollen sockets.

He stumbled back away from the body, trying not to retch. He had to keep moving. If he stopped, they'd both die, and he couldn't allow that. He'd already failed so many times, so many people. He couldn't fail this time. He wouldn't survive another loss.

He veered around the corpse and kept going down the trail. The death was horrendous, but the body wasn't burned. The fire hadn't come this far yet, so this path should be safe. He would bring his burden home and everything would be well.

He'd gone another fifty feet when something in the undergrowth caught his foot, and he nearly fell. Catching his balance, he looked to see what had tripped him up. Booted feet lay across the path. He followed the legs up to a body, but he knew right away there was no hope for life. Half the chest was torn away. Nobody could have survived such a wound. Hoping for some identification, he rolled the body over, only to lose his battle with his stomach.

Ian's eyes were closed, but there was no mistaking his red hair and freckles, or the sweet curve of his lips.

He had to get away. He had to get to safety. He picked up his burden again, running this time despite the weight he carried. The forest was dangerous even without the fire. First the body that had been hanged and now this one, torn apart by a roadside bomb or landmine. They couldn't stay here if they wanted to live. They had to get back to base, to safety and treatment and the possibility of salvation.

The trail curved off to the right ahead of him. He frowned at that. The fire was to his right. They couldn't go that way, but he didn't see a path going any other way, and they couldn't go back. Danger lay behind them. The fire lay to their right. He would have to take the trail anyway and hope the turn was only a short one to avoid some obstacle ahead of them. He followed the path only to find a line of bodies laid out next to it. Their hands were tied behind their backs and they each had a single bullet wound to the back of their heads. Executions, then, not that it made seeing the bodies any easier. Most frightening of all, though, they all had familiar short red hair. He knew without needing to look that every body in that row bore Ian's face.

He sprinted past them, desperation riding him hard. The base had to be right ahead. He'd been carrying the body on his back long enough now. The forest blurred as he ran, tree trunks blending together in a crazy kaleidoscope of colors and sensations. Flashes of red against the green and brown of the trees tried to catch his attention, but he ignored them. He couldn't see another body bearing Ian's likeness. He couldn't stop. He had to get his teammate to safety.

With a final burst of speed, he made it through the door of the base just as it swung shut behind him. Carefully, so very, very carefully, he eased the body off his shoulders onto the cot in the medical ward. Ian's eyes were closed, but Thorne wasn't deterred. He called for the doctor as he felt for a pulse. It was weak but present, so he hovered at Ian's side until the doctor got there and started checking him for injuries.

They searched every inch of his body, but they couldn't find a single mark to explain Ian's unconscious state. No wounds, no contusions, nothing to give them any hint of finding a cure. He simply lay there unmoving, his breaths coming more and more slowly. The doctor started an IV, pushing fluids or medicine or who knew what into Ian's body, but nothing changed. And then the breathing stopped, and his chest went motionless. Thorne sprang into action, breathing into Ian's lungs to keep them moving, putting his fingers on the pulse at Ian's neck to monitor his heartbeat. That, too, was painfully sluggish, but still there, so he kept breathing for both of them. He could do this. He'd do it for as long as it took. The doctor would find the cause and fix it, and Thorne would provide breath and even a pulse for Ian until that time. He wouldn't lose him. Not again.

The pulse flickered out and Thorne started CPR. Thirty compressions, two breaths, thirty compressions, two breaths. He had no idea how long he worked to give the doctor time to find a solution, but his arms grew tired and his lungs burned from the strain. Hands pulled at his shoulders, trying to drag him away from Ian, but he resisted. Couldn't they see? Didn't they understand? Ian wasn't dead. He was just sleeping. Thorne just needed to wake him up.

The hands pulled again, succeeding this time in separating him from Ian. As the medics covered his body with a sheet, Thorne threw his head back and howled in defeat.

The sound of his own shout brought Thorne out of his nightmare and back to the present. His heart pounded frantically in his chest, and he gasped for breath as he tried to dispel the dream images and reconnect with reality. He was lying on Ian's couch, the blankets so tangled around him he could barely move. It was still dark outside, although Thorne thought it must be getting close to morning, but the light from the lamp he'd left on when he fell asleep made it hard to judge the quality of the darkness. He was safe and whole, if a little battered. His back stung where the rocks had cut it the day before, but that was a minor annoyance in the grand scheme of things. The book he'd been reading before bed sat on the table still, waiting for him to pick it up again. In short, his nightmare had been just that: a hypnagogic amalgam of his worst experiences with death and dying, Ian's face superimposed over the faces of men he had seen murdered, executed, or killed in battle, and finally on Walker's face. He knew Nick wasn't dead. Thorne's stuff was at Nick's apartment, but he'd nearly died, and Thorne would carry the memory of that frantic flight through the forest for the rest of his life.

He could have done without the nightmares, though.

He'd had enough experience with bad dreams and his reaction to them to know he wouldn't be able to get back to sleep, so he untangled himself from the covers, folded them neatly, and went to shower. He'd clear the cobwebs from his head and get an early start back to the fire line. He couldn't change the past, but he could bloody well make sure Ian had a home to come back to when the doctors released him in a few days.

"ANYBODY seen Thorne this morning?"

"No, why?" Neil asked, looking up from his breakfast.

"Because he didn't come back to the main house last night, and his ute isn't with the others," Caine said. "Did he come back to the station at all?"

"He did," Neil said. "I heard him go into Ian's place last night. Maybe he parked by Ian's house instead of with the other utes?"

"I don't think so," Caine said, but he went to the window to check. "No, I don't see any sign of him."

Neil frowned. Thorne had risked his life yesterday to save Ian, winning Neil's loyalty almost as fully as Caine had it for saving Neil's own life. "Bloody hell, I hope he hasn't gone and done something stupid."

"Is that a concern?" Macklin asked, joining Caine at the window.

"Maybe." Neil gestured for them to join him. Ian wouldn't appreciate Neil revealing any of what he was about to say, but it would be even worse if he shared it with the whole canteen. "You know Thorne's got issues, right?" Caine and Macklin nodded. "Well, he's apparently latched on to Ian as someone safe. Two nights ago, he almost lost it again, and he let Ian stay with him while he calmed down. They talked for a while and Thorne slept on his couch. Maybe it doesn't mean anything, but when Thorne found out Ian was missing yesterday, he was like a madman. Ian's my best friend, but I wouldn't have gone back into that hellhole to look for him. I wouldn't have known where to start, for one thing. Thorne threw himself down into the inferno like it was nothing, and he came back with Ian. And…."

He hesitated a bit now. What he'd told them so far was pretty much public knowledge, things Neil had observed, not things Ian had shared in confidence, but to continue would break Ian's confidence. He looked at the two men sitting across from him. If anyone on the station needed to know what Ian had said, it was these two, because any kind of long-term relationship would require their blessing. "And I think Ian likes him. I mean, is interested in him."

Macklin raised his eyebrows in surprise. "Ian?"

"Yes, Ian," Neil said. "I've known him a long time, and he's never shown any interest in anyone. I don't know Thorne well enough to know if he returns it, but he saved Ian's life. I kind of feel like we owe it to Thorne to make sure he gets the chance to make up his own mind."

"Not to mention you'd like to see Ian happy," Caine said.

"Yeah, there's that too. He has a smile for everyone and a kind word, but have you ever looked at his eyes?" Neil asked. "He's always alone, even in a crowd. Even with me. If Thorne can take that look away, I'll do whatever it takes to let him."

"But you think he's gone and done something stupid," Macklin said.

"Maybe I'm wrong," Neil said, "but while I'm thrilled with the results, going after Ian yesterday was pretty much the definition of something stupid, and he stayed at Ian's place again last night instead of going back to the guest room that has to be more comfortable than Ian's couch. I'm not even going to guess at what's going through his head, but I'd put money on it not being rational."

"So what do you suggest?" Caine asked.

"Keep an eye on him," Neil replied. "Maybe I'm wrong and everything will be just fine, but if I'm right and he starts doing stupid shit, maybe we can make him see it, and if we can't, maybe we can protect him from himself."

"There are kids on the station," Macklin said. "We can't have him here if he's a threat to them."

"I know," Neil said. "One of those kids is mine, and about to be two, but the kids can learn to respect his boundaries just like adults can, and he didn't actually hurt Laura. He saved Ian's life. Isn't that worth giving him the benefit of the doubt?"

"Yes," Caine said before Macklin could reply, "but there's still a line he can't cross, and if he does, we'll have to ask him to leave."

"That's fair," Neil said. "Thank you. I'm going to grab a passenger and head back to the fires. I don't like the idea that he's out there by himself."

"You know the other Firies are out there too," Macklin said.

"Yeah, but I don't know them. I trust our men to watch his back."

"We'll meet you there as soon as we can," Caine said.

"Thanks," Neil said. He grabbed his hat and the keys to one of the utes and found a jackaroo who'd already finished his breakfast. The other man grumbled a little about being pulled away, but Neil was the foreman. None of them would argue with him for long.

THE fire had moved from where they'd been fighting it before, Thorne discovered when he reached the base camp. The flames in the deadfall and surrounding woods had burned out overnight for the most part, although Captain Grant had ordered a crew to check for hot spots and put them out if possible. The firebreaks had worked on one side, but it had jumped the break on the other side and was creeping through the fields to the west of the ridge where they'd fought the day before.

"We've got to put it out," Thorne said. "It's not enough to try to contain it. Each time we do, it jumps the firebreak and keeps going."

"I don't have the men or the equipment to fight it directly," Captain Grant protested.

"You will," Thorne said. "When the Lang Downs folk get here again, their utes can go into the grasslands. They were useless in the woods, but they won't be out in the open. Have them start at the firebreak and work inward, dousing the fire as they go. If they maintain a fairly tight line, they should be able to put a huge dent in the fires."

"That's asking a lot of them."

"It's their lives and their livelihoods at stake," Thorne said. "I don't see them saying no."

"Fine, I'll ask," the captain said, "but until they get here, I want everyone working to widen the firebreak."

Thorne didn't acknowledge the order. He should have. He knew it was the logical thing to do with so few people and such a powerful fire, but he couldn't make himself retreat that way. Every inch of grassland the fire burned was an inch closer to Lang Downs and Ian's home. Thorne had failed at protecting Ian. He wasn't going to fail again. He grabbed one of the portable foam sprayers and joined a crew heading toward the firebreak.

No one looked at him askance since they often soaked the firebreaks with foam to decrease the likelihood of the flames catching any lingering fuel in the breaks, but when they got to their destination, Thorne didn't stop. The foam worked well as a flame retardant, but it would also work to smother the flames at their source.

He heard shouts behind him, but he didn't turn back. They could follow orders or come with him as they pleased. He intended to keep putting out the fires directly.

AN HOUR later, Thorne headed back to the firebreak to switch out the tank on his back. He couldn't say he'd stopped the fire completely, but he'd done his damnedest to put a dent in it. The other Firies watched in resignation as he switched the container and turned back toward the open grasslands. He'd gone ten feet when someone grabbed his arm, spinning him around. His fists came up automatically, but he stopped the instinctive punch when he saw Neil's face.

"Where the fuck do you think you're going?" Neil demanded.

"To do my job," Thorne replied shortly. "The fire is out there, not here."

"So you're just going to march out there by yourself with no backup? Are you bloody stupid?"

"I know what I'm doing," Thorne insisted.

"And who's going to explain it to Ian when you get yourself killed?" Neil shouted. "You're going to make me walk into that hospital room and tell my best friend the first person he's ever been interested in went and did something stupid and is laid up with burns or worse, and when that happens, I'm going to forget how grateful I am you saved his life and fucking kill you myself."

"I promised him I wouldn't let the fires win," Thorne protested even as he reeled at what Neil's words had revealed. "He's lost so much already. He can't lose his home."

"He won't lose his home," Neil replied. "Even if the buildings burn to the ground, he won't lose his home, because Lang Downs isn't a collection of buildings in a valley. It's the men and women who live there, who believe in everything it represents, and if you can't see that, maybe you don't belong there after all."

"What?"

"I went to bat for you this morning," Neil said. "I told Caine and Macklin you belonged on the station and asked them to watch your back the way they watch our backs. I told them I thought you could be good for Ian, but if you can't see the most basic fact about who we are and how we work, then maybe I was wrong."

Thorne had to stop and process that for a moment. He couldn't believe his ears—first that Ian had said something to Neil about him, and then that Neil had translated that into the potential of staying at Lang Downs, of actually having a home again. It sounded almost too good to be true. More importantly, it was too much to deal with right now.

"Listen, the captain is being conservative. He's trying to contain the fire instead of putting it out, and with a limited number of men, that's not a bad plan, but with all the utes and tanks and men from Lang Downs, we can be more aggressive. We can put the fires out instead of trying to contain them as they burn themselves out. We couldn't do it in the forest. There was too much fuel and not enough space, but the fires don't burn as hot or as fast in the grasslands. They smolder and inch along instead of blazing up like they did yesterday. If we string a line of utes together and work our way forward, spraying down the flames as we find them, I think we can beat this thing. Just by myself, I was able to stop a section of it, but it's too much to finish alone."

"I'll try it," Neil said, "but it's not my decision alone. Let me talk to the others."

Thorne nodded and went back to his ute. He'd leave the foam sprayer there and ride out with one of the utes from Lang Downs. He could spray water from there, and he knew where the fire line was. He'd be able to get them there as efficiently as possible.

"You didn't listen to your captain's orders this morning."

Thorne spun around to see Macklin coming toward him. He forced down his reaction, because Macklin didn't look in any mood to deal with it, and Thorne suddenly had a reason to want to leave a good impression on the man in front of him.

"They weren't good orders," Thorne replied.

"Maybe they weren't, but you deliberately did something reckless on your own without backup," Macklin said.

"And Neil's already yelled at me for it."

"And probably said more than he should have, if I know him," Macklin said with a shake of his head. "His temper will get him killed one of these days. I'm not going to yell. I'm just going to say this: sometimes risks are necessary, but I can't have someone on my station who puts people at risk by being reckless. There is a difference, and you'd better learn it if you plan on hanging around for long."

Macklin's words cut even deeper than Neil's had. Macklin had the power to make it possible for Thorne to stay at Lang Downs with Ian, to give them the time and space to see if they could build something together beyond the frantic kiss they'd shared in the smoke the day before. Macklin also had the power to send him away and deny him that chance. He didn't give a fuck what the captain thought of him, but Macklin's good opinion was suddenly critical.

"I'll be more careful," he promised, "but I have a plan. An actual workable plan. Yes, there's a risk, but I don't think it's reckless. The captain's strategy isn't working. We've got to try something else."

"I'm listening," Macklin said. He still had his arms crossed over his chest, nothing in his body language particularly receptive, but Thorne forged ahead. This was his chance to show Macklin he could think under pressure, that he could analyze a situation and balance risk and gain. He hadn't done it this morning when he'd stormed away from the firebreak by himself, but he *could* do it. He'd done it for years with the Commandos. It was time to put it on display again.

By the time Thorne had finished explaining his plan, Macklin had relaxed and was nodding.

"All right, here's what we're going to do."

Macklin outlined the safety guidelines he considered essential to the plan, all of which Thorne accepted. These men were Ian's friends. He didn't want to have to tell Ian they'd been hurt any more than Neil wanted to tell Ian that Thorne had been hurt, especially if Thorne could do something to prevent it.

ELEVEN

THORNE dragged into the hospital after dinner, but while his body was exhausted, his smile was victorious. His plan had worked and the fires they had set out that morning to combat had been significantly reduced. They'd encountered a few areas where they hadn't been able to get the utes close enough to spray the flames. Thorne had been all for going in on foot, but a single look from Macklin had quelled the suggestion before it could leave his mouth. They'd have to keep an eye on those spots to see if they burned out or if they spread back into areas where the fires were now out, but it had been the first day of what Thorne considered significant progress in weeks.

Even more importantly, Thorne had felt like part of a team again today. At the height of his career, with a team of men he trusted, he'd been one cog in an incredibly successful machine. He hadn't realized how much he'd missed that feeling of camaraderie until he had it returned to him today. Macklin ran the operation with all the skill of any drill sergeant Thorne had ever known, keeping everyone in place, directing utes from one area to another as they encountered varying intensities of fire, and the men under his command had reacted instantly, with a level of teamwork and trust that Thorne envied.

It seemed Neil had been right. They weren't some motley collection of jackaroos, no matter how much they might look that way. They were a team, held together by the year-rounders who hardly even needed to talk to communicate. He'd seen them react to a gesture, even to a look, and he knew that kind of rapport didn't happen in a few days or weeks. It took years to learn to work together like that, years they had obviously spent together.

He wasn't one of them yet, but they'd included him. They'd even listened to him when he'd pointed out problems in their approach. As long as he explained the logic in his suggestions, they were willing to go with them, only overriding him when the danger outweighed the potential benefits.

Neil's words echoed through Thorne's head again: *"Lang Downs isn't the buildings. It's the people who make it what it is."*

He'd spent the day protecting and being protected by those people, and he yearned for that to continue with a depth of need he couldn't begin to plumb.

The key to that continued acceptance lay behind the door in front of him. Neil had made it very clear why they were so willing to accept Thorne as one of them. He'd saved Ian's life, and that meant he deserved a chance at winning their respect and securing Ian's interest. He only hoped he could be worthy of both.

He wished he'd had a way to clean up before coming to the hospital, but he hadn't had time to go back to Lang Downs and still make it before visiting hours ended, so he'd just have to be a mess. At least he wasn't sporting any new cuts or scrapes this time. He might be sweaty and covered in soot, but he wasn't bleeding.

After taking a fortifying breath, he pushed the door open and walked into Ian's room.

"Hi," Ian croaked from the bed.

Thorne smiled. Ian no longer wore the oxygen mask, although it hung from a hook next to his pillow. He was wearing his own clothes today, and all the soot was gone from his face and hair, so they'd obviously deemed him stable enough to get up and move around.

"Hi, how are you feeling?"

"Better today," Ian said. "I still get short of breath, but they let me off the oxygen for a few hours to see how I'd do."

"I'm glad I'm here when the mask is off," Thorne said.

Ian flushed a little. "I asked if I could wait until dinner to take it off so I wouldn't be wearing it when you were here. If you were able to come, of course."

"I promised, didn't I?" Thorne said.

"Yes, but sometimes people don't keep their promises, even with the best of intentions. Life sometimes gets in the way."

Thorne wondered who had broken promises to Ian in the past and where he could find them to take the sadness in Ian's eyes out of their hides. "Give me your number," he said impulsively. "That way if I can't be where I promised to be, I can at least call you and explain. It won't be quite the same, but you won't be left wondering and worrying."

Ian gave Thorne the number, and Thorne programmed it into his phone. He swore nothing short of the apocalypse would keep him from keeping a promise to Ian, but if the unthinkable happened, he'd have a way to let him know.

"How was your day?" Ian asked. "Sorry, that was a stupid question. I can see by the soot all over you."

"It's not a stupid question," Thorne said. "We had a really good day. The Lang Downs crew helped make a significant dent in the fire. There are only a few hot spots left burning where we couldn't get at them with the utes. Another few days and the fires could be out."

"Oh, that's good news," Ian said, looking crestfallen. The expression was so out of sync with Ian's words that Thorne began to hope Neil was right. "What will you do then?"

"Go to Wagga Wagga for a day or two," Thorne said. "All my things are at a friend's apartment there. Walker said I could leave them there until I found a place of my own, but I don't want to impose on his generosity, especially since he should be getting back from his deployment soon."

"You've found a place, then?" Ian asked.

"Maybe," Thorne said. "Neil and Macklin seemed to think I might stay at Lang Downs. If you want me to."

"You want to stay?"

Thorne nodded. "I've been drifting since I left the army, not feeling like I fit in anywhere. I thought maybe the Firies would be better, that we'd be a team, but nobody really knows each other. They're all volunteers too. They're good blokes, but it's not the same as being part of a team. Watching Macklin and Neil run the operation today, I was part of a real team again, and it felt like coming home."

Ian didn't say anything for so long Thorne started to get nervous. "Unless you'd rather I go. I shouldn't have presumed when I kissed you, but you kissed me back and—"

"Thorne, stop," Ian interrupted gently. "You didn't presume, and I did kiss you back. And I wanted to kiss you again last night. This is…. I don't do things like this, but that doesn't matter because I'm doing it anyway. Yes, I want you to stay, but…."

"But?" Thorne prompted when Ian didn't finish his sentence.

"But I meant it when I said I don't do things like this. I've never had a relationship like this. Things weren't great for me before I came to Lang Downs, and while they got better on the station, I never imagined I'd meet someone. I didn't know about Macklin until after Caine came to the station, and by then, I was resigned to being alone. It's not all that unusual on a station. But then Caine came, and Neil met Molly, and Kyle and Linda got married, and suddenly I was the only one not with someone. But I still didn't think I'd find anyone. I'm not wired that way. Except then I met you."

Thorne refrained from whooping with delight, but he couldn't stop the smile spreading across his face.

"I don't think I've ever seen you smile like that," Ian commented. "It looks good on you."

"I haven't had a lot of reason to smile in my life," Thorne said, "but maybe that's about to change, and you aren't the only one who doesn't know what he's doing. I spent twenty years in the military straight out of high school. My last relationship ended the day I enlisted. It took us some time to realize it, but he went from being my best friend to being my boyfriend to being a total stranger in less than six months, and you've already seen how bad things can get for me. I don't know how to be a civilian."

"Then I guess we'll have to figure it out together," Ian said. "I…. I don't want to rush anything, okay? We're still practically strangers in so many ways."

"Not a lot we can do besides kiss a little while you're stuck in that bed, anyway," Thorne replied, "but I'm not a horny kid ruled by his hormones. We can take things as slow as you want. I don't know a lot, but being on a team of Commandos taught me one thing: building trust takes time, and no relationship can go anywhere without it. Right now, you have no reason to trust me and every reason not to. I hope that will change, and when it does, other things will follow."

"I do have a reason to trust you," Ian insisted. "You came after me yesterday when everyone else had abandoned me. Nobody else did. Just you."

"Don't agree to anything out of gratitude," Thorne said immediately.

"I'm not," Ian replied. "Really, I'm not. I was already thinking about you before all that happened. You can ask Neil if you don't believe me. Seeing you coming out of the smoke to save me just proved I chose well."

Neil had already said as much, although he hadn't specified when Ian had expressed his interest. Still, it was good to have it confirmed.

"So when do you think you'll go to Wagga Wagga?" Ian asked.

"Not until you're out of the hospital, for sure," Thorne said. "The last note I had from Walker said he'd be home by Christmas, but I haven't been able to check e-mail recently to see if he's got any updates. I'd like to see him while I'm there. He's the only one left of my original team."

"Where are the others?" Ian asked.

Heavy, humid air clogging his nostrils with the scent of death and decay, warning him even before he reached the squad what awaited him.

"Dead."

Ian flinched at the tone of his voice. Thorne took a deep breath and tried to school his expression to impassivity. He would never feel impassive when he thought about the senseless deaths, but he could project it. Ian didn't deserve the anger that still burned inside him

"My commander ordered me to evacuate Walker for medical treatment. When I returned to their position, they were all dead. Walker and I were the only ones who survived."

"How do you even cope with something like that?" Ian asked incredulously. "I can't begin to imagine how strong you are."

Thorne didn't feel strong. He felt miserably weak every time he thought about those deaths or any of the others on his conscience. His hands were stained with blood, and no amount of atonement could change that. He didn't deserve someone untouched by those horrors, but he was selfish enough not to refuse when life handed it to him.

"You learn to live with it," Thorne said when he realized Ian was actually waiting for an answer.

Images from his nightmare flashed before his eyes, the bodies lined up execution-style, and he grimaced.

"Or at least not to think about it," he amended. "I still see them in my nightmares sometimes."

Ian held out his hand and Thorne moved closer to the bed. Ian coughed a little. "Are you okay?" Thorne asked.

"Yes," Ian said as he reached for a cup of water. He took a couple of sips. "I can smell the smoke on your clothes."

"I didn't think about it until I got here," Thorne said. "I'll bring a change of clothes with me tomorrow so I can change before I come in. I don't want to set back your recovery. Maybe I should sit across the room."

Ian shook his head. "I can't kiss you if you're over there, and I really want to kiss you right now."

Thorne took his time leaning in to capture Ian's mouth. Their first kiss had been hard and fast, rife with adrenaline and fear. Thorne didn't regret it, exactly, since it led to them being here now, but he needed Ian to trust him, and that meant showing he was capable of restraint.

This kiss, though, this kiss had to be perfect, and so Thorne lingered over the barest of contact, their lips hardly touching. He felt Ian's breath against his beard, little puffs of air with only the slightest hint of a rasp from his smoke exposure. Thorne lifted his hand, intending to cradle Ian's cheek in his palm, but the memories of his dream were still fresh. He could see the blood staining his hands, and he couldn't sully Ian with that.

Ian had no such reservations, grabbing Thorne's hand and pressing it to his cheek, so Thorne gave up questioning what he'd done to deserve such a treasure and went with it, curving his fingers along Ian's jaw so that the tips barely touched his ear. Ian shivered and leaned closer. Thorne took that as an invitation and increased the pressure of their lips, not asking for more, just brushing their mouths together, lingering, parting for breath, only to linger once more.

Thorne felt the motion of Ian's shoulder as he lifted his hand up to Thorne's tangled hair. He'd lost his tie at some point during the day and had given up trying to keep his hair back. Ian didn't seem to care as he hummed into the kiss. A moment later, his other hand joined the first, carding through the jumbled strands, easing out the knots and massaging Thorne's scalp.

Thorne groaned softly at the sheer luxury of it: a private room with a closed door, Ian's mouth soft and pliant beneath his as he leaned into Thorne's hand, Ian's hands in his hair, stroking and caressing like he couldn't imagine being anywhere else. Thorne pulled back for a moment, resting his forehead against Ian's. Ian opened his eyes and met Thorne's gaze, and Thorne could have wept for the joy and wonder he saw on Ian's face. A kiss, a simple, practically chaste kiss, had earned him that look, and he would do whatever it took to keep it.

He nuzzled Ian's cheek, letting his beard brush against the hint of stubble along Ian's jaw. Ian sighed and leaned into the contact, so Thorne brushed his lips over Ian's cheekbone and across the bridge of his nose. Ian's hair was too short to run his fingers through, but he curved his hand around the back of Ian's neck, letting the bristle tickle his palm. With his hand that way, his thumb rested right below Ian's ear. When he stroked that patch of skin, Ian shivered and sighed again.

Thorne couldn't resist that sound. He needed to swallow it from Ian's throat, so he kissed him again with parted lips, though he kept his tongue to himself.

Perfect, he reminded himself. *It has to be perfect.*

When he repeated the caress, Ian repeated the sigh, and Thorne thought his heart would burst right then. He had done nothing to deserve Ian's trust, but Ian seemed to be giving it to him anyway. He inhaled sharply when one of Ian's hands tugged a little roughly on a tangle in his hair, the smell of hospital disinfectant overridden by the slightly woodsy scent of Ian's skin. Carley must have brought Ian's own toiletries from the station, because the hospital soap certainly didn't smell that good.

Wanting more, he buried his face in the crook of Ian's neck and simply breathed Ian in.

"Oh," Ian breathed out, and Thorne wasn't sure how to interpret the sound. He started to pull back so he could ask, but Ian held him in place. Thorne smiled and nuzzled a little more, making sure his beard caressed Ian's skin as much as his lips did.

"That shouldn't feel so good." Ian's breathless tone would have brought Thorne to his knees if he hadn't already been sitting. Ian had implied he didn't have much experience, but surely someone had taken the time to appreciate him.

If no one had, well, all the more reason for Thorne to make this kiss as perfect as possible. Ian deserved to be cherished. He deserved to be kissed like the treasure he was. If no one had seen that before, it made Thorne the luckiest son of a bitch in New South Wales, because he had Ian now, and he wasn't letting go.

Ian tugged at his hair until Thorne lifted his head, and this time Ian dove into the kiss with no guidance from Thorne. Thorne returned it but left Ian in control. If he wanted to play for a bit, Thorne wouldn't complain.

The touch of Ian's lips was hesitant after the first burst of enthusiasm, like Ian didn't quite know what to do with Thorne now that he had him there. Thorne didn't press, content to share lazy kisses while Ian decided what he wanted. If this was as far as he was willing to take things, Thorne would stop there without complaint. He wouldn't spoil the mood of the moment by asking for more than Ian was willing to give.

Ian didn't deepen the kiss, but he didn't stop either, running his fingers through Thorne's hair and over his beard, tracing the line where the beard stopped and smooth skin began both on his neck and on his cheeks, and generally taking his time exploring Thorne's face.

The soft, almost teasing caresses were far more potent than any more sexual touch as far as Thorne was concerned. If all he wanted was sex, he could find it in any bar from here to Melbourne, but not one of those encounters would give him even a fraction of the intimacy that came from the tentative brush of Ian's fingers over his skin.

He set up a rhythm with his thumb, back and forth across the smooth patch of skin behind Ian's ear. Anything else might disrupt either their continued kisses or Ian's exploration of his face, but Thorne couldn't stop touching entirely. He wanted Ian to feel the same blossoming intimacy that had him more overwhelmed than he'd been since he lost his virginity.

He pushed that thought away to focus on Ian again. Memories of Daniel would only spoil the moment.

Finally Ian sat back, looking at Thorne with lust-darkened eyes, and Thorne felt like he'd won the prize to beat all prizes. "I never knew kissing could feel like that," Ian murmured.

Thorne closed his eyes briefly, humbled and horrified in equal parts by Ian's words. He had somehow earned Ian's trust enough to be able to share this moment, and yet the years of emptiness those words represented struck him to the very core. Thorne might not have had a relationship since Daniel, but he hadn't lived such an isolated life that he didn't know how good a kiss could feel. "I'm happy to repeat the experience anytime you want."

Ian grinned at him, quick and bright. "You might regret saying that."

"Never," Thorne swore.

"The blokes at the station don't know about me," Ian said. "There was never a reason to tell them."

"Do you really think they'll have an issue with it?" Thorne asked. "With three other gay couples living openly on the station, why would it make a difference to them?"

"Because I didn't trust them with it even when it was obvious it wouldn't make a difference," Ian said. "Michael wouldn't tolerate slurs of any kind in his hearing, and we heard a few back then, mostly against Kami rather than about anyone being gay, because no one was open about it. The few times it came up, Michael shut those comments down just as fully as he did the racial ones, but he couldn't control what he didn't hear, and while Kami had his defenders in the bunkhouse, nobody said anything about the homophobic slurs."

"That's not the case now," Thorne said. "Neil warned me the first night I arrived."

Ian laughed, although it didn't strike Thorne as a happy sound.

"Yes, I'm sure he did. Neil is incredibly loyal. Almost to the point of stupidity."

"What's that got to do with anything?" Thorne asked.

"Neil was the worst about the comments when Michael wasn't around. When he found out about Caine, he was as nasty and cutting to him as he could be. I don't honestly know why Caine didn't fire him, except that he was still getting his feet underneath him at the station and so maybe didn't feel like he had the authority to do that yet," Ian explained. "And then we had a series of bad storms, and Neil got trapped on the other side of a gully with no way to get anywhere safe and dry. As cold as it got by the time the storms passed, Neil would have died of hypothermia if he hadn't drowned trying to cross the gully to get home. Caine refused to lose a man, even Neil, and tied a rope around himself so he could ride across the gully to get another rope to Neil and lead him across safely. Neil's attitude toward Caine did a complete reversal after that, but I was never sure how much that extended beyond Caine."

"His brother's gay too, isn't he?" Thorne asked. He thought he'd got the relationships among the senior jackaroos straight, but he wasn't completely sure.

"Yes, and the struggle there wasn't even because Sam was gay, but because Sam ended up falling in love with Jeremy Taylor," Ian said. "It's not rational, but the fear of his reaction was still there. Caine saved his life, Sam's his brother; his loyalty would keep him from turning on them."

"And you're his best friend," Thorne said. "He tore me a new one in the field today when he thought I was taking unnecessary risks."

"He and Caine have that in common," Ian said. "He wouldn't want anyone hurt on his watch."

"That's not why he yelled at me," Thorne said. "He yelled at me because if I got hurt, it would upset you."

Ian opened this mouth to respond, but no words came out, only a harsh, dry cough. Thorne grabbed the cup of water and pressed it to Ian's lips, but although he swallowed a few sips, that didn't settle his cough like it had before. Growing worried, Thorne caught Ian's chin in a gentle hand. "How can I help?"

Ian fumbled for the oxygen mask hanging by his bed. Thorne helped him put it on and turned on the flow of air. He didn't know how far the nurses had opened the valve on the tank before, but he opened it two turns, hoping that would be enough. When he was sure Ian wasn't going to choke, he would get a nurse and have her come adjust it to the appropriate level.

Ian's coughing eased a little, but his eyes were still watering. "Should I get a nurse?" Thorne asked.

Ian nodded, so Thorne rushed to the door and called for a nurse. One came in, all bustling efficiency, and set the flow of oxygen and then gave Ian another dose of something in the breathing tube. That seemed to help, but Thorne was acutely aware again of the smell of smoke on his clothes. Staying would only make Ian's symptoms worse. When the nurse left them alone again, he squeezed Ian's hand once. "I'll come back tomorrow, in clean clothes this time. You should get some rest."

Ian frowned at him, but Thorne didn't let that dissuade him. He *couldn't* put Ian's health at risk. He stopped at the door and turned back for a moment to appreciate how even beneath the oxygen mask, Ian's lips were visibly swollen from their kisses, his neck and jaw slightly red from Thorne's beard. It was a delectable look on him, and one Thorne wouldn't mind reproducing when Ian wasn't stuck in a hospital bed with a compromised pulmonary system.

He blew one last kiss in Ian's direction, feeling silly until Ian caught it and pressed his hand to his heart. He smiled and shut the door behind him. Now he just had to get through another day, and then he could come back and visit Ian again.

TWELVE

IT TOOK a long time after Thorne left for Ian's breathing to return to normal. His pounding heart was probably as responsible for that as anything else, but he couldn't very well explain that to the nurse. He ran his fingers over his cheeks and around the edge of the mask, feeling the tingling that remained from the gentle scratch of Thorne's beard. The few guys he'd kissed before coming to Lang Downs had all been clean-shaven, so that had been a revelation. He'd felt the whiskers when they kissed before, of course, but it had been so sudden and over so quickly Ian hadn't really had time to do more than realize they were kissing before it was over. Not so today. Today Thorne had lingered over their kisses, seemingly content with the tender contact. Not once had he hinted in any way that he wanted more or that their kisses somehow weren't enough.

It was a good thing, too, because those kisses had been all Ian could handle without being a prelude to something more. His few fumbling forays hadn't prepared him for the depth of emotion Thorne's kisses evoked in him, the wonder that this magnificent man would want such a thing with him. Thorne hadn't hurled accusations of teasing or worse at him. He hadn't groped him. He'd simply touched Ian's face and neck like he was the most precious thing in the world. If their first kiss had been desperate and full of fear, like Han kissing Leia before being encased in carbonite, their kisses tonight were more like their reunion after she rescued him on Tatooine: tender and full of promise.

He'd outgrown his obsession with Han and Leia about the time he'd decided boys were more interesting than girls, but they had defined romance for him from quite the tender age. Sioned's vision of herself and

Rohan in the flames had perhaps superseded that since then, but the imagery remained with him still.

Whichever comparison he chose, Thorne fit right into the role, a thought that warmed Ian's heart even as it sped his pulse. He coughed a little behind his mask as his elevated pulse made breathing more difficult. As much as he wanted to dwell on the memories of the time spent kissing Thorne, he wasn't sure it was a good idea. He'd have time enough to remember—and repeat—the experience when he could go for more than a few minutes without coughing.

With a smile on his face, he picked up *Dragon Prince* again and allowed his imagination to replace the familiar faces of his favorite characters with the mental image of Thorne and himself.

IAN had just finished lunch and had been told by the nurse to leave his mask off for a while when Molly and Dani arrived.

"Uncle Ian!"

Dani ran across the room as fast as her three-year-old legs could carry her, which was far faster than Ian had ever been able to explain, given how short they were. He caught her as she threw herself at him and lifted her up onto the mattress with him.

"Hello, Danibelle," he said. "Can I have a kiss?"

She gave him a smacking kiss on the cheek. He blew a raspberry on her neck in return, making her giggle wildly.

"How are you?" Molly asked as she pulled the chair up to the bed.

"Doing better," Ian replied. "How's everything at the station?"

"Everything's fine, if you don't count everyone being worried about you."

"I'm fine," Ian said automatically.

"You're not," Molly retorted, "or you wouldn't be here."

"I will be fine," Ian amended. "They just want to keep me for another day or two until they're sure I won't have an asthma attack out on the station. I'm not in danger anymore."

"Uncle Ian sick?" Dani asked.

"I am. I breathed in too much smoke and it made me sick," Ian said. "But the doctors are taking good care of me, and I'll be home before you know it."

"Come home today," Dani demanded imperiously.

"You'll have to talk to the doctors about that," Ian said. "I think they want me to stay a little longer. But I'll come home as soon as I can."

Dani pouted, so Ian tickled her until she laughed again.

"What are they doing about the fires?" he asked Molly.

"They went back out to keep an eye on the hot spots," Molly said, "but Neil seemed to think it was a precaution more than a necessity. He said the fires were out in all but a few isolated locations, and that they'd probably burn out in another day or two without any help, so as long as no new ones start, the worst has passed."

"Did he say… anything else?" He glanced at Dani. Neil wouldn't have said anything about him and Thorne in front of his daughter, no matter his own feelings. He was raising her to love and accept her Uncle Sam and Uncle Jeremy without blinking. Ian had heard the brothers talking one night, and Neil had sworn to Sam he wouldn't be the kind of father they'd grown up with. That didn't mean he hadn't said something to Molly in private.

"He mentioned that Thorne might be staying longer than planned," Molly replied. "Something about sleeping on your couch?"

"The other choice is the guest room in the main house, and that means listening to Caine and Macklin."

Molly chuckled. They'd all heard stories from Chris about the challenge of staying down the hall from their bosses. During the day, in the sight of the jackaroos, they were completely circumspect, and if one didn't know about them, one might miss their relationship entirely. At night in the privacy of their own home, they were apparently much less reserved.

"Is it a good thing that he's staying?" Molly asked.

Ian considered his answer for a moment. The very idea of Thorne staying on his couch and in his life pushed him far out of his comfort zone, but every time he got nervous, he remembered the way they'd kissed the night before, and especially the way Thorne hadn't even tried to do more than kiss. He hadn't abused Ian's trust last night, so Ian was willing to trust him a little more. "I think so," he said finally. "I've never done anything like this."

"Just remember you aren't doing it alone," Molly said. "You have people who love you and who will be there if you need to talk or if you need someone to go beat him up for you."

"Not sure how good an idea that is," Ian said with a laugh. "He's pretty highly trained."

"Dani can take him," Molly said. "Can't you, sweetheart?"

Dani put up her little fists and looked at Ian with perfect seriousness. "I take him." She looked back at her mother. "Who I taking?"

Ian burst out laughing, long peals of sound, until he couldn't breathe and started choking. He wiped the tears from his eyes as he reached for the oxygen mask. Molly started to apologize, but he waved her silent. He grabbed his pad and wrote, *It feels good to laugh.*

DESPITE his confident words to Molly, Ian was glad of some time alone after she and Dani left and before Thorne arrived. Thorne had talked about staying on the night before, had asked Ian's opinion on the possibility, and hadn't been put off by Ian's concerns, but Ian had had time to think since then, and he wasn't sure he liked what he'd come up with. Staying on the station would mean starting over completely for Thorne. Ian didn't know if he could ride a horse or if he knew the first thing about sheep. Ian loved every aspect of life on the station except maybe shoveling out the sheep sheds in the winter, but he'd spent fifteen years listening to jackaroos complain about one aspect or another of the job. He'd watched people swear never to spend another minute on a sheep station by the end of a summer. Even if Thorne chose to stay now, it didn't guarantee he'd stay forever. He could well end up so bored he'd decide to leave, especially if Ian couldn't get over his own fears. What good was a relationship if he couldn't do more than kiss his lover?

The word was enough to make Ian shudder. What did he know about that kind of relationship? His father had disappeared around the time he was born, and his mother's string of live-ins had been as likely to take a swipe at him—or her—as do anything else. Once the Department of Child Services had become involved, he'd been moved from one foster family to another so quickly as they tried to find a place for him that he hadn't had a chance to learn much of anything from them, and then had come his last foster family, and that had been a disaster from beginning to end. He still had nightmares about the first night his foster father had come to his room "to make sure he was settling in."

He wanted this to work. He wanted Thorne to be happy on the station and to stay with him and to keep looking at him like he'd done the night before. And maybe to keep kissing him like he'd done the night before. If only he had the slightest idea how to do that, he'd be a little happier about the prospect, because the idea of having Thorne and losing him was far too horrible to contemplate. If he did this, he had to do it for keeps, and if he didn't, he needed to decide that soon. It wouldn't be fair to Thorne otherwise.

Not to mention that the longer he waited, the harder it would be to keep his heart whole if Thorne left.

No, he had to commit to this. He was already in too deep to back out without consequences to his own heart. He took a deep breath and tried to consider what that would mean and how he could satisfy a lover without triggering his own panic attacks. Thorne had enough of those for both of them.

IAN lit up like a Christmas tree when Thorne came in a couple of hours later, which was appropriate, since Christmas was only about a month away. Thorne's answering smile was everything Ian could have hoped. He looked genuinely happy to see Ian.

"I changed before I came," Thorne said. "No smoky clothes today."

"Good," Ian said, patting the mattress beside him in invitation, "although I'm doing better today. I've had the mask off most of the day and only had one coughing fit when I had to put it back on. Molly and Dani made me laugh and I couldn't stop."

"That sounds delightful. She's a precious child." Thorne came and sat next to Ian on the bed.

"She's a little demon is what she is," Ian said, "but she's the apple of everyone's eye. She's going to pitch a fit when her little brother makes an appearance. She won't want to share the spotlight." He reached for

Thorne's hand and pulled him closer. The smell of smoke hadn't entirely evaporated from Thorne's hair, but it was less noticeable than the day before. Ian didn't think it would trigger a coughing fit, but he'd be glad when the fires were out and Thorne no longer smelled of smoke at all. Ignoring the memories triggered by the smell, he leaned up and kissed Thorne softly. "Hi."

"Hi yourself," Thorne said. "So you're feeling better?"

"The doctors say if I do well tonight without the mask, they might let me go home tomorrow." He paused for a moment. "I'm ready to be home. I'm not used to staying in bed all day."

"I could think of a few good reasons to spend all day in bed."

Ian flinched at the suggestion alone. He could spend all day kissing Thorne, he was quite sure, but if they were in bed, a real bed with no worry about nurses barging in to check on him, kissing wouldn't be enough for Thorne, and that still made Ian uncomfortable.

"How are the fires?" he asked instead of addressing his fears. "Molly said there were only hot spots left."

"There were a couple of small flare-ups today, but nothing major," Thorne said. "I think the worst is over."

"I hope so," Ian said. "I hate the idea of you out there in danger."

Thorne looked surprised at that. "I've spent so much of my time in danger I don't think about it anymore."

"Well, start thinking," Ian said. "If you're going to stay on Lang Downs—" He swallowed hard. "—with me, I need to know you're going to think about your own safety. I want you to come home every night."

"There's a difference between being in danger and being stupid about it," Thorne said. "I always take every precaution I can to stay safe and still get the job done. I don't have a death wish."

"No job at Lang Downs is worth risking your safety," Ian insisted. "If you don't believe me, ask Caine. Buildings can be rebuilt, sheep replaced, but not lives. The only reason to risk your life is to save the life of someone else."

"I got yelled at for that too," Thorne admitted. "Captain Grant didn't agree with my decision to go after you, but I'm fine and you're alive. I respectfully told him where he could stuff it."

Ian snickered. "Respectfully?"

"Very respectfully," Thorne replied. "I told him I'd make sure these fires were out because they threatened someplace important to me, but to consider this my resignation from the RFS. Your life is worth more than any regs."

Ian couldn't do anything after a declaration like that except lean into Thorne and kiss him. Thorne's beard rasped against his lips, driving home to Ian just who he was kissing. This wasn't some random guy in a bar or some faceless fantasy. This was Thorne, with his lush beard and long hair. That thought was enough to make him lift his hands to burrow into Thorne's hair. He luxuriated in the sensation of the silky strands moving over the back of his hands as he pulled Thorne closer. He wanted to dive into Thorne and never leave.

Thorne broke the kiss and nuzzled Ian's jaw again as he had done the night before. Ian gasped and tilted his head back, offering Thorne his trust as he offered him his neck. He sighed at the tender caress that followed, licks and nibbles and kisses all along his neck, all punctuated by the constant tickle of Thorne's beard. Ian relaxed into the contact, content to let Thorne lavish attention on him.

With that moment of surrender came a crashing realization. He didn't just want more kisses. He was getting turned on. For the first time, he was with someone else and aroused despite his lingering fears. Suddenly eager, he used his hand in Thorne's hair to guide his head back up so they could kiss again. He kissed Thorne with all the joy and wonder in his heart and as much of the rising passion as he dared. His inhibitions wouldn't give up that easily, but even so, Ian pressed their lips together and then daringly nibbled on Thorne's lower lip. He felt more than heard Thorne's gasp at that, and then Thorne swept his tongue across his lips, surprising Ian into retreating for a moment.

"No?" Thorne asked.

"Yes," Ian answered, his need getting the better of his nerves. Thorne had asked. He'd held himself back at the first sign of hesitation and had waited for Ian's approval before continuing. He'd proven Ian could trust him.

Ian pulled Thorne to him again, parting his lips in invitation this time. He could take this risk. Thorne would stop if he asked. He could sit here in this hospital bed and kiss this wonderful, amazing, *arousing* man and not worry about what came next.

Thorne tasted like peppermint, Ian discovered as Thorne deepened their kiss, making Ian wonder if he'd popped a breath mint before coming to the hospital or if he was like Michael, who always had peppermints in his pocket for when he needed a "pick-me-up." The answer didn't matter except to make Ian smile into the kiss.

"What?" Thorne asked.

"You taste like peppermint. It bought back good memories."

"An old boyfriend?"

"No," Ian said, "none of those in my closet. Michael Lang always had one or a dozen in his pocket. He went through so many in a day that he always smelled of peppermint. He started it when he quit smoking, but that was before my time. By the time I got to Lang Downs, the cigarettes were a thing of the past and only the peppermints remained."

"They remind me of my mother," Thorne admitted. "She always had one in her pocket or purse. After… after she died, I started carrying them as a way to remember."

"I'm glad you have good memories of her and a way to keep them," Ian said.

"It was a long time ago," Thorne said.

"All the more reason it's important," Ian insisted, drawing Thorne in for another kiss.

The contact was still languid, neither of them showing any inclination to rush, but this kiss was deeper now, openmouthed as they took turns exploring each other. The whole time, Thorne cradled Ian's head in his hands as he'd done the night before, caressing that spot behind Ian's ear that shouldn't have been so sensitive but was.

Experimentally, Ian tried caressing Thorne the same way, but while Thorne tilted his head into Ian's hand, it didn't earn him the same reaction. As he moved his fingers, they brushed over the nape of Thorne's neck, and that elicited the reaction Ian had hoped for.

"Right there," Thorne murmured against Ian's lips.

"There?" Ian asked as he repeated the caress.

"Yes."

"That's not where I'm sensitive," Ian mused aloud.

Thorne smiled and kissed him softly. "No, but that's the joy of discovering a new lover: finding all the places that feel good to him."

"I thought…." Ian trailed off, not wanting to reveal his complete ignorance.

"The guys you were with in the past were complete drongos if they didn't take the time to find this little spot." Thorne brushed his thumb over Ian's skin.

"It never got that far," Ian admitted. "They'd kiss me and then start groping and that would be the end of that."

"Drongos, every one of them," Thorne said. "I won't make the same mistake."

Ian nodded even as a shiver of desire curled through him, and he stroked the nape of Thorne's neck again. "Nor will I."

THIRTEEN

"THANKS for coming to pick me up, Molly. I know the drive can't have been easy to make twice in a week," Ian said as they arrived back at Lang Downs. The sheep still crowded into the valley, but Thorne had told him the day before that they were still watching hot spots, so it made sense Caine would play it safe. Much longer, though, and they'd have to bring hay in to feed the sheep, and that would get expensive. Hopefully the danger would be passed before then.

"You're welcome, Ian. Just don't overdo it before you're ready. I don't want to have to take you back."

"I've got a nebulizer and a rescue inhaler," Ian said. "I'll be fine."

She didn't look convinced, but she didn't follow him across the station as he walked toward his house either. It would be good to sleep in his own bed, to make it through the night without interruption, and to be back at work tomorrow. He didn't expect to be let anywhere near the fires again, but he could find plenty to do in the valley. He'd see if Neil would leave Max with him. The kelpie worked with Neil best, but he'd listen to Ian if Neil wasn't around, which was more than he could say for Arrow, Jeremy's dog. Arrow had eyes and ears for Jeremy and Sam alone.

He neared the house and wondered if Thorne was back yet. Thorne had come to see him every night he was in the hospital, and they'd spent far more time talking than they had kissing. Of course they'd done quite a bit of that too, but Ian felt like he had a better sense of the other man, his military past, and his reasons for retiring when he did. He didn't know details, but a lot of those were classified and he might never know. It wasn't the details that mattered, anyway. He just wanted to know the man Thorne had become because of those experiences.

He was looking forward to evenings spent together in his living room, just time to be together and relax from the day. He hoped to teach Thorne about the station and living there, to show him the beauty in the stark landscape and hidden copses, to introduce him to the majesty of a storm breaking across the tablelands. He pushed open the door to the house and stepped inside, only to be brought up short by majestic beauty of an entirely different kind.

Thorne stood in the middle of the living room in nothing but a towel that barely closed around his hips.

Ian had known Thorne was a big man, but he hadn't really known what was hiding under Thorne's clothes. His shoulders were broad and heavily muscled, the black ink of tattoos dark against each bicep, although Ian couldn't tell what they were from this distance. He was golden brown all over, either his natural skin tone or the result of time spent outdoors in a very small swimsuit (or nothing at all). His chest was covered by a thick black pelt shot through with silver like his hair and beard, but that only added to the appeal. His torso narrowed to the hips, which was probably a good thing or the towel wouldn't have covered anything, not that it hid much. Thorne had managed to knot it at his waist, but it opened again below the knot, so Thorne's hip and upper thigh were uncovered. If he'd turned, Ian suspected he'd get a glimpse of arse as well.

"Like what you see?" Thorne drawled, making Ian's face flame in embarrassment.

"Sorry," he stammered. "I didn't mean to stare."

"You can stare all you want," Thorne replied. "I don't mind."

Ian's cheeks heated even more, because despite his best intentions, he couldn't make himself look away. Common courtesy dictated he go into the kitchen or the bedroom or somewhere to give Thorne some privacy while he dressed, but the rivulets of water working their way down Thorne's chest had caught his attention, and he couldn't stop tracing their tracks with his gaze. He itched to touch, but Thorne hadn't given permission for that, only to watch.

Ian swallowed hard as Thorne turned his back and grabbed a pair of white boxer briefs. He stepped into them and pulled them up his legs and underneath the towel. Ian's breath caught in his throat as he watched. He knew Thorne wasn't putting on a show for him, but damn if it didn't feel that way. Then the towel slipped, giving Ian a glimpse of sharply defined buttocks the same golden brown as the rest of Thorne's body. A second later, Thorne pulled the briefs into place, not that the clingy fabric did anything to disguise the muscular curve of flesh. The only real difference was the color.

"What did the doctors say about continuing care for your lungs?" Thorne asked as he turned back around.

The words didn't even begin to compute in Ian's head. He was still too busy assimilating the view. Ian was pretty sure Thorne was even more dangerous now with his underwear snug over his body than he'd been when the towel was threatening to fall. The towel at least had been loose, leaving some things to the imagination. Thorne's briefs framed his package, practically begging Ian to stare.

"What?" he said, forcing his gaze up to meet Thorne's, except Thorne was pulling a T-shirt over his head.

Good, Ian thought. *Maybe now I can stop making a fool of myself.*

"I asked what the doctors' orders were concerning continuing care," Thorne repeated. He grabbed a pair of jeans and pulled those on as well.

"Oh, um, take it easy for a few days, ease back into work, use the nebulizer at night, and keep the inhaler on me at all times because other things besides smoke could contribute to an attack," Ian replied absently, still taken by the vision of Thorne standing nearly naked in his living room.

Now fully dressed, Thorne crossed to where Ian was standing. "You okay?" he asked as he ran his thumb over the sensitive spot on Ian's neck. Ian leaned into the caress.

"Yeah, just a little…."

Thorne grinned. "I'd apologize, but you don't seem to mind. If I'd known you were home already, I would have taken my clothes into the bathroom with me."

"No, I don't mind," Ian whispered, amazed at his own boldness. He'd hated living in the bunkhouse because he'd always been bothered by the lack of privacy, but Thorne wasn't some random jackaroo, and Ian's staring wasn't unwelcome. He pushed up on his tiptoes and kissed Thorne softly. He'd known Thorne was taller than him, but when they were sitting side by side on the bed at the hospital, it hadn't seemed like that much of a difference. Now Ian felt positively dwarfed next to him. "How tall are you, anyway?"

"Six foot four," Thorne said. He bent his head so their lips met again. Ian threaded his fingers into the wet hair and made sure to find Thorne's own sensitive spot in retaliation—or gratitude—for Thorne's attention to the patch of skin behind his ear.

Thorne sucked lightly on Ian's lower lip, making Ian's head spin even more than the sight of him nude had already done. He gasped into the kiss and held onto Thorne's shoulders like a lifeline. Having seen the breadth of them, he thought maybe they were wide enough to bear that burden.

Ian couldn't say what might have happened if the bell hadn't rung for dinner. For the first time in his memory, Ian was willingly in someone's arms and not freaking out because of it. Seeing Thorne had him so turned on he might have actually done something about it, but as it was, his stomach rumbled with Pavlovian precision.

"Let's get dinner," Thorne said as he drew back. "We can pick up here later."

FOUR hours later, Ian slumped at the kitchen table, absolutely exhausted. Dinner had gone exactly as he would have predicted if asked. Everyone had come over to check on him, and once they were sure he was cleared, they'd insisted he come to the bunkhouse after dinner to have a "welcome home" beer. One beer had turned into several, until Ian was pleasantly loose. Even better, Thorne hadn't left his side since they'd walked out his door to head to the canteen. For that matter, Thorne was still right there, hovering over Ian as he set up the nebulizer. "Sit down," Ian grumbled when he finally had everything ready. "You're ruining a good buzz."

Thorne glared at him but sat down in the other chair, so Ian figured that was acceptable progress. He could have done without the glare, but he could live with Thorne being protective, even if he didn't really need it. He couldn't talk while he used the nebulizer, so before he started, he looked up at Thorne and said, "Tell me about your day. It'll make the treatment go faster."

Ian listened in silence as Thorne talked about the situation with the fires and the number of hot spots they were still worried about. He mentioned more fires farther to the north and how the captain had diverted resources there. Ian worried for a moment, but Thorne smiled at him. "I told him I was staying here, with the Firies or on my own, it didn't matter. He didn't tell me not to, so I guess that means I'm still one of the Firies until the last men are called north. Then I'm all yours."

The words sent a heady rush through Ian's system that had nothing to do with the medicine or the beer and everything to do with the man sitting across the table from him. He wasn't sure he was ready to contemplate everything involved in Thorne being "all his," but he wanted it no matter how bad it ended up being. Thorne was nothing like Ian's foster father. Whatever they were doing, it wasn't about power and pain like it had been back then, and Ian wasn't the scrawny helpless boy he'd been at sixteen.

"You have the strangest look on your face," Thorne said. "Did I overstep my bounds?"

Ian shook his head. He didn't want to explain his past or the memories Thorne's words had stirred up. They didn't have any bearing on the matter at hand.

"Are you sure? I can leave if you want."

Ian shook his head again and reached for Thorne's hand. He didn't know a lot of things about how this would work, but he knew one thing: he didn't want Thorne to leave.

Thorne smiled at his gesture, the expression taking years off his face, and Ian resolved to make him smile more often.

Finally he finished with the breathing treatment. He put the supplies away and flopped onto the couch. Thorne joined him a moment later.

"Tired?"

"I shouldn't be," Ian said. "I haven't done anything all week."

"Except recover from nearly dying, and I've been in the hospital before. I know how restful they are—nurses coming in every few hours to check on you, noises out in the hallway at all hours."

"Not very," Ian agreed.

"Not at all," Thorne insisted. "You don't have to stay up and keep me company. It's already late."

"I haven't got my kisses yet," Ian said with a pout.

"That's because you wanted to go to the bunkhouse," Thorne said. "I could have come back here right after dinner and kissed you all night."

Ian thought that sounded wonderful, but he yawned before he could say so.

"Go to sleep," Thorne said. "I'll be here in the morning."

"Are you sure the couch is comfortable enough?"

"It's better than a bedroll on hard ground," Thorne replied. "So unless you're inviting me into your bed, baby, you need to stop tempting me, because I'd really love to carry you in the other room and hold you all night long, but I promised we'd go slow, and I'm trying to keep that promise."

A curl of warmth moved through Ian's heart and belly, but he knew he wasn't ready. He could sit on the couch with Thorne all night. He could probably even sleep in Thorne's arms on the couch, but someone in his bedroom, in his bed, had always ended with him bleeding and begging for it to stop.

"Thank you." Ian gave Thorne a soft kiss before rising from the couch.

"For what?"

"For not pushing."

"There is more to life than sex," Thorne said. "I don't know how you got to be your age, looking like you do, and still skittish, but while I hope you'll trust me with that story someday, it doesn't need to be now. Regardless, I'm not ruled by my dick. We won't do anything that makes you uncomfortable."

Ian tensed a little at how close Thorne had come to guessing his secret. He supposed it wasn't hard to figure out the bare bones of it. He just hated the idea of anyone actually knowing what had happened. He knew intellectually that he hadn't done anything wrong, that he hadn't asked for what happened to him, but it didn't stop the embarrassment that still lingered or the sting of the filth his foster father had heaped on his head when he came to Ian's room.

SLEEP was a long time coming after Ian stripped down to his underwear and climbed into bed. He'd shut the door, as he did every night, but that thin piece of wood suddenly seemed like no barrier at all. Images of Thorne flashed though his mind: appearing through the smoke to rescue Ian like some majestic hero from any of a hundred quest fantasies, playing with Dani at dinner so Neil and Molly could eat, laughing with the other jackaroos in the bunkhouse as he nursed his one beer, giving Ian that intimate smile of his when Ian had said he wanted Thorne to stay. Mostly, though, he saw Thorne in that *bloody* towel, looking good enough to eat and dangerous enough to set off every one of Ian's warning bells. Ian wasn't a big guy, not like Thorne. He was five foot ten in his boots, which meant Thorne had six inches on him. Ian lived a very active life and was as strong or stronger than the average man his size, but Thorne wasn't average. He could have been carved out of the stone beneath their feet, and he was bigger. Ian had no hope of getting away if he had to.

"He wouldn't do that," Ian said aloud, forcing away the doubts that wanted to crop up. "He isn't like that. He all but said tonight that he'd be fine if we never had sex."

That was the problem, though, and Ian knew it. Thorne might be fine with that now, and he might even remain fine with it, but Ian wasn't. He finally had the chance at a relationship with a man who might be capable of respecting Ian's limits, and Ian couldn't take the first step.

"That's not true," he muttered to himself. "I did take the first step. I kissed him. I've kissed him quite a bit."

They'd been amazing kisses too, every single one of them, even the hard, fast one as they escaped the wildfire. And for once, kissing had led him to wanting more as much as he feared it. He wanted to be pleased with that, but it only added to the terrible sense of uncertainty. He'd never allowed anyone else to touch him intimately since he was old enough to leave DoCS custody. He'd never met anyone he trusted to touch him intimately.

Until now.

Ian's stomach churned as he let the thought settle into him. He wanted to know how it would feel to touch Thorne. He was getting hard just thinking about the eyeful he'd got earlier, when he'd walked in on Thorne getting dressed. The man was gorgeous, with heavy, powerful muscles under the dark pelt of fur across his chest, and Ian wanted to touch. He didn't think Thorne would turn him away, but he wasn't sure he could handle what would come next. If Ian gave in to his desire and explored Thorne's body the way he wanted to, Thorne would want to reciprocate. No sex was not at all the same thing as one-sided sex, and that was what it would be.

He rolled onto his side and concentrated on his breathing. He wasn't accomplishing anything by going through this repeatedly in his head. He needed to sleep. Everything else would wait until morning.

HE MOVED his hands slowly over the hard body, the mat of fur tickling his palms. The gesture elicited a gasp and a smile from the man below him, lying back so trustingly as he explored. He was safe. As long as he was here, he was safe. No one could touch him with Thorne around.

He leaned down to kiss his lover and sucked eagerly on his lips. When Thorne swept his tongue across Ian's lips in retaliation, he drew it into his mouth and sucked on it instead. Thorne liked that, to judge by the way he bucked beneath Ian. Ian liked the way their bodies felt rubbing together, so he rested a little more weight on Thorne's chest and rubbed a little more purposefully. Thorne rumbled something beneath him, but the words were too indistinct for Ian to make them out. It didn't matter anyway. They hadn't been a sound of protest, so Ian took the seductive sound as encouragement and pressed even closer, splaying his legs wide across Thorne's hips.

Heavy hands settled on Ian's hips, startling him and stilling his movement at the same time. "Don't rush."

Ian woke with a sharp cry. Even before he could get his bearings or really register that he was alone—*safe*—he heard a knock at the door.

"Ian? Are you all right?"

Bile rose in Ian's throat. He swallowed it down. "I'm fine. Just a strange dream."

"You're sure?" Thorne asked.

"Yes, I'm fine," Ian repeated, heart pounding as he waited for the door to open, but it stayed closed.

"All right. If you need anything, just give a shout. I'm here."

Ian felt his pulse return to normal slowly. Thorne had listened. He'd taken Ian's words at face value and hadn't insisted on coming in to check on him. He'd respected the closed door.

He took a deep breath and tried to settle again after his dream. Even his subconscious, it seemed, had accepted that Thorne wouldn't rush him. Dream Thorne had touched him, yes, but only to slow things down between them when Ian got carried away. Not that Ian had felt carried away in his dream until Thorne slowed things down.

He'd never dreamed like that, and certainly never about a specific person. He'd had nightmares with his foster father's face in them, but this had been no nightmare. He hadn't been scared, hurt, or forced. He'd been the one in charge, the one making Thorne feel good, even as he got more and more aroused himself.

Now that he thought about it, he was still half hard, even with Thorne coming to check on him and the dream fading. He still had no idea how any of this would work, but he was becoming more certain he needed to try.

FOURTEEN

THORNE tensed as Dani came running across the grass toward him. It would have been much less stressful if the road hadn't been between them. Thorne didn't see any cars, but that wasn't the point. Dani had no sense of self-preservation, and Thorne just knew one day she'd walk up behind him, trigger a flashback, and get hurt. The thought made him sick to his stomach. Dani didn't deserve that, but even worse, Macklin would be justified in ordering Thorne off the station if that happened, and that would mean losing Ian. Things were going well between them, but Thorne didn't delude himself. If it came to choosing between Lang Downs and Thorne, Thorne would lose in a heartbeat. Furthermore, if it came to that, Ian's choice would be the right one, however much it hurt. Ian deserved someone he could trust in his life and in his home.

"Hi, Dani," he said, scooping her up into his arms. "You should be more careful running across the road."

"Mum said no cars," Dani replied as she gave him a smacking kiss on the cheek above his beard. "No cars, safe to cross."

"If you say so," he said.

She wrinkled up her nose. "You stinky."

"Not after today," Thorne promised. "The fires are out. I don't have to go back and smell like smoke anymore."

"Good. Smoke stinky."

Thorne chuckled. "Were you a good girl for your mum today?"

"I watched her for Molly today."

The unexpected voice behind him sent Thorne's instincts into hyperdrive. He spun around, curling his body protectively around Dani.

"Laura!" Molly scolded before Thorne could react further. "What did we tell you about walking up behind Thorne?"

"Sorry," she said. "I forgot."

"That's a dangerous rule to forget," Thorne warned her. "You remember what happened the last time?"

"Thorne scared?" Dani asked, putting her tiny hands on his cheeks and turning him to face her.

"Scared something was coming to hurt you," Thorne replied honestly.

"Nobody hurt me. Only snakes, but they only go in sheds," Dani said.

"I know Laura wouldn't hurt you," Thorne said. "But it startled me and that made me want to protect you."

She squirmed in his arms to be let down. He set her on the ground, and she scampered over to Laura. "Say sorry."

"I already did."

"Say again," Dani demanded imperiously.

Thorne stifled a chuckle. Dani had picked up her mother's ability to run the world, it appeared.

"I'm sorry," Laura said again. "I really didn't mean to surprise you again."

"Good. Come play." Dani dragged Laura off before Thorne could say anything else.

"Thanks for that," Thorne said to Molly after the girls had left. "I was holding Dani, so I think the need to protect her outweighed the instinct to lash out, but it was still better for someone else to talk to her about what she did."

"There's nothing wrong with protecting a child," Molly said. "Just make sure she needs protecting first."

"That's easier said than done," Thorne admitted. "That hair-trigger reaction saved my life more than once. It's hard to unlearn that lesson."

"So don't unlearn it. Just learn to temper it," Molly said. "I'm not saying it'll be easy, but it has to be better than living in fear of how you'll react if someone startles you."

"How did you get so wise?"

Molly laughed. "Years of dealing with Neil."

Thorne laughed at Molly's reply and tried to imagine still being on Lang Downs five or ten years from now. It was remarkably easy to think about, provided he didn't do something to screw up his standing with Caine and Macklin. More than the ease of imagining it was how powerfully he desired it. He'd had a roof over his head in the Commandos, but he'd been homeless in all the ways that really mattered for a long, long time. Now he had a chance at a place of his own. He just had to keep it together so he wouldn't lose this one too.

"You okay there?" Molly asked.

"Yes, sorry, I was just thinking."

"Thinking is good. Neil should do it more often, but sometimes you have to ignore your brain and go with whatever your gut is telling you," she said. "I know you're new here, but we're a family. You never have to deal with things alone unless you want to."

"Several people have mentioned that," Thorne said.

Molly smiled ruefully. "You aren't a stockman, but it looks like the military did the same number on you that the outback did on most of them."

"And what number is that?"

"Hard as granite, convinced emotions are worse than a mulga, and determined to keep everything inside if it kills you." She laid a gentle hand on his forearm. "It won't kill you to let people help you. We won't abuse your trust."

Thorne wanted to believe her, but he wouldn't even know where to start talking about all the crap in his head. More than that, these people didn't deserve the crap in his head. They didn't deserve the death and misery that lived in his soul. That chapter of his life might have ended, but the effects lingered on.

"Do I need to bap you the way I do Neil?" Molly asked.

Thorne summoned a smile for her. "No, I heard you. I just don't know where to start."

"Wherever you hurt the most. You don't have to talk to me, but talk to someone, Thorne. Ian or Macklin or Kami, if you want. He's a surprisingly good listener, and he won't judge you or tell anyone what you said. Sometimes I think he's the station's confessor."

Thorne couldn't help smiling at that image. He didn't know the station cook beyond seeing him at dinner and sometimes at breakfast, although Sarah served breakfast most days. He didn't seem particularly approachable, but maybe that was his appeal. If he really wasn't one to talk, any secrets confided in him would be safe from idle gossip.

"I'll keep it in mind," he promised. "I should shower before dinner."

She let him go then, so he hurried back to Ian's house. He didn't know if Ian would be there yet, and even if he was, Thorne didn't expect anything different than the kisses they'd shared in the previous evenings since Ian had come home from the hospital. He didn't like to think about the possible reasons why Ian was so skittish, but he'd resolved not to do anything to make it worse, and he intended to keep that promise.

He stopped in the mudroom to take off his boots, noticing as he did that Ian's were already there, along with the long-sleeved shirt Ian had been wearing that morning. He wondered if that meant Ian was walking around with no shirt on. Probably not. He was probably wearing an undershirt. Thorne had already learned that Ian veered toward the modest side of the scale when it came to his body. Years in the military had cured Thorne of any such issues, but he respected Ian's choice. He'd even taken to carrying his own clothes into the bathroom with him when he showered so he wouldn't distress Ian.

"I'm home, Ian," he called as he walked into the living room to get his clean clothes, so he'd be ready when Ian finished his shower.

"Oh, you're back sooner than I expected."

Thorne looked up from his duffel to see Ian standing in the hallway between his bedroom and bathroom in dirty jeans and nothing else, a clean pair of trousers draped over his arm. His mouth started to water as he stared. Ian wasn't bulky, but Thorne could see the evidence of wiry muscles beneath the pale, freckled skin. From what he could see at this distance, there wasn't an inch of fat on Ian anywhere. His stomach was flat and toned, bisected by a thin line of red hair arrowing down into his waistband. Covering his staring with a cough, Thorne looked up at Ian's face and gave him a lopsided smile. "Captain Grant declared the fires all out. He pulled the Firies out, and I didn't see any reason to stay when there wasn't anything left to do. As of this afternoon, I'm officially done with the RFS."

"So that means tomorrow I can show you the station?" Ian picked nervously at the waistband of the clean pants, but he had answered, so Thorne kept the conversation going.

"That's what it means," he agreed. "Be gentle with me, though. I'm as much a novice as your newest jackaroo."

Ian grinned at that. "I've been teaching blow-ins how to survive for fifteen years. I think I can keep you from making too many mistakes, especially since all the other blow-ins know what they're doing for the most part now. They've had three months to learn and don't need constant supervision anymore."

Thorne wanted to keep Ian talking just so he could keep staring at his bare chest, but they both needed to shower, and Kami didn't hold dinner for anyone. "Get cleaned up. You can tell me what to expect over dinner."

Ian flashed that grin again and disappeared into the bathroom, leaving Thorne to sit on the couch and will away the erection he couldn't do anything about, not when Ian still looked like a stunned mullet every time some new intimacy arose between them.

"COME on," Ian said, tugging playfully on Thorne's hand after breakfast the next morning. "I've got things to show you today!"

"Can't a bloke even finish his coffee?" Thorne retorted, but he was smiling, so Ian ignored the protest as Thorne left his coffee cup—empty, Ian noticed—in the bin with the other dirty dishes.

"So what's on the agenda today?" Thorne asked as they headed toward the utes parked near the shearing sheds.

"It should be getting the sheep back to the outer paddocks," Ian said, "but you're a blow-in and I'm still on light duty, so we won't be riding out with the mob."

"Good thing," Thorne said. "I don't know how to ride."

Ian grinned. When they were in the ute, he said, "We can fix that. Titan doesn't have a regular rider right now, so once all the sheep are back where they belong, we can use him and teach you enough to get you comfortable on a horse. For now we're checking fences and drovers' huts. Caine doesn't think the fires did any damage, thanks to the Firies, but we're going to make sure and also to check the drovers' huts for supplies."

"Sounds tedious," Thorne said.

"A lot of what we do is," Ian admitted as he drove them out of the valley, "but I try to look at the contributions each piece makes. Sure, it's boring driving along klicks of fences, but if it keeps us from losing sheep, then I've contributed to the well-being of the station as a whole. Stocking the drovers' huts is tedious work, but if it means someone has food and water when they need it, I'm making sure my friends are safe and cared for."

"A lot of my work in the Commandos was the same," Thorne said. "Months of legwork for the greater good, and then moments of excitement to break up the boredom."

"I think my moments of excitement are safer," Ian replied with a grin. "The occasional dingo or snake, a grassfire if I'm really unlucky. Nothing compared to bullets and guerrillas."

"Be glad for it," Thorne said, a shadow passing over his face.

"I am," Ian said.

"Are we headed back toward the fire zone?" Thorne asked.

"Only to the property line," Ian replied. "We'll drive the fences and repair any damage we find, whether from the fires or other causes. There are a couple of huts out that way, so we'll check them too."

"So the huts are temporary shelter?" Thorne asked.

"Pretty much," Ian said. "They're little one-room cabins stocked with water and nonperishables. We use them if we're out with the mob overnight or if there's an emergency. I've waited out more than one storm in them. Everyone knows to bring replacements for what they use, but Caine still likes to check them systematically two or three times a year; switch out the blankets, make sure there's plenty of water and food, restock the firewood, refill the first-aid kit, that sort of thing. In an emergency, it could make the difference between surviving and dying."

"You don't have to sell me on what we're doing," Thorne said. "I was a soldier, remember? Give me an order and I'll follow it. Especially when I see the logic in it like I do this one."

"But I'm not an officer," Ian said, feeling vaguely uncomfortable at the idea of giving Thorne orders. He'd been thrilled when Macklin asked Neil, not him, to take the foreman's job. Ian would have done it if asked, but he was far more comfortable as a crew boss or even simply a jackaroo who didn't need to be told what to do. "And this isn't the military."

"No, but there is order and routine and discipline to it," Thorne said. "Neil or Macklin or someone gives orders, and everyone else carries them out. When you're out with a crew, you have a job to do and you get it done. That's very much like in the military. The only difference is that it's not always a matter of life and death."

Ian hadn't thought of it like that, although it made sense when Thorne said it. "I know I started feeling more comfortable here when I understood why I was being asked to do different things. I try to extend the same courtesy to others."

"You mean you didn't know this was home the minute you stepped foot on the station?" Thorne teased. "It seems like everyone else did."

Memories of his early days on the station washed through Ian. He'd been on his own for two years by that time and had learned not to trust anyone, not that he'd been terribly trusting already after what his foster father had done. He'd been sullen and hard to work with. Macklin wasn't foreman yet, just a crew boss, but he'd rubbed Ian the wrong way from the very beginning, every order raising Ian's hackles until he nearly snapped. He'd been ready to quit when Michael had summoned him to the station house.

"No, it wasn't an easy adjustment for me," Ian admitted. "When I lived with my mum, we moved around a lot, mostly hiding from her exes or from creditors, and once I ended up in DoCS custody, they had a hard time placing me with a foster family. I wasn't young and cute. I was an angry teenager with an attitude the size of Uluru. By the time I got here, I was an angry twenty-year-old with an attitude. I didn't know what it meant to have a home, so of course I didn't recognize Lang Downs for what it was."

They reached the gate for the upper paddock. Without waiting to be told, Thorne jumped out of the ute and opened the gate. Ian drove through and waited for him to climb back in before turning the ute along the fence line and continuing the conversation. "Michael finally got sick of it. I was sure he was going to fire me, but instead he sat my butt down and told me I had a choice in life. I laughed in his face. I hadn't had a single choice in my entire life up until that point, as far as I was concerned."

"He obviously changed your mind about that," Thorne observed.

"He said he couldn't change what had happened before I got to Lang Downs, and neither could I, but that it was up to me what happened now that I was here," Ian explained. "He said I could hold onto my bad attitude and leave at the end of the season with everyone else, or I could accept that life had dealt me a shit hand up until then, let it go, and make a place for myself here. I didn't believe him, to be honest. Nobody else had ever wanted me. Why would he? He was an old man already, and he was still too in love with his partner to be interested in me. I wasn't a particularly good jackaroo because I'd been too busy being a pain to actually learn much. It didn't make sense."

"How did he convince you?"

"He didn't, really," Ian said. "I mean, not by anything he said. I didn't believe him, but he got me thinking, and so I started looking around at the other year-rounders and listening to the other jackaroos talk, the ones who came back year after year even if they left in the winter. That's when I started hearing things. They called the year-rounders Michael's Lost Boys. I scoffed at that. Peter Pan was only a fairy tale and this wasn't Neverland, but I kept listening, and before long I realized maybe it was, and if it was, if Michael's offer really was genuine, I'd be a fool to pass it up. When the season ended, Michael called me to the station house again and asked me what I'd decided. I asked him if I could stay."

"He obviously said yes."

Michael had said yes, on one condition. He needed to know exactly what had brought Ian to him, but Ian didn't tell Thorne that part. He'd acceded to Michael's request and poured out the whole sordid story, but he didn't want to go through it again. Fortunately for Ian, a break in the fence drew his attention.

"Yes, he did," Ian said, putting the ute in park. "Let's go. We've got a fence to fix."

FIFTEEN

"GOOD news," Thorne said when he joined Ian in the living room of Ian's house after dinner. "I got a call from Walker. He's back in Australia. He'll be in Wagga Wagga next week, so I thought I'd drive down and get the rest of my things one day next week. It's probably too long to drive there and back in one day, though."

"I think we can spare you for two days," Ian replied. He forced a grin even as he fought the sudden surge of jealousy. "Or even three if you want to catch up with your friend."

"That'll depend on his schedule," Thorne said. "I don't know that he'll have much time off other than in the evenings. I'll probably drive down, spend the evening with him, and drive back the next day. I want to see him and get my stuff, but I don't want to be gone too long."

Ian felt the jealousy subside. "So tell me about him."

"About Walker?" Thorne asked. Ian nodded. "There's not much to tell that I haven't already told you. We were in the Commandos together. We've been friends for a long time."

"What will he think of you staying here on the station?" Ian asked. It wasn't what he really wanted to know, but it was the best he could come up with to ask.

Thorne pulled the book Ian had been reading out of his hands and set it on the coffee table. He cradled Ian's cheeks in his hands and kissed him. Ian leaned into the touch, completely addicted after the two weeks they'd spent doing this. "Is that what you really want to know, or are you asking what he'll think of me being with you?"

"Both," Ian admitted, feeling his cheeks flush from the kiss and from being caught out.

"He'll probably be surprised about the station," Thorne said. "I don't know how he'll react to me being with you, but it doesn't matter. It's not his decision to make, and his reaction, good or bad, isn't going to keep me from coming back to you. Yes, he's a friend, one of the few people I'd actually give that title to, but he's not a threat to you."

"Sorry," Ian said. "I shouldn't be so clingy."

"You can be as clingy as you want, baby," Thorne said as he leaned in to kiss Ian again.

Ian let him take control of the kiss. He'd found it easier and easier to trust Thorne over the past two weeks when they sat together in his living room kissing, and today had only added to that. Thorne had been a model student out in the tablelands, doing everything Ian asked him to and only needing Ian to explain things once. The first time they'd stopped to fix a fence, Ian had to show him how to do it, but the second time, they worked like a team.

Ian tilted his head into Thorne's hands, trusting their support. Thorne didn't let him down, and before long, Thorne had wandered away from Ian's mouth and along his jaw, his beard providing an erotic prickle that always made Ian gasp.

He'd watched Thorne today and had seen the strength in his hands and arms. Pulling a fence was hard work, something a lot of the seasonal jackaroos never managed to do on their own, but Thorne had figured it out the first time Ian had shown him, and then he'd done it with such powerful efficiency that Ian hadn't been able to stop staring at his forearms. Feeling bold now, he traced the line of muscle in Thorne's arms with tentative fingers. He didn't move above Thorne's elbows yet, not wanting to rush and miss any part of the experience. The skin on Thorne's arms was covered in hair like his chest, soft black strands that matched the hair on his head, and beneath that, rock-hard muscle. Thorne murmured something incomprehensible against Ian's neck, but Ian figured Thorne wasn't telling him to stop, so he took his time with his exploration.

The inside of Thorne's wrists were exquisitely sensitive, Ian discovered through trial and error, and it made him smile to hear the gasps that escaped each time he dragged his nails over the smooth skin, one of the few patches not dusted with that wonderful dark pelt.

"I wondered if you'd find that spot," Thorne said between gasps, and Ian smiled even wider to think he'd discovered something about Thorne through his own initiative. It made him wonder what other spots he could find if he were bold enough to look.

He could have simply asked, of course, but he suspected the search was at least half the fun for both of them... as long as he had the courage to follow through.

Thorne still nuzzled his neck, but Ian could tell he was waiting, too, to see what Ian did next. The moment stretched between them, pregnant with significance. Ian could pull back or continue doing what he'd already done, and Thorne would resume his usual attentions, or Ian could try something new and see what kind of reaction that got. He took a calming breath and then another one, reminding himself how Thorne had always respected the limits he set. Thorne would never pressure him to do more than he was comfortable with, but as Ian glanced down at where his hands rested on Thorne's arms, he realized he wasn't done. As attractive as Thorne's forearms were, there was still so much more of him to explore. Maybe he wasn't ready for everything, but he could move to Thorne's biceps. That wasn't much more of an intimacy than what he'd already undertaken.

He cupped Thorne's elbows in his palms before running his hands up Thorne's biceps until he reached the edge of Thorne's T-shirt. He stopped there and worked his way back down over the strong muscles.

"I can take it off," Thorne offered.

Ian froze at the words. He'd seen Thorne shirtless, but only from across the room. Since his first day home from the hospital, Thorne had been careful to take all his clothes with him into the bathroom and come out fully dressed after his shower. He waited until Ian went to bed at night to strip down to whatever he slept in, and he was always up and dressed when Ian came out of his room in the morning. He knew Thorne had made the effort for Ian's comfort, not for his own, and that helped settle his nerves and make up his mind. "If you want."

Thorne shook his head, the gesture rubbing his beard against Ian's skin again. Ian moaned softly at the contact. "It's not what I want, Ian," Thorne said seriously. "It's what we want, and right now, that's determined by what you want. I know you've been hurt in the past, and I won't be the one to make it worse."

Ian's first reaction was to deny it, but the look on Thorne's face stopped the words in his throat. Thorne didn't pity him, but he also wasn't going to take any bullshit about how nothing bad had happened. He wasn't demanding answers, but he wouldn't accept a lie. Ian nodded slowly, trying to go back to the question at hand. What about his shirt? He'd certainly admired Thorne's chest before, and he didn't have to do more than look even now just because Thorne took his shirt off. It didn't obligate him to do anything. "Maybe in a minute," he said finally before drawing Thorne back into their kiss.

Thorne came willingly enough, and that gave Ian the courage to move his hands over the cloth-covered breadth of Thorne's shoulders. It wasn't a daring caress, but it felt like a victory to Ian. Instead of burying his hands safely in Thorne's hair, he let them wander over Thorne's back, feeling the strong muscles beneath his T-shirt. When Thorne reciprocated, though, he froze. Immediately Thorne removed his hands and leaned back on the couch away from Ian.

"I won't touch you unless you ask," Thorne promised, "but I hope you won't stop touching me."

Ian gulped hard once and then a second time as he stared at Thorne laid out on the couch in front of him. With his hands locked behind his head, his chest puffed forward, making him seem even broader than usual. Ian raked his gaze over Thorne's body, flushing hard when he saw the bulge in Thorne's jeans. He'd done that, or rather, kissing him had done that to Thorne. Yet even aroused, Thorne put himself completely at Ian's command. It was a liberating realization.

He reached out again and rested his hand on the curve of Thorne's chest. He couldn't meet Thorne's gaze as he waited for a reaction—he didn't have that much boldness in him—but the sound of Thorne's sharp intake of breath reached his ears. "You're going to be the death of me," Thorne said, his voice a rumble in his chest that Ian swore he felt as much as heard.

"Will it at least be a good way to go?" Ian asked, plucking up his nerve.

"The best," Thorne replied.

The words sent warmth of a different kind through him. This wasn't just lust, although that was a part of it. This went beyond that to something deeper. Thorne tugged at him in a way no one else had ever done, both physically and emotionally.

"Can I…?" He couldn't get the words out.

Thorne cupped his cheek with his hand again, drawing Ian's gaze up to his face. "You can do whatever you want, Ian. I'm all yours, remember?"

Ian swallowed hard and nodded as he reached for the hem of Thorne's shirt. Thorne sat up enough to rip the cloth over his head before returning to his reclining position on the couch. "Whatever you want," he repeated.

Ian took a moment just to stare. He'd seen Thorne from across the room, but this was different. At this distance, he could see the scars that lurked beneath the pelt of dark hair and the details of the tattoos that adorned Thorne's shoulders under the cover of his T-shirt, a sword through a boomerang on one side and a series of numbers on the other. He didn't ask, but he committed the black lines to memory. Another time, perhaps, he'd find the courage to ask the significance of the numbers. If they were dates, as they appeared, the oldest was from more than twenty years ago. The scars told a different tale: a pucker beneath Thorne's collarbone, a sharply ridged line along his ribs, what looked like the jagged edge of a handsaw disappearing into the waistband of his pants, the shiny remnants of a burn wrapping around his waist to his back. The details drove home to Ian just how hard a life Thorne had lived. Ian had a few marks on his hands and legs from life on the station, where barbed wire had caught him once when he was still a blow-in and had more bravado than brains. Macklin had torn him a new one when he'd found him tangled in the wire and bleeding in more places than he had intact skin, but only a few of the puncture wounds had left scars. Thorne hadn't been as lucky, it seemed, or if he had, he'd been hurt far more often than Ian.

"They're all old and long since healed," Thorne said softly, as if reading Ian's thoughts. "Line of duty, for the most part, and nothing that bothers me now. I'm not going anywhere unless you ask me to."

"You're sure they don't hurt?" Ian hesitated with his hand above the pucker on Thorne's upper chest. He wanted to touch, to feel for himself that the wound had healed, but he didn't want to cause Thorne any pain.

"I'm sure," Thorne replied, "but if it'll make you feel better, I promise to tell you if you do anything that hurts."

"You'd better," Ian demanded fiercely. He knew what it felt like to be hurt, and he would cut off his hand before he did such a thing to anyone else.

"I will," Thorne said, "but you aren't going to hurt me like this. Believe me, it all feels wonderful." He rested his hand on top of Ian's. "When you're ready, maybe you'll let me show you too."

Ian swallowed back the automatic denial that sprang to his lips. He'd already done so much more with Thorne than he'd ever imagined doing with anyone. Maybe he would be ready at some point. For now, though, he had the acres of Thorne's chest to explore, and so he let his fingers wander over the thick chest, enjoying the way the muscles twitched beneath his fingers and the sounds of Thorne's ragged breathing. When he glanced up at Thorne's face, his own breath caught in his throat at the passion he saw burning in Thorne's sapphire eyes. He swore Thorne's eyes weren't that dark usually, but now his pupils were blown, leaving only a ring of dark, dark blue around the center, and all that fire was focused on Ian. He felt heat rise in his cheeks again and looked down, needing to escape the intensity of Thorne's gaze. The view that presented him with did nothing for his composure. If there had been a bulge in Thorne's jeans before, now Ian could see the outline of his cock beneath the fly, a fence post to rival the ones they'd driven along the property line earlier in the day. He gulped and nearly pulled away, but Thorne's voice stopped him.

"Nothing you don't want, remember? That's my problem, not yours."

Ian wanted desperately to believe him. Thorne hadn't gone back on his word yet and had gone beyond the call of duty to protect Ian. He'd come by the hospital every day, even when it was out of his way, and he'd spent the past week on Ian's couch, never pressing for more than Ian was willing to give him. Today he'd worked tirelessly at Ian's side, doing whatever Ian asked, no matter how demanding or how trivial. They'd set fence posts, pulled barbed wire, and carried packs of batteries and lamp oil into drovers' huts, and Thorne had done each task with the same careful determination. Taking a deep breath, Ian nodded and let himself trust.

Thorne had returned his hands to their resting place behind his head. Ian could give himself this time to explore.

Thorne's skin was hot beneath his hands as he ran his palms over the broad expanse of naked flesh. Ian avoided Thorne's nipples, not sure he was ready for something that would be deliberately arousing instead of simply exploring, but the little buds of flesh peaked despite the lack of direct stimulation, pushing through the mat of hair to draw Ian's attention. Cautiously he reached out to touch, then snatched his hand back when Thorne inhaled sharply.

"No, don't stop," Thorne urged. "It feels good."

It hadn't felt good when his foster father had twisted his nipples while forcing him onto the bed, but Thorne's face showed no sign of pain, so Ian rubbed his thumb over the taut bud.

"Yessss," Thorne hissed. "Again."

Ian liked the sound enough to follow Thorne's command and repeat the caress. Thorne arched into the touch and gasped again. The noises urged Ian on, but more than that, they fed his own awakening need. He'd never imagined he could feel such desire, nor that he would take such pleasure in touching someone else, in bringing pleasure to someone else. Leaving his hands where they were, he leaned forward to kiss Thorne again, reveling in the slightly chapped lips beneath his and the way Thorne's beard abraded his lips ever so slightly. When Thorne licked across the seam of his mouth, Ian didn't hesitate to open to the silent request this time. Thorne still tasted of peppermint, but Ian didn't question it now, sucking Thorne's tongue into his mouth and enjoying the crispness the sweet candy had left behind.

Ian reveled in the kiss and the feel of Thorne's chest beneath his hands, but something was missing. It took him a moment to realize what it was, but then he saw Thorne's hands still clasped behind his head. "There's a lot I'm not ready for," Ian said, "but I love the feel of your hands in my hair."

"Since you asked," Thorne said with a smile. He curled his hands around Ian's head again, stroking that spot that made Ian moan, and Ian renewed the kiss, dipping his tongue into Thorne's mouth this time. Thorne let him and sucked lightly in return.

Ian shivered and pulled back a bit, then rested his forehead against Thorne's. His cock ached for attention, but he wasn't ready for Thorne to take care of that for him, nor to take care of it himself where Thorne could see. He imagined Thorne must be in the same sorry state or worse, but he simply lay there and let Ian rest against him. Ian wanted to give some explanation for stopping, but he didn't know where to begin. Thorne didn't ask, though, simply rubbing his fingers over Ian's scalp. The gesture reminded Ian of the way Sam would rub Hawk's ears. The jackaroos teased Sam mercilessly for turning the kitten of a mostly feral barn cat into a pet, but Ian had listened to the way the little ball of fluff would purr at Sam's attentions, and he thought he finally understood. He wished he could purr to let Thorne know how good the caress felt.

"I should let you sleep."

"Only if you want to go," Thorne said. "You're welcome to stay here as long as you're comfortable."

Ian hated to admit they were reaching the limits of his expanded comfort zone, but Thorne deserved the truth. "I think I won't be comfortable staying much longer, at least not like this."

"Then sit up and we'll read for a while if you aren't ready for bed," Thorne said. "I haven't even made a dent in your bookshelf."

Ian smiled and then had to smother a yawn. "It's getting late, and tomorrow will be another early day."

"Are there any not early days around here?" Thorne asked.

"Everyone gets a day off a week," Ian said, "although not everyone takes it. It's not like there's much to do with a day off. Boorowa isn't exactly next door. I go into town if I need something, but that's once or twice a season, honestly."

"So you don't run into town to have a drink or let off steam?"

"I can have a drink here, and whoever has the supply run will pick up more for me if I run out, and I'm not exactly one to let off steam," Ian replied. "I haven't gone to town just to go to town since I decided to stay on the station permanently. Everything I need is right here."

"Then I'd say that makes you a very lucky man," Thorne said. "Would you want to come to Wagga Wagga with me? It would mean taking an extra day off, but from the sound of it, you've built up enough days to take an extra one."

"It doesn't work that way," Ian said "There's work to be done, and if I leave, Caine and Macklin are shorthanded. That's not fair to them or the people who have to take up my slack while I'm gone."

"Haven't you taken up their slack in the past?" Thorne asked.

"Probably, but it's not like I keep track," Ian protested.

"Do you want to come with me?" Thorne asked. "If missing work weren't an issue, would you come help me get my stuff and meet Walker?"

"If work weren't an issue," Ian said. "But it is."

"I know it is," Thorne said, "but I've met your family. I thought maybe you'd like to meet the closest thing to family I have left. I know things are moving fast, but what we're doing together doesn't feel casual."

It wasn't, not for Ian.

"I'll talk to Neil," Ian said. "If he thinks they can cover for me for an extra day, I'll go with you. If not, maybe we can go in the fall after we're done with the shearing. There isn't as much work once April rolls around."

Thorne sat up and gave Ian another quick kiss. "Thank you. It means a lot that you'd even ask Neil about it." He stretched his arm along the back of the couch, and Ian relaxed underneath it, pressing his cheek against Thorne's side. Thorne leaned forward and snagged the books they'd been reading the night before and handed Ian his.

Ian took it and found the page he'd bookmarked. As he fell back into the story, he thought this might be the most comfortable he'd ever been in his own skin.

SIXTEEN

"YOU look happy," Neil said when he cornered Ian in the paddock three days later.

The comment surprised Ian. He would never have said he was unhappy before Thorne arrived, but for the past two weeks, he'd been floating on air. "I guess I am," Ian replied.

"Good. He seems to be settling in well."

"A lot better than most of our new jackaroos do each spring," Ian agreed. "We need to figure out his day off each week. He needs to go to Wagga Wagga to get his stuff from his friend's place."

"I gave him the same day off as you," Neil said. "I do that for Chris and Jesse, and for Kyle and Linda. I figured you deserved the same courtesy, but Wagga Wagga isn't a one-day trip."

"No, I know it isn't," Ian said, "but at least if he starts with that day, he'll only have to miss one day of work instead of two. He mentioned me going with him, but I was off work for a week and then on light duty for a week. I can't take another day off again so soon."

Neil snorted. "You do realize this is me you're talking to, right? When was the last time, not counting when you were in the hospital, that you actually didn't work for a day?"

Ian had to stop and think about it. "Maybe Christmas last year?"

"Exactly," Neil said. "If we're counting who owes days to who, the station owes you far more days than you've taken being sick—which doesn't count—or that you'd take by going with him to Wagga Wagga. If you don't want to go for some reason, that's fine. I'll be the bad guy and say you can't have the extra day off, but that's bullshit and everyone will know it."

"I don't know what I want to do," Ian admitted after a moment. "Thorne's right that he's already met everyone important to me. The guy in Wagga Wagga is his best friend, pretty much the closest thing to family he has."

"That's a pretty big step, going home to meet the parents," Neil said. "Are you ready for that?"

"That's exactly the problem," Ian replied. "I don't know if I'm ready for it. I don't know if I'll ever be ready for it."

"It's your call, of course, but I'd built up meeting Molly's parents to be much worse than it actually was," Neil said. "And this guy is his best friend, not his parents, who might actually stop him from doing something."

"They were on the same team in the Commandos," Ian said. "Thorne saved his life. I got the impression they were pretty close."

"Close like you and I are close? Or close like Chris and Jesse are close?" Neil asked. Ian couldn't quite hide the smirk at the thought that Neil referenced Chris and Jesse, not Sam and Jeremy.

"Close like you and I are," Ian confirmed. "I don't think Thorne told anyone he was gay while he was in the military."

"Probably the safer choice," Neil said. "Is he going to tell the guy now?"

"He said he was. That's part of my concern. If there's a scene, I don't want to make it worse by being there," Ian said.

"You might make it better by being there," Neil said. "It's harder to air dirty laundry when someone else is around."

"If I'm there, he has to tell him," Ian countered. "He can't read the cues in the situation and decide to explain later. That isn't fair either."

"Maybe, maybe not," Neil said, "but he asked you to go with him."

"You think I should go."

"I think you shouldn't refuse to go without a real reason other than just being nervous," Neil amended. "He took a huge step in asking you to go with him. You shouldn't dismiss that lightly."

"I'm not dismissing it," Ian said, "but it feels like a huge step to be taking with a man I've only known for a month."

"Time moves differently around here," Neil said. "You've spent far more hours with him than you would have if you lived in Melbourne, met someone there, and started dating. You've eaten together, worked together, hell, you bloody near died together. I don't think you can use time as an excuse."

"How long did it take you to know how you felt about Molly?" Ian asked. He'd known Neil was falling for her, but he hadn't paid all that much attention at the time. Caine had just arrived on the station and everything had still felt unsettled, and Neil's infatuation with the pretty jillaroo hadn't seemed of much importance until Neil had announced their engagement.

"I knew almost immediately that she was the one I wanted," Neil said, "but Michael had just died and everything was up in the air, so I didn't say anything the first summer she worked here. When she came back the next year, though, I figured it was a sign, and I did everything I could to convince her to marry me."

"You know Thorne and I can't get married," Ian said.

Neil rolled his eyes. "Not the point, drongo. There are a lot of things I don't know, but if there's one thing Caine and Sam have taught me, it's that love isn't defined by the gender of the person you care about. Sure, it sometimes still makes me uncomfortable if I think about it too much, but Sam loves Jeremy the same way I love Molly. If you get the chance to have that with Thorne, you need to grab it with both hands and not let go."

"We should get to work," Ian said. Neil was right, Ian was sure, but he needed time to think about it, and that couldn't happen with Neil standing there looking at him expectantly.

Neil shook his head. "Get Titan and teach your blow-in how to ride. You'll reap the benefits of it later."

Ian's cheeks flamed. The only benefit he'd reap of Thorne learning to ride was an extra jackaroo to help with the work, but Neil didn't know that. Ian hadn't ever told him, and he wasn't going to tell him now. He grabbed Titan's halter and fled, Neil's teasing laughter following him all the way to the shearing shed where they kept the tack.

"WHAT are you doing in my kitchen?"

Thorne looked up in surprise as Kami glared at him from across the room. "I came to get some water," Thorne replied. "Ian's been teaching me how to ride and it's hot outside. He said I could get some water in here."

"Out in the canteen," Kami grumbled, "not in the kitchen where I'm working."

Before Thorne could apologize and leave, Kami had slammed a cup of water down in front of him. "Thank you."

"Don't thank me," Kami said. "Sit down."

Thorne almost balked at Kami's tone of voice, but if he'd learned one thing while in the military, it was not to piss off the person responsible for dinner, so he sat and took a long drink of his water.

"You're spending a lot of time with Ian during the day and sleeping with him at night."

"Sleeping on his couch," Thorne corrected.

That drew Kami up short for a minute, surprise crossing his face before being replaced by that glare again. "Something wrong with his bed?" Kami demanded.

"I wouldn't know," Thorne said. "I haven't been invited into it, and I'm certainly not going there uninvited."

"Good to hear," Kami said. "He's the one year-rounder whose story I don't know, but I know he has one. I remember him when he first came, and he had all the signs of a wounded animal."

"He hasn't told me either," Thorne admitted, "but he doesn't need to. I can guess enough of it, and even if I couldn't, I'm not the kind of man to force anyone into bed."

"So what kind of man are you?" Kami demanded.

Thorne wasn't sure how to answer that question, in part because he wasn't sure what Kami wanted to know. "I'm a soldier," he said slowly. "Retired, maybe, but it's still who I am."

Kami stared at him for so long that Thorne squirmed uncomfortably on his chair. "Not a soldier," he said finally. "A warrior."

"Same thing," Thorne said.

"No, it's not," Kami insisted. "Anyone who joins the army is a soldier and when he leaves the army, that's over. It's a job, nothing more. You're different. You were a soldier. You were in the army, but it's deeper than that for you. It's in your nature to fight for what's important, to spend everything you have and are to protect those you love."

"Hell of a lot of good it ever did me," Thorne muttered.

"That only makes you a wounded warrior," Kami replied. "It doesn't change your heart."

"I'm not wounded," Thorne replied automatically.

"Not all wounds are physical," Kami said. "You flinch when someone walks up behind you. You shy from unexpected touches or loud noises. Your body might be as strong as ever, but your heart is bruised."

Thorne opened his mouth to deny it, but Kami cut him off. "Don't say it," Kami said. "Don't lie to yourself. You don't have to talk to me about it. You don't even have to talk to Ian about it, but he doesn't deserve to live with your lie."

"So what do I do?" Thorne asked.

"Help each other heal," Kami replied like it was the most obvious thing in the world.

"How?" Thorne asked, because he'd do whatever it took to help Ian, but he didn't really know where to start.

"That's a question for you and him," Kami said, "but I'll tell you the two things Sarah has taught me: love him unreservedly and have patience with his scars."

Thorne froze. He hadn't let himself think about love. It wasn't in the cards for him, not as fucked up as his head was, but the minute Kami put words to it, he knew the emotion rang true. Sometime in the past month, he'd fallen in love.

"I can do that," he said in a choked voice. "If he'll let me."

"I'm quite sure he won't," Kami said sardonically. "That's where the patience comes in. I've seen it before, with Macklin, with Jesse, with Sam, with Neil. They don't believe they deserve to be loved and so they try to reject it when it comes. No reason Ian should be any different. No reason to expect you to be any different either. You might be new here, but you'd be one of Caine's strays if Ian hadn't got to you first."

"Your wife mentioned that the station has a tradition of taking in people in need of a home," Thorne said neutrally.

"You're sleeping on Ian's couch," Kami pointed out. "I think you fit the description, but yes, Lang Downs has always taken in the people no one else knew to value. You belong here as surely as the rest of us do."

"As long as I don't put anyone in danger," Thorne said bitterly.

"So don't," Kami said with a shrug. "Do what you need to do to put your past to rest, so it doesn't threaten anyone."

"I wouldn't know where to start," Thorne admitted.

"Then maybe you'd better figure that out."

THORNE collapsed onto Ian's couch with a sigh after dinner. If anyone had asked, he would have said riding a horse couldn't be all that hard on the rider since the horse was doing most of the work. He'd never been so wrong in his life. Every muscle in his lower body hurt, and he wasn't sure his thighs would ever close again. He feared he'd be permanently bowlegged.

Ian laughed at him unrepentantly, but Thorne didn't care. His bruised dignity aside, it had been another wonderful day spent in each other's company learning the skills he would need if he intended to stay on the station. Even more, it had been fun. Ian was a patient teacher and Titan was a docile horse, and by the time Ian had released him from lessons for the day, Thorne had grown comfortable with the basics of riding. He just couldn't walk now.

"I was thinking about Wagga Wagga," Ian said as he joined Thorne on the couch. "We both have Wednesday off, and Neil said he could spare us on Thursday as well if that suits your friend."

"You're coming with me?" Thorne asked, feeling like a kid on Christmas morning.

"If you still want me to," Ian said. "I don't want to be in your way or anything, but you asked, and, well—"

"Of course I still want you to come," Thorne interrupted. His muscles protested as he sat up and turned to face Ian, but he ignored the soreness. He'd dealt with worse. "After what you said the other night, I didn't think you'd want to, and I'd be fine if that's what you decided."

"I thought about it," Ian admitted. "Neil even offered to be the bad guy so I'd have an excuse not to go."

"What changed your mind?" Thorne was thrilled at the thought that Ian really did want to go with him. Whatever had brought that about, he needed to do more of it.

"Neil convinced me I had more to gain by going with you than I had to lose," Ian said. "Maybe it'll be a disaster, but you asked me to come, so I'll go meet your friend."

Thorne couldn't stop the smile that spread across his face as he pulled Ian closer. He nuzzled his cheek and then bent his head to kiss Ian tenderly. He was tempted to deepen the kiss, but this wasn't about passion, and Kami's words still rang in his head. *Love him unreservedly.* Instead he touched their foreheads together and tried not to imagine what it would feel like to tug Ian's shirt out of the way and lick and kiss all over his torso. Ian had made it visibly clear he wasn't ready for that kind of intimacy, and Thorne wouldn't push, no matter how much he wanted to know if Ian's skin was as smooth as it had looked the other night or to see if the delightful blushes that sometimes stained his cheeks extended down below the collar of his shirt.

Ian might not be ready to take his own shirt off, but he had no qualms getting his hands underneath Thorne's shirt, not that Thorne was complaining. The minute he felt Ian's hands on his waist, he lifted his arms to facilitate his disrobing. It had been torture of the most amazingly pleasurable kind, having Ian run his hands over him and not being able to make Ian feel the same mind-blowing pleasure, but it was torture he would willingly endure if it helped Ian trust him more. Not unexpectedly, Ian took advantage of Thorne's position to strip off his T-shirt, leaving Thorne bare to the waist. He leaned back as he had done before, letting the arm of the couch bear his weight so Ian could look and touch his fill.

"Tell me about your tattoos?" Ian asked, tracing the one on Thorne's left shoulder.

"It's the emblem of the Commandos," Thorne said.

"And the others?" Ian asked.

"Dates I don't ever want to forget," Thorne said. He hoped Ian wouldn't ask what the dates represented. He didn't want to talk about his parents, his squad, or even leaving the Commandos right now. He wanted to focus on Ian. Fortunately his answer seemed to satisfy Ian's curiosity because he nodded and turned his attention to exploring Thorne's chest.

Ian's hands were hot on his skin and rough with calluses from years of hard work. Thorne hadn't expected life on the station to be easy, but he hadn't realized just how physically demanding it was until he started spending his days with Ian. Up before dawn, working until nearly dusk, pulling fences, setting fence posts, riding horses and watching the sheep, and all that was while Ian was still on light duty. Thorne didn't even want to think about what would happen when Ian was fully back at work. Then Ian carded his fingers through Thorne's chest hair, coming tantalizingly close to his nipples, and all extraneous thought disappeared. Thorne's world narrowed to the touch of Ian's hands and the heat of his body. He was rock hard already, and they'd barely started. He felt like he was fifteen again, but he blamed that on how worked up he was by the end of the evening, with no true satisfaction in sight. He'd relieved himself in the shower, but it wasn't what he wished he could have. He wouldn't pressure Ian, though, not when Ian leaned against him so trustingly now, not worried, like he'd been the first night, that Thorne would press for more.

He curled his hand around the nape of Ian's neck and pulled him in for a kiss. Whatever else would or wouldn't happen between them tonight, Ian had become as eager to kiss Thorne as Thorne was to kiss him. When Ian shifted to mate their mouths more easily, he settled his palms directly on top of Thorne's nipples, and Thorne gasped into the kiss.

Ian started to pull back, but Thorne shook his head and kept Ian close. It took a minute, but Ian settled back into the kiss. He didn't move his hands away, which Thorne took as a victory, but neither did he do anything to stimulate Thorne more. Then again, given how having Ian in his arms kissing him made Thorne feel, he didn't need stimulation.

Ian shifted again until he was practically lying on top of Thorne, a position not well suited to hiding how hard he was. Ian hadn't said it, and Thorne honestly didn't want to hear it, but he suspected Ian had been raped. Kissing was safe and easy, as was making out like this on the couch, and Thorne didn't want to ruin that because Ian realized how hard he was. Thorne shifted his hips, trying to get Ian to lie down next to him instead of nearly on top of him, but Ian didn't take the hint, so Thorne ran his hands down to Ian's shoulders to urge him to the side. He felt Ian's muscles tense through the fabric of his shirt, and a spark of anger flared in him. No one deserved to be hurt, least of all Ian, and Thorne felt a burning hatred for the faceless man who had left Ian with such insecurities. When he jerked his hands away so as not to make Ian uncomfortable, Ian shook his head.

"You don't have to stop."

Thorne wished that meant he could roll Ian beneath him and make love to him all night long, but he knew better than to think that. He did let his hands roam over Ian's back, though, feeling the wiry strength of his body through the cloth. Ian hummed and returned to kissing Thorne, and Thorne took what he was given and was grateful for it.

SEVENTEEN

THEY hadn't left the station as early as they'd planned, so by the time they reached Wagga Wagga, it was nearly dinnertime. Thorne had told Walker they'd be there in time for dinner, so they didn't have time to go by the hotel where they'd be staying before they went to Walker's flat.

"I wanted to make a good first impression," Ian muttered as they pulled into the car park.

"Relax," Thorne said. "He's just got back from six months in East Timor. Compared to the way everyone looked and smelled there, you're positively fresh."

"Gee, thanks." Ian rolled his eyes. "That's exactly the comparison I wanted him to make."

"Ian, relax," Thorne repeated. "He isn't going to care that we came straight here, and we're probably going out to a local, anyway, where people will be coming straight from work. It's not going to be a problem. I promise."

Ian wasn't sure that was a promise Thorne could keep, but he hadn't let Ian down yet, so he relaxed into the reassurance as requested. They left the safety of the car and walked up to Walker's apartment.

The door opened moments after their knock. "Getting shaggy there, Lachlan," the man who answered the door said as he pulled Thorne into a tight hug. "Civilian life agrees with you."

Thorne laughed, the sound sending a spike of jealousy through Ian. He'd spent nearly a month with Thorne and knew how rarely the other man laughed, but one offhand comment from Walker and Thorne was laughing like a loon.

"Ian, this is my old Commando buddy, Sergeant Nick Walker. Walker, this is Ian Duncan. He's one of the crew bosses at Lang Downs, the sheep station where I'm working."

"Nice to meet you, Duncan," Walker said, offering his hand to Ian.

"Please, call me Ian," Ian replied as he shook Walker's hand. "I'm not the kind to stand on formality."

"You're welcome to call me Nick too, although I won't promise I'll answer. After all these years in the military, I answer to Walker more than to Nick." He opened the door wider to invite them both inside.

"How long have you been in?" Ian asked for lack of anything better to say.

"Nineteen years next month," Walker said. "I have one year left and then I have to decide if I'm going to stay in or get out. I don't have the rank to get stuck in a desk job like Lachlan would have, so I can re-up and stay in the field if I want."

"What would you do if you got out?"

"That's the problem," Thorne said. "For the people who do a short stint, they have time to get other training, but for us career soldiers, it's a different situation entirely."

"We serve our time, and then we're pretty much left adrift unless we want to sign on again to serve more time," Walker agreed.

"Sounds like you already know what you're going to do," Ian commented.

"I don't know. Lachlan found something else to do with himself," Walker replied. "Maybe there's room for one more on that sheep station of his."

Another surge of jealousy washed through Ian, but he'd learned Michael's lessons too well to assure Walker they didn't need any more help. "That's not my decision to make, but I've never known Lang Downs to turn away someone in need," he said instead. It was both honest and noncommittal. The ball was in Walker's court now. If he showed up in a year, Ian would have to decide what to do about it and whether it was worth fighting Thorne's best friend to keep what he hoped was the tentative beginning of something real and lasting.

"So, what are you doing for Christmas, Lachlan?" Walker asked. "You coming down here like you did last year?"

"No," Thorne replied, much to Ian's relief. "I'm going to stay at Lang Downs with everyone there."

Walker's surprise showed on his face. "You said you were working there. You didn't say you'd decided to stay."

"We haven't exactly had a chance to talk since I got there," Thorne retorted. "I'll tell you everything you want to know, but Ian and I have had a long drive. We could use a pint and something to eat."

"Sure, mate. Let me just grab my keys."

They took Walker's car to the local pub, and it was obvious from the way they were greeted that Walker was a regular when he was in town. He introduced Thorne and Ian. Thorne got the same hero's welcome Walker did, and Ian reminded himself he'd done nothing to deserve it and not to be jealous. He was going to kill Neil when he got back to the station. This had been an unmitigatedly bad idea, but before he could think of an excuse to bow out of the evening and find a way to their hotel, Thorne squeezed his arm and pulled him into the conversation.

Maybe the evening would still be a complete disaster, but Thorne wanted him there. Ian would cling to that.

"WHAT'S the deal with the stockman?" Walker asked Thorne an hour later, after Ian had excused himself to go to the loo. "Are they afraid you'll go AWOL or something?"

"It's a sheep station, not the military," Thorne replied. "If I didn't go back, I wouldn't get paid, but nobody would come after me. That's not the way it works."

"It was a joke."

"A bad one," Thorne retorted. "I like it there, Walker. It's peaceful and quiet and restful. I haven't had a lot of that in my life. Sure, it's hard work, but it feels good to be part of building something instead of always destroying."

"We did a lot of good all those years," Walker insisted.

"Yes, we did," Thorne agreed, "but the good we did for some was always bad for someone else. If we killed a guerrilla and protected a village, the villagers were safe, but the guerrilla was dead and his family lost a son, brother, father, whatever. The good of the many is supposed to outweigh that, except it never fully did. There's no downside on the station. The sense of building something isn't accompanied by the knowledge of having destroyed something else."

"You got a girl on the station?" Walker asked. "You're talking like a bloke with a soft heart."

"Not a girl," Thorne replied as he braced himself for the moment of truth. "I've got Ian."

"Wait, what?" Walker said. "Ian, as in the bloke who just went to the restroom?"

"Yes," Thorne said distinctly. "You got a problem with that?"

"No," Walker said immediately, "but… when did this happen?"

"I met him a month ago, when I got sent to Lang Downs to warn them about the grassfires," Thorne said. "I told you that."

"No, not that part," Walker said. "The part where you like blokes."

"That happened when I was a kid," Thorne said. "I just didn't tell anybody about it."

"And in all that time and with everything we've been through, you couldn't have told me before this?"

"There was never a reason to tell you," Thorne said. "I hadn't met anyone, I didn't know if I ever would, and you know how it is with secrets. As soon as you tell anyone, it's not a secret anymore."

"Like I'd do anything to put you in danger! You saved my fucking life, remember?"

"Is everything okay?" Ian asked as he rejoined them at the table.

"Stupid fucker kept secrets from me for nineteen years," Walker spat. "No, everything is not okay."

Thorne could have punched Walker right then for the look the comment put on Ian's face. "Don't take it out on him," Thorne said. "If you're angry at someone, be angry at me."

"Damn straight I'm angry at you." He turned to Ian. "You work on a team on the station. You know how it is. You have to trust the men you're out in the paddocks with to do their job and to have your six. Now I find out he lied to me all these years. What am I supposed to think?"

"That he did his job and had your back all those years," Ian replied quietly. "I don't know how it is in the army, but I know how it is in the outback, and telling the wrong person you're bent is a good way to have nobody watching your back ever again unless it's to take a stab at it. If it makes you feel any better, my best friend's brother and both of our bosses are gay, but I didn't say anything to any of them until a couple of weeks ago. I'd kept the secret for so long I didn't say anything until I didn't have a choice anymore."

Walker didn't look convinced by Ian's passionate defense, but the heartfelt words warmed Thorne. He squeezed Ian's knee beneath the table.

"Look, I didn't tell you to cause problems or to make you uncomfortable," Thorne said. "You're the closest thing to family I have left, and I wanted Ian to meet you, but I can see that's a bad idea now, so we'll just get my boxes from your place and get out of your hair. If you reach a point where you're comfortable with us, you know how to reach me, but I won't bother you again."

"Sit down," Walker snapped as Thorne started to stand "I'm angry as fuck, but you're not getting out of it that easily. You're stuck with me, remember?"

"I never wanted it any other way," Thorne said, "but I'm not going to listen to homophobic bullshit."

"You think that's what this is about?" Walker retorted. "I don't give a shit who you fuck. I'm pissed because you didn't tell me the truth. I went out with you. I watched you pick up girls. Hell, we shared those twins in Saigon. That's not omission, like your boyfriend said. That's an outright lie."

"A necessary one," Thorne insisted. "You weren't the only one watching all those nights. Maybe you wouldn't have cared, but you *know* we served with men who would have, and stories like the twins in Saigon made sure I was safe from the rest of them."

"Any other secrets you're keeping from me?" Walker demanded.

"No," Thorne promised, "this was the only one. I mean, there's stuff we haven't talked about since I've been out, stories we haven't had time for me to tell you, but nothing secret."

"That's something, anyway," Walker grumbled. He turned to Ian. "Sorry about the outburst. It's not about you. You get that, right?"

Ian didn't look convinced, as far as Thorne was concerned, but he nodded and gave Walker a halfhearted smile.

"So tell me about East Timor? Are things getting any better?" Thorne asked, hoping to change the subject.

They spent the rest of dinner trading stories of shared and separate missions, reminiscing and remembering lost friends. Thorne worried Ian would feel excluded, but he hoped it would give him some insight into Thorne's past. He didn't feel comfortable trying to recount his service in any kind of coherent fashion, but this rambling walk down memory lane served the same purpose in a far less studied fashion. Ian laughed at the funny stories—and Walker made sure to drag out every story that made Thorne look like a Galah—and squeezed Thorne's hand beneath the table when the conversation turned to lost friends and dark missions. By the time they left the pub to return to Walker's apartment, the tension between Thorne and Walker had dissipated, leaving them laughing like they always did when they were together for any period of time.

"You want another beer?" Walker asked when they got back to his apartment. "Tomorrow is my day off, so I don't have to get up early."

"You don't, but we do," Thorne reminded him. "We have to drive back several hours past Boorowa tomorrow instead of lazing around in bed all day. We can't afford to be hungover."

"Has your tolerance really dropped that much in a few months?" Walker teased. "You used to be able to drink me under the table without even trying."

He could probably still fake it, like he had all those years in the military, but Thorne had told Walker no more secrets. "That's because I was really good at making it seem like I drank more than I actually did. Most of those nights I drank you under the table, I'd only actually had one drink. Everyone just thought I'd had more."

"More secrets?" Walker asked, but he didn't seem as upset as he had earlier, so Thorne just shrugged.

"Sleight of hand. My best friend in high school was the son of an alcoholic, often an angry one. We swore we'd never be like him," Thorne explained.

"You can drink without getting drunk," Walker said.

"And he can choose not to drink if that's his preference," Ian interrupted. "If you want us to stay longer, we can, but we can have coffee, or water, for that matter. We don't need to keep drinking to have a good time."

"Kitchen's in there," Walker said to Thorne. "If you want something, help yourself. I want a word with your boyfriend."

Thorne tensed, but Ian waved him toward the kitchen, so Thorne went to put on a pot of coffee. He'd been here enough times when they were still serving together to know where everything was.

IAN tensed when Thorne left the room. He didn't think Walker meant him any harm, and even if he did, Thorne was a shout away, but it didn't make the moment any less nerve-racking.

"I've known Lachlan for a long time," Walker said.

"I got that impression," Ian said wryly.

Walker grinned, although the expression didn't reach his eyes. "Smartarse. I like you already. In all that time, I've never seen him happy. Satisfied with a mission well done, relieved to be alive, replete after a night of fucking, even excited about the prospect of leave—and doesn't that make more sense now—but I've never seen him happy. Too much shit in his past for that. Has he told you about his parents?"

"Only a little," Ian said. "I know they're deceased."

"That's not my story to tell, but ask him about them at some point. You'll see what I'm talking about with the whole happiness bit. You, however, make him happy. I'm not quite sure how I feel about that, to be perfectly honest, but he's my brother-in-arms, and nothing changes that."

"That's good to know," Ian said, relaxing a bit. "I want him to be happy."

"So do I," Walker said. "I grew up on a sheep station, you know. Not in NSW, but enough to know what it's like and the kind of prejudices he could be facing."

"Not on Lang Downs," Ian said immediately. "Not with Caine and Macklin owning the place and Neil running it. I know that doesn't mean anything to you, but I watched Neil fire a man last summer because he wouldn't let up on the comments about the bosses. If he'd kept his mouth shut after the first time, or probably even after the fifth, Neil might have let it go, but he's loyal to the bone, and he won't stand for any kind of ignorant comments about the bosses or any of the other couples on the station. The same will apply to Thorne and me. Not that Thorne can't look after himself; I'm pretty sure whatever he'd choose to do in his own defense would be far worse than losing a job."

"He could, but he won't," Walker said, "not unless he's attacked physically, or maybe if you are. He's trained enough to kill in his sleep, but he's disciplined enough to keep all that under wraps unless there's a bloody good reason to let it out."

Ian thought about the moment in the paddocks with Laura and the times since then when he'd seen Thorne come close to reaching his breaking point. He wondered how aware Walker was of Thorne's current condition, but before he could ask for clarification or advice, Thorne came back in with two cups of coffee—one black, one light and sweet, just the way Ian liked it—and a beer for Walker.

"Everything okay in here?" he asked as he set the drinks on the low table in front of the couch.

"Everything's fine," Ian said, realizing as he spoke that he actually meant it. "Thank you for the coffee."

"I know how you get," Thorne said with a grin, and Ian couldn't help his answering smile. Thorne *did* know him after a month spent together working and living on the station. Judging from Walker's expression, that was another sign of something different—something good, Ian hoped. He took a sip of the coffee and swallowed hard as an epiphany struck him with all the subtlety of a stampede: he'd fallen in love with the burly wounded warrior sitting next to him on the couch.

Thorne and Walker kept the conversation going, thankfully, because Ian was too shell-shocked to do anything but sit there and stare blindly at the wall of Walker's apartment. He couldn't be in love with Thorne. Thorne didn't deserve someone who couldn't even contemplate taking his shirt off in the same room with another man. He deserved someone who could love him without reservation, but the thought of what that might entail still left Ian feeling sick to his stomach. His hands trembled as he sipped his coffee, nearly sloshing the hot liquid over the rim of the cup. He took a deep breath, trying to steady himself, but the shaking got worse, and he had to put the cup down before he spilled it all over himself and the couch.

"Ian?" Thorne asked when the cup clattered against the table. "What's wrong?"

Ian shook his head and tried not to hyperventilate.

"Ian, you're scaring me."

"Can it, Lachlan," Walker snapped. "You've been around enough blokes straight out of the field. You should recognize a flashback when you see one."

Ian wanted to deny it, to insist he was perfectly fine, but he couldn't form the words. A moment later, he felt Thorne wrap a thick blanket around his shoulders. It should have been stifling in the mid-December heat, but Ian felt frozen all the way through, even with the blanket encasing him. He didn't protest when Thorne pulled him onto his lap and added his own body heat to the mix. The circle of Thorne's arms did more to steady him than anything else. He was safe with Thorne, safe in his arms, safe with those big hands covering his back and shutting out everything that might come to hurt him. All he had to do was relax and trust them and he'd stop shaking. He'd be able to breathe right again. He'd be able to smile and assure them it wasn't anything serious, just a bad memory. They might even let it go at that. They had moments they didn't want to relive. Surely they'd understand Ian just wanting to put this behind him.

In the seventeen years since he'd escaped, he still hadn't put it behind him.

Bile rose in his throat. He buried his face against Thorne's neck, letting the smell of cedar and granite remind him where he was. His foster father had always smelled like cheap pomade and often of whiskey, never like this, and he'd never worn a beard, so the familiar rasp of Thorne's facial hair against Ian's forehead was another layer of reality separating him from the past. He had to get himself under control or they'd ask for explanations he couldn't give. He couldn't admit to what had happened. Shame roiled through him, choking him with its intensity.

He had to get out of here. He had to get somewhere safe.

"—safe. I've got you. You're safe."

Thorne's words finally penetrated the panicked haze of Ian's mind.

"Look, Walker is standing guard at the door, and I've got you in my arms. Nobody's getting anywhere near you. You're safe."

Ian wanted to tell them he'd never be safe again, but he forced himself to picture his foster father realistically. Compared with a sixteen-year-old boy, he'd been large and intimidating, but Ian wasn't sixteen anymore, and the men in the room with him towered over him. They were close to the same age his foster father had been then, which meant they were fifteen or more years older than him, powerful, highly trained soldiers in the prime of their lives. Even if somehow his foster father found him again and tried to take him, he'd stand no chance against either of them, much less against both of them. He was safe.

He slumped in Thorne's arms, all tension leaving him as that feeling settled into his very bones. As long as Thorne was there, he was safe.

"Sorry about that," he said sheepishly.

"Don't apologize," Thorne insisted. "You helped me the last time I nearly lost it to flashbacks. I can help you in return."

"We've both been there," Walker agreed. "We might not have the same nightmares stalking us, but we'd be lying if we said we slept easy at night. Lachlan, take him back to the hotel and make him forget everything but your name. That'll help him feel better."

Ian shuddered. He wished that were a possibility. He'd love to be able to forget, but it wouldn't happen the way Walker suggested, not when that was the cause of his nightmares in the first place.

"I'll take care of him," Thorne promised. "I was going to pack up the ute tonight so we didn't have to come back in the morning, but now I'm not sure that's such a good idea."

"It's just a few boxes," Walker said. "I'll carry them down now and that way you can sleep in and get on the road tomorrow when you're ready."

"I'm sorry," Ian said again when Walker had left with the first of the boxes. "I've spoiled the evening."

"You haven't spoiled anything," Thorne insisted. He nuzzled Ian's cheek, the tickle of his beard another reminder that Ian was safe and protected. "Walker is right. We've both been there. I wish you'd tell me what caused it, but I won't push. I know talking about it doesn't always help."

"Not now," Ian said. "Maybe… maybe someday, but not tonight." *Not here.*

Thorne nodded and held him a little tighter. Ian closed his eyes and just breathed in the scent of safety. Eventually the blanket became overly warm, probably a good sign, given the ambient temperature, so he shrugged it off his shoulders, but he made no move to escape Thorne's embrace. He couldn't think of anywhere he'd rather be than snug in Thorne's arms.

He'd have to deal with both the immediate and underlying causes of his panic attack at some point, but for right now, he could pretend Thorne's care meant he felt the same way Ian did. Ian didn't delude himself into thinking that would last beyond the revelation of his past, but he would take what he could get. Memories of his time with Thorne would keep him warm through the winter of his future.

He heard the door open and shut several more times as he sat there with Thorne murmuring in his ear, but he didn't look up. Thorne wasn't worried, so the sounds had to be Walker coming and going with Thorne's boxes.

"Everything's loaded," Walker said eventually, breaking Ian's reverie. "I'll see you next time you come to town."

"Don't expect it to be soon," Thorne said.

"I won't," Walker replied. "It doesn't matter how long it is. Just keep me posted."

"I will. Thanks, Walker."

"Take care of him, and let him take care of you."

"As much as he'll let me."

Ian felt like he ought to say something, but the panic attack had left him exhausted. He rose at Thorne's urging, but it took Thorne's arm around his waist to keep him steady. They made it down the stairs and into the ute, but Thorne had to fasten the seat belt around him. He fell asleep before they'd even left the car park.

EIGHTEEN

THORNE hated to wake Ian up when they got to the hotel, but he didn't think carrying him inside was really an option. Fortunately, Ian woke without fuss or fear, even summoning a genuine smile for Thorne.

"Sorry. I didn't mean to fall asleep like that."

"No worries," Thorne said. "Are you feeling better?"

"A little," Ian said. "I just hope my impromptu nap doesn't keep me from sleeping tonight."

"Let's get checked into the hotel and you can go straight to bed," Thorne suggested. "If we hurry, maybe you won't wake up all the way and can fall back asleep easily."

Ian nodded and followed Thorne into the lobby of the hotel. The clerk gave them two keys and directions to the rooms. They were on the same floor, but on opposite ends of the hall, which made Thorne uneasy. If Ian had nightmares, Thorne wouldn't be close enough to hear him.

He paused at the door to Ian's room. "Are you going to be all right by yourself? I don't like leaving you alone after a panic attack like you had earlier."

Ian hesitated for a moment before replying. "I think a spot of company would be good. If you don't mind. I can't... what Walker said—"

"Not like that," Thorne assured him before he could even finish his sentence. "Just to make sure you can sleep. He meant well, but he doesn't understand."

"And you do?" Ian asked.

"Enough to know that making love to you would hurt more than it would help," Thorne replied honestly. "No matter how much I might like the idea, I'm not going to do anything to hurt or upset you. Ever."

"I… thank you."

Thorne wasn't sure he'd ever been prouder of hearing those two words. He was only doing what any decent man would do, but it seemed Ian hadn't known many decent men before now, at least not ones who were interested in him. To have earned Ian's trust to the point that he would believe Thorne's assertion felt like a feat far more worthy of praise than anything he'd done with the Commandos.

"I'll step out while you get ready for bed," Thorne said, "and then I can sit with you until you fall asleep."

"Like a child afraid of the dark," Ian said bitterly.

Thorne caught Ian's arms and pulled him into an embrace. "No, like a man who just had a panic attack and is now having to sleep in an unfamiliar room in an unfamiliar city without anything to ground him if something triggers another one." He tipped Ian's chin up so he could meet his stormy green gaze. "You're not the only one who has them. You saw me barely fight one off the first night I spent at your place, and believe me, the only reason I managed was because you were there keeping me steady and giving me a place to feel safe. If I can do the same for you now, I'll count myself lucky."

"I don't know how to handle it," Ian admitted. He pulled away and Thorne let him go, watching helplessly as Ian started to pace. "I thought it was all behind me and then…."

"If you want to talk about it, I'll listen," Thorne offered quietly. "Whatever haunts your nightmares, it might be an easier burden if it's shared. I know it helps sometimes just to remember that I'm not alone, that whatever nightmare I'm dealing with, Walker was there with me."

"Not tonight," Ian said. "All I want tonight is to sleep. Ask me again after Christmas, and I'll tell you anything you want to know."

Thorne frowned. Christmas was only a week away, so that was hardly so far in the future that it would make much difference in the grand scheme of things, but Thorne hated the idea of Ian suffering alone even that much longer. He'd known Ian had a rough past. Kami had told him that much, even if he didn't know details, although Thorne could guess at some of what that was, given Ian's hesitancy where anything sexual was concerned, but he'd thought it was limited to that. Whatever had triggered his panic attack tonight, it hadn't been sexual. They'd been sitting on Walker's couch talking, not even close enough to touch, and for once, the conversation hadn't been laced with innuendo. Walker had used the word "boyfriend" a couple of times, but not immediately before Ian's meltdown, so that wasn't it. Ian's fears clearly went beyond the scope of what Thorne had guessed.

"If that's what you want," Thorne said.

"I don't want to fuck up the holidays," Ian said. "Don't say I won't. You can't know that, and I won't take the risk. After Christmas, we'll talk, and if you still want me then, we'll see how things go."

Thorne froze. He couldn't imagine anything Ian could tell him that would change the way he felt, but then Ian didn't know how Thorne felt. Now wasn't the time to tell him, though. He wouldn't believe it if Thorne said it, or if he did, he'd worry his revelations would change it. Thorne couldn't think of anything Ian could tell him that would change the way he felt. He knew Ian had been abused to the point of having hang-ups about sex, whether he'd been raped or had resorted to prostitution to keep himself fed. Thorne would gladly kill the man or men who'd left him so shattered, but he didn't blame Ian for it, no matter which it was. For that matter, Thorne wouldn't blame him if Ian revealed he'd killed to protect himself.

"It won't change anything, but I'll wait," Thorne said. "Come on, it's bedtime. You still look completely wrung out. I'll step outside and you tell me when I can come back in."

"You don't have to leave," Ian said. Thorne could practically see him struggling with himself as he began unbuttoning the long-sleeved shirt he'd worn even in the ute to protect his fair skin. He wore a sleeveless T-shirt underneath it, so Thorne only got a glimpse of his arms and shoulders, not his chest, but the T-shirt clung to lines of Ian's chest, hinting at what it concealed. Ian reached for the button on his jeans, but he didn't undo it, resting his hands on the waistband as if he was wrestling with himself. Taking pity on him, Thorne turned his back, giving Ian the illusion of privacy, if nothing else. He heard the sound of Ian's jeans hitting the floor and then the rustling of covers. "You can turn back around now. Thank you."

Thorne turned to see Ian bundled under the thin sheet all the way up to his neck. It was too hot for anything else, even now that the sun had gone down. "You're welcome," Thorne said as he settled in the chair across the room. "Turn the light off and go to sleep. I'll keep watch until I'm sure you're out."

Ian clicked off the lamp, plunging the room into darkness. It took a few minutes for Thorne's eyes to adjust, but he'd always had exceptional night vision, and enough light came in through the open window that before long, he could trace the outline of Ian's body on the bed. Ian lay unmoving, but Thorne could tell he hadn't relaxed. Unfortunately, he didn't know if that was because of the lingering effects of the panic attack or because of Thorne's presence in the room. However much Thorne wanted to represent safety to Ian, he knew enough about the tricks the mind could play in a compromised state to understand that his good intentions might not be enough. Despite everything, with Ian feeling vulnerable, Thorne could well represent a threat.

He couldn't make himself offer to leave, though, not while there was a chance Ian might need him. He'd go if Ian asked, but not before.

THE chair across the room creaked.

Ian sighed and rolled over. Thorne still sat there, far less alert than he'd been earlier, which probably accounted for the creaking chair. When he'd first sat down, he'd been eerily still, every muscle motionless as he'd stood watch. Now, though, he appeared to be dozing, and Ian felt guilty. He didn't know what Thorne was waiting for or why he'd decided to stay, but he wasn't going to get any rest nodding off in that chair.

"Thorne," he said softly.

Instantly Thorne came awake, his whole body on alert.

"What is it? What's wrong?"

"The chair creaks, and you're going to get a crick in your neck. Come to bed."

The words were out before he realized he'd intended to say them, but he didn't try to take them back. Having Thorne in the room steadied him, except when the noise kept him awake. He could deal with having Thorne closer.

He expected to be more nervous as Thorne removed his shirt and jeans and came toward the bed in only his underwear, but he wasn't. To the depths of his marrow, he knew Thorne wasn't a threat to him. He would lie down next to Ian and stay completely on his side of the bed, if that was what Ian wanted, or he would hold Ian tight all through the night if that was what he asked for, and come morning, he would kiss Ian sweetly and go on as if this were an everyday occurrence.

As soon as the thought occurred to him, Ian knew he wanted it to be. He wasn't ready for Thorne to follow Walker's suggestion and make love to him until he couldn't remember his own name, but he could take this step. He could sleep in Thorne's arms and let that closeness soothe some of the rough edges of his soul. He only hoped it did the same for Thorne.

He lifted the covers in invitation, and Thorne lay down on the other side of the bed, exactly as Ian had known he would. Ian shifted a little closer and sought Thorne's hand. Thorne entwined their fingers immediately but left it at that. Ian smiled and rolled onto his side, tugging Thorne's arm over him so their joined hands rested against Ian's breastbone.

"Are you sure?" Thorne whispered.

Ian snuggled a little closer, the hot, hard line of Thorne's body behind him like a mountain protecting him from everything outside their bed. "I'm sure."

Thorne was silent after that, and Ian relaxed even more. Between the warmth of Thorne's body and the sense of safety he radiated, Ian felt sleep stealing over his senses. He should have been nervous when Thorne shifted a little on the bed and his groin pressed against Ian's arse, but Ian knew even without thinking about it that the movement posed no threat. Thorne was getting comfortable, not gearing up to force himself on Ian. Ian nestled a little closer and let himself go completely limp, his grip on Thorne's hand his anchor as he drifted off into sleep.

THORNE woke up the next morning fully hard and in desperate need of the loo, but getting out of bed would mean disturbing Ian, who had wrapped himself around Thorne like a rather large koala. He hated to wake Ian, but he would have to get up soon or he'd embarrass himself, not to mention he had no idea how Ian would react to feeling his morning erection.

If that weren't enough, he could feel tendrils of memory curling around the edges of his mind, susurrations of doubt that reminded him what had happened the last time he slept with a man this way. He pushed the thought away, but the damage was done. He couldn't stay here any longer, even if he woke Ian to get away.

He did his best to disentangle himself gently rather than throw Ian's arms away from him. Ian wasn't the source of his discomfort and didn't deserve that kind of treatment. He'd taken a huge step in trusting Thorne enough to sleep in the same bed with him last night. Thorne certainly didn't want them to backslide, but he had to get up.

Now.

"Thorne?" Ian mumbled.

"I need the loo," Thorne said, wincing at how sharp the words sounded to his own ears. Ian seemed a little taken aback, but he let Thorne up. Thorne pulled on his jeans but didn't bother with his shirt as he left the room as quickly as he could.

He locked himself in the loo and tried to steady his breathing. He had to get it together or Ian would come looking for him before long. If he'd been smart, he would have told Ian he was going to take a shower. Then he'd have an excuse to be gone for ten or fifteen minutes. He'd never had that kind of time in the shower in the military, but Ian wouldn't necessarily know that. As it was, he had a minute or two at most before Ian would wonder where he'd gone to or what was wrong.

He really did need the loo, so he took care of business and pulled the façade of control that had saved his arse so many times in the Commandos around him before he walked back to Ian's room. If he was lucky, Ian would've rolled over and gone back to sleep.

He wasn't lucky.

"Is everything okay?" Ian asked as soon as the door closed behind Thorne.

Thorne almost lied and assured him everything was fine, but Ian was looking at him with such an open expression that Thorne couldn't make the lie form. "You don't really want to hear my sob story, do you?"

"I'm sure it's not a sob story," Ian said, "but even if it is, yes, I want to hear it. Anything you can share with me."

Thorne couldn't help noticing the choice of words. Not everything, but anything you can share. Either because it was classified or too painful to discuss, Ian would accept the gaps in the tales Thorne told, but this one wasn't classified, and if it was too painful to discuss, maybe that meant he needed to say it aloud, to lance that memory the way one lanced a boil.

"Last night was only the second time I've slept that way with someone in my arms," Thorne said. "The first time... ended badly."

"What happened?" Ian asked, a stricken look on his face.

"Nothing like what you're thinking," Thorne said immediately, remembering the weekend after he finished high school. "Daniel was my best friend. We'd just got our HSCs, and I'd told my parents I was going to stay over at his house so we could celebrate. We did that so often that they didn't think anything of it. They didn't know we'd managed to sneak a box of condoms and had decided that was the big night. We were going to lose our virginities together and then we'd be real men. We thought we were in love. It was going to seal our relationship forever."

Thorne could still remember the way it had felt to touch and kiss Daniel. It had been sly and secretive, but it hadn't felt shameful. Not then. The shame had come later.

"We fell asleep after it was done, curled around each other like we didn't have a care in the world," Thorne said. "Daniel's mother woke us up before dawn the next morning. I'd never seen her cry until then."

"Because you were together?" Ian asked, horrified.

"No," Thorne said. "I wish it had been that simple. She came to tell me there'd been a fire. It destroyed my house and killed my parents and younger brother. While I was at Daniel's house getting laid, they were dying."

Thorne hated how detached the words sounded, but he'd spent so long forcing all that behind a solid wall that he recounted the story now like an outsider rather than someone who had lived it. He didn't even know how to hurt for them anymore.

"Your being there wouldn't have changed anything," Ian said softly. "Except you would have died with them. I'm sorry you lost them that way, but I can't be sorry you're still alive. I just can't."

Thorne had been. He'd taken one look at the desolation his life had become and he'd considered ending it right there. It would've been so easy, which was probably why Daniel's mum insisted he stay with them for a few weeks. At least that way someone was checking on him, making sure he ate and slept and bathed. He'd had to borrow Daniel's clothes because his had all been destroyed in the fire. It had taken him a month to realize he had to do something for himself. He'd joined the military the next day and had refused to look back.

"You don't know that," Thorne said. "I might have still been awake. I might have woken them up before they burned to death. I might have saved them."

"You might have," Ian said. "You certainly would if it happened now, but you were eighteen. You were a kid. It wasn't your responsibility then, and you shouldn't feel guilty for living now."

Thorne nearly snapped at Ian for that, but as angry as it made him, Ian was right. He couldn't have done anything except die with them, and he liked to think he'd lived a life worth being proud of in the Commandos. His parents would have wanted him to make something of himself, even if a career in the military wasn't what they would have chosen. They'd still be proud if they could see him, because he'd made a difference in the world.

"It's not as easy as saying that," Thorne said instead.

"Believe me, I know," Ian said. "My list of issues because of my family is as long as my arm, and I'm not even going to pretend I have them under control. I just hate to see you beating yourself up over something you couldn't have changed. Come back to bed. It's still too early to be awake."

Thorne chuckled. "This from the man who gets up before dawn every morning to go to work?"

"Just because I *can* do it when I have to doesn't mean I want to do it when I have the chance for a lie-in," Ian retorted. "Come back to bed."

Thorne had started back toward the bed, already in the process of taking his jeans back off, when doubt took him. It was one thing last night, when they were both too exhausted to do anything but sleep. It was another thing entirely this morning.

"Don't be a drongo," Ian said. "I'm going back to sleep and you should too, and you'll be more comfortable without your jeans. I trust you."

The import of those three little words was not lost on Thorne. If they weren't quite the words he wanted to hear, they were nonetheless important, possibly more important. Ian couldn't love him if he didn't trust him. He tossed his jeans on the floor and climbed back into bed, intending to pull Ian against him as he had the night before, but Ian had other ideas, tugging on Thorne's shoulder so he ended up with his cheek pillowed on Ian's chest, his nose buried in the crook of Ian's neck.

Ian sighed contentedly and kissed the top of Thorne's head. The simplicity of the gesture and the pure acceptance of the moment left Thorne fighting tears. He hadn't let himself cry for his losses since he'd signed the papers for the army. He'd been the strong one, the dependable soldier, the leader at times. He'd been the one everyone else took their cue from even when he wasn't the one in charge of a mission. He'd buried his heart deep and become the poster boy for military control and precision. It had saved his life more times than he could count, but it had taken a different kind of toll, and now he had a lifetime of grief built up behind those walls. His heart wanted out so it could take everything a life with Ian had to offer, but Thorne was afraid what else would be unleashed if he took down those walls.

He had a chance at a real life, a real family again. The seasonal jackaroos would come and go, but he'd seen the way the year-rounders had already started including him, as if his staying with Ian was a foregone conclusion. Neil and Molly, Chris and Jesse, even Caine and Macklin didn't want him for his skills. They'd watched Ian teaching him things the youngest child on the station already knew. Dani already knew which snakes were dangerous, but Ian had to warn Thorne. Laura rode like she'd been born in the saddle, and Thorne could still barely keep his balance at anything faster than a trot. Patrick's son Jason had arrived home from uni and whatever veterinary internship he was currently doing for the Christmas holidays a few days ago, and watching him with Polly, his dog, was exactly like watching Jeremy and Arrow. Thorne didn't even know the most basic commands. They didn't need him, but they had made him welcome anyway because they recognized a kindred spirit.

He had enjoyed that kind of brotherhood with his first Commandos team, but after their massacre, he'd held back from investing to the same degree. He'd worked with his new team, fought to protect them, and trusted them to protect him, but it hadn't been the same. For the first time since he carried Walker to med evac, he felt the same stirrings of family he'd lost when he'd returned to find his team dead, and this time, he could accept those outstretched hands with little risk. Life on Lang Downs might never be predictable, but it didn't come with the inherent risks that dogged any Commandos team. Thorne could be part of their family without having to worry about a group of guerrillas or a stray bullet from friendly fire taking it away from him. He could trust them the way Ian trusted him.

He muffled the sob that wanted to escape against Ian's throat. Ian didn't say anything; he just tightened his grip on Thorne and waited, giving him the space to come to terms with this epiphany. Thorne only hoped that when Ian finally opened up about his own past, he could offer the same kind of solace and peace.

NINETEEN

THE return to Lang Downs was anticlimactic in a way that only reinforced Thorne's feeling that this could be home. Nobody seemed surprised to see him. Nobody made any comment about how much, or how little, he'd brought back with him from Wagga Wagga. Neil just told him to stow his gear and get to work. He didn't even say that much to Ian.

Not that Ian needed Neil to say anything to him. He'd already grabbed his duffel bag and tossed it on the veranda and was changing his boots from the "good" ones he wore to town to the grubby ones he wore in the paddocks.

"Neil said to get to work, but he didn't tell me what to do," Thorne said. "Any suggestions?"

The barking of dogs drew their attention before Ian could reply. When Thorne looked back at Ian, Ian had a grin on his face. "As a matter of fact…." He whistled sharply, drawing the attention of the dogs and the man standing with them.

"Ian, you're back!"

As the man drew nearer, Thorne recognized Jason, Polly and Arrow cavorting at his feet.

"Just now," Ian said. "I need to go check in with my crew, but Thorne doesn't ride well enough yet to head out with me."

"Want me to give him a riding lesson?" Jason asked. "I taught Seth."

"Actually, I was hoping you'd teach him to work with the dogs," Ian said. "One of the bitches is expecting a new litter, and I was thinking about claiming one. I haven't had a dog of my own in a while, and it seems like a good time to get one. Thorne should know how to work with it too."

"Sure," Jason said. "Polly and I'll get him all sorted. He can't be any more clueless than Caine was when we started."

"I wouldn't count on it," Thorne said. "I'm pretty clueless about anything that doesn't involve military procedures."

"Next to that, this is a breeze," Jason assured him. "Come on. We'll see if there are any sheep in the sheds for us to practice on."

"Maybe we should just start with basic commands," Thorne said. "I'm not sure I'm ready to deal with real sheep."

"We don't have a training course set up," Jason explained, "although with a new litter on the way, I imagine Neil and Macklin will build one. Polly's a work dog, not a show dog. If you give her commands that have no purpose, she's going to get annoyed with you. When she hears something, she expects to act a certain way with the sheep, not just for the hell of it."

That made sense, actually. Thorne had always hated the training exercises that had them going through empty motions. "Okay, but don't let me do anything that would hurt her or the sheep."

"She's too smart to get into trouble with the sheep," Jason said. "Don't worry about that. If you give an order that doesn't make sense, she'll let you know."

Thorne wasn't sure how he felt about a kelpie being smarter than him, but he figured somebody had to be in this situation. "So where do we start?"

An hour later, Thorne had an even greater respect for the men and women he worked with, not to mention for the dogs they used to help manage the sheep. Jason was the epitome of patience when it came to teaching, and Polly obediently followed Thorne's orders except when he gave an obviously wrong one, but Thorne still felt like that happened far more often than it should have.

"If it makes you feel any better," Jason said as he climbed over the fence and joined Thorne in the middle of the paddock, "everyone who works with the dogs has gone through exactly what you're going through. I taught Caine when he first got here, and he got mixed up and turned around and sent Polly all the wrong places too, and back then, she was still learning and didn't know to ignore the mistakes. And if you think that was bad, you should have seen Seth learning."

"Seen me learning what?" a voice interrupted.

Thorne spun around, senses leaping to high alert, but Jason didn't wait for him to assess the situation. He took off running toward the fence, vaulting over it like it was inches tall instead of nearly up to his chest. The kid on the other side of the fence—*only a kid if you're an old man*, his conscience pointed out snidely—braced himself for the impact of a hundred and fifty pounds of muscle when Jason barreled into him in the guise of a hug. They didn't fall, but to Thorne's eye, it seemed like a close thing.

"You're home! Chris said he didn't know if you'd make it for Christmas," Jason said.

"I haven't missed Christmas yet," the kid said. "I'm not going to start now. Who's the blow-in?"

"Thorne, come meet Seth," Jason called.

Thorne crossed the paddock to the fence as Jason led Seth toward him. "Seth, this is Thorne Lachlan. He's staying with Ian. Thorne, this is Seth Simms, Chris's brother."

"Nice to meet you," Thorne said, offering Seth his hand. Seth shook it with a solid grip that Thorne appreciated.

"Cheers, mate," Seth said. "I didn't think Ian had any family outside the station."

"He doesn't," Thorne said, although he wasn't completely sure that was true. Ian had said he didn't stay in touch with anyone, but that didn't mean there wasn't anyone.

"So why are you staying with him?" Seth asked bluntly.

"Because he offered me a spot on his couch when the guest room in the main house got a little too…."

"Say no more. The day Neil and Molly moved into the foreman's house and Chris and I got Neil's old house was a very good day," Seth said with a laugh. "I feel your pain. Why were you in the guest room and not the bunkhouse?"

"Because I didn't hire on as a jackaroo," Thorne said. "I came with the Fries to fight the grassfires."

"And then Caine adopted you," Seth said. "Wonder where I've heard that before."

"Actually, Ian adopted me, but Caine and Macklin were kind enough to agree to it," Thorne said.

"Ian?" Seth parroted. "Really?"

"Yes. Why are you surprised? He's been nothing but kind to me." He'd been a whole lot more than just kind, but Thorne wasn't ready to tell Seth and Jason that.

"Because Ian has always been a loner," Jason explained. "He's friendly with everyone, but he's only friends with Neil and Kyle. He makes furniture and stuff for everyone on the station. He'll bring food or beer to every station gathering, but he never invites anyone to his place, which is okay, because his place is small compared with Neil and Molly's house or Mum and Dad's house, and if it's something big, like Christmas or a birthday party, we'll have it in the canteen, but the point remains. Nobody here has ever seen Ian take to someone like he seems to have taken to you. That's usually Caine's job."

Polly yipped behind them, drawing the attention of all three men.

"I'm teaching Thorne how to work with the dogs," Jason explained.

"And you didn't ask Caine to pretend to be a sheep?" Seth teased.

"I'm not fourteen anymore," Jason said. "I'm allowed to work with real sheep now."

That sounded like a story Thorne wanted to hear, but he found the slight flush on Jason's cheeks even more interesting than the possibility of a story. Up until now, Jason had been the epitome of a confident stockman, younger than Ian or Neil or some of the others, but much more at home than the seasonal jackaroos. Now, with Seth teasing him, Jason looked like a kid again.

"So, Seth," Thorne said, changing the subject entirely, "I know what Jason's doing that keeps him away from the station for most of the year, but I haven't heard what you're doing."

"Studying mechanical engineering," Jason said before Seth could answer. "You should see him. He's a genius with machines. Even my dad says so, and I used to think nobody knew more about engines than my dad."

It took Thorne a minute to work out the relationship, but then he remembered Patrick, the station's head mechanic, was Jason's father.

"I like knowing how things work," Seth said with a shrug and a flush on his face now at Jason's praise. Thorne wondered if he'd ever been that young and clueless. Then he remembered how long he and Daniel had danced around each other before admitting they were interested in something more than friendship. He suspected Seth and Jason hadn't reached the admitting stage yet.

"Do you have plans for after you graduate?" Thorne asked.

Seth shrugged again. "Depends on a lot of things. The engineering stuff is interesting, but mostly I like the down and dirty application side of it. I like getting in the machines and working on them. I really could have got an apprenticeship with a mechanic and been just as happy, but Chris wouldn't hear of it."

"I don't imagine there's a lot of call for mechanical engineering on a sheep station," Thorne said.

"You'd be surprised. There's machinery to maintain, of course," Seth replied, "but Caine's looking at ways to improve the paddocks, with windmills to bring water to the troughs instead of depending on rain or having to fill them from the utes. He's talked about trying to put solar-powered generators in some of the drovers' huts, because even with a fire going, they're pretty miserable in the winter. Those are all design projects that would be right up my alley."

"I guess I haven't seen that side of things yet," Thorne said. "It sounds like you have it all planned out."

"We'll see," Seth said.

"He's got this girlfriend," Jason said with a scowl. "She's a city girl through and through. She'll never agree to come live out here on the station, and she'd be miserable even if she did."

"I can see that being a problem," Thorne agreed. He couldn't imagine being miserable on Lang Downs, but then he wasn't city-bred, not after twenty years in some of the remotest places on the planet. Lang Downs felt like the lap of luxury after some of the places he'd bivouacked with his team. Then again, he already knew his was a unique perspective.

"I need to go unpack," Seth said. "I'll let you get back to your lesson, and I'll see you at dinner."

Seth headed back toward the collection of houses scattered along the north side of the road through the valley, and Thorne watched the way Jason followed him with his eyes. "I think I've hit information overload," he said, taking pity on the kid. "We can call it a day for now if you want to go help Seth get settled."

"Are you sure?" Jason asked. The hope that shone in his eyes was all the confirmation Thorne needed.

"I'm sure. I'll find something else to do. There's never a shortage of work around here."

"Thanks," Jason said.

"Jason!" Thorne called before Jason could run off. "Don't hassle Seth about staying in the city. He'll figure out what's important. You just have to give him time."

"Lang Downs wouldn't be home without him," Jason replied.

"Give him time," Thorne repeated.

Jason nodded and whistled for Polly before sprinting after Seth. He couldn't stop a smile at the way Seth bumped his shoulder against Jason's as they walked down the road together.

Leaving them to their reunion, he wandered around the sheds and toward the bunkhouse, looking for someone to give him another job, but he didn't see any of the crew bosses. With nothing more productive to do, he decided to head back to Ian's house to unpack a little. He wouldn't unpack all his boxes, in case he didn't end up staying in Ian's house permanently, but he could get out his Kindle and a few things like that. Ian had been generous with his library. Thorne could return the favor now. He'd have to go to the canteen if he wanted to buy anything new since Ian's house didn't have Wi-Fi. Come to think of it, Thorne hadn't seen anything even vaguely electronic other than Ian's cell phone and one of the radios they all carried when they left the valley for the upper paddocks.

He dug through the boxes until he found his Kindle and set that aside to charge before digging back through the boxes. He couldn't honestly remember what was in all of them. He'd picked up odds and ends over the years in various places they were stationed, mostly cheap tourist stuff to remind him of where he'd been, but a few of the pieces were of better quality, either from longer missions or from a place or a people who had touched him more deeply. He left all of those wrapped for the moment. He didn't want to presume on Ian's generosity. He was pretty sure of his welcome after a month, but he was still sleeping on the couch without an explicit invitation to make their current living arrangements permanent.

Of course, that was before they'd spent the night in the same bed. Thorne didn't want a repeat of whatever had given Ian his panic attack, but he certainly wouldn't complain about a repeat of the rest of the night. It had felt right in a way that defied words to sleep with Ian in his arms, to curl protectively around Ian's slimmer body and put himself as a wall between Ian and the rest of the world. He'd spent twenty years fighting to protect his team and whatever place or group of people his commanders decided to send them to, to the point that the need to protect was ingrained, but he'd never had someone of his own. If he thought he was driven before, it was nothing compared to what he felt toward Ian, and increasingly toward Lang Downs. Anyone who thought to threaten his new home and family had another think coming.

The sound of footsteps on the gravel path alerted Thorne that he had company. He looked up and smiled when he saw Ian on the veranda taking off his boots. He set the boxes aside and went to greet him.

"Hi," Ian said when Thorne joined him on the veranda. "I thought you were working with Jason and Polly."

"I was," Thorne said, "but Seth came home, and that was the end of Jason's interest in working with me."

Ian laughed. "Yeah, that would do it. They've been best friends since they first laid eyes on each other seven years ago. Can't pry them apart with a stick when they're both on the station. I swear Jason finished his HSC a year early because he wanted to do the same classes Seth was taking, never mind that they're interested in two completely different things."

"I was going through the boxes we brought back," Thorne said, "but I didn't want to unpack too much without asking first. I didn't want to presume."

Ian drew Thorne back inside and kissed him the moment the door closed behind them. "You still have to ask after last night?"

"I will always ask," Thorne replied fiercely. "You will always have a choice with me."

"You have no idea what that means to me," Ian said before giving Thorne another kiss.

Thorne didn't need any more details of Ian's life to know he'd had the right to choose taken from him too often. This was Ian's home now, and Thorne wouldn't allow it to become another place where choices were taken from him. He kissed Ian back with all the determination that burned in him to see Ian happy and safe. He hoped to still be doing it in another forty or fifty years.

"Let's go see if we can find space for your things," Ian said. "If we can't, we'll figure out what we need and I'll order the wood from Paul and someone can pick it up on the next trip to Boorowa. We might have to squeeze things in for a bit, but I can make whatever we need."

Thorne couldn't resist. He pulled Ian back into his arms and kissed him again. Comments like that were tantamount to a declaration of love as far as Thorne was concerned. He still hoped to hear the words—not that he could talk, since he hadn't worked up the courage to say anything either—but he could live with the proof that Ian intended him to be around for a long time even without the words.

When they separated, Ian looked as dazed as Thorne felt, which did nothing for Thorne's self-control. He took a deep breath and stepped back enough to put some space between them. Ian trusted him because he could keep himself in check. Now was not the time to blow it.

"So show me what's in the boxes," Ian said a little breathlessly.

Thorne opened the nearest box and unpacked his prized possession, a teak mask a Timorese carver had given him after he'd saved the man's young son from a band of guerrillas. "This is from East Timor," he said, showing it to Ian. "It's probably the most valuable thing I own."

"It's beautiful," Ian said. "The craftsmanship is stunning. May I?"

Thorne held it out to Ian, trusting that the hands capable of the woodwork in the house would treat the mask with the care and respect it deserved. Ian carried the mask to the window so he could study it in the light. "Absolutely stunning," he repeated. "The time it would have taken to create the details…. I hope you paid the artist well for this and didn't buy it in some cheap shop that takes advantage of native craftsmen."

Thorne knew all too well the kind of shops Ian was referring to. He tried to avoid them for anything of real value, but in this case, it hadn't been an issue of payment. "It was a gift," he said. "The mask represents protection. The man who made it said it would watch over me since I'd saved his son."

"I don't have anything to hang it with," Ian said, "but we can get something the next time someone goes to Boorowa. We'll find a place to display it. Something this precious deserves to be seen, not hidden away in a box."

"The box seemed safer when I was moving around every few months."

"Of course, but you're here now. This puts my little hobby to shame. We have to find a place for it," Ian said. "Do you have anything else like this?"

"Nothing that fine," Thorne said. "If I was stationed somewhere for a short time, I picked up a little kitschy thing to remind me of the visit. If I stayed for several months, I got something nicer, but this is definitely the crowning glory of my collection of memorabilia."

Ian brought the mask back to Thorne. "Until we find a place to hang it, we can stand it on the chest in my room if you want," he offered. "It won't be as visible if anyone comes to visit, but we'll see it and it will be safe from harm."

As far as Thorne was concerned, it could stay in Ian's room forever if that meant Thorne got to be there with him. He couldn't think of anywhere he'd rather have the protective spirit holding sway. "I think that sounds perfect."

He took the mask back and followed Ian into his bedroom, the one room in the house he hadn't gone into until now. It was furnished in much the same way as the rest of the house, hand-carved wooden furniture and soft, muted colors. A beautiful earth-toned quilt over the foot of the bed drew Thorne's attention. "Do you quilt as well?"

"No," Ian said with a laugh. "Carley made that for me when I wouldn't let her pay me for the bed I made Jason when he decided he had to have a bunk bed. Somehow I think I got the better end of the deal. The bed wasn't anything out of the ordinary."

Thorne didn't think anything Ian made could be "ordinary" even when it was purely functional, because it was all handmade and unique.

Ian stood the mask up on the chest of drawers opposite the foot of the bed. "There," he said. "Now it can watch over you as you sleep."

"It can watch over us both," Thorne corrected.

Ian smiled and leaned in for another soft kiss, which Thorne gave willingly.

"I should clear some space for your clothes too," Ian said when he pulled back. "Go get your duffel and bring it in here while I do that."

TWENTY

CHRISTMAS started as early on Lang Downs as any other day, Thorne discovered when Ian's alarm went off at the same ungodly hour as every other day. But it was still Christmas, and Thorne was pretty sure it would be the best one in twenty years. No other Christmas had started with him waking up next to an incredibly attractive man with the relative assurance of being able to do so again the next day, and the day after, and the day after that. No other Christmas had started with soft kisses and tender fingers running through his hair. No other Christmas had started with the man he'd fallen in love with on a station he finally believed he could call home.

"We'll miss breakfast if we don't get up," Ian murmured between kisses.

"It's Christmas," Thorne protested.

"Yes, I know," Ian said. "That's why we don't want to miss breakfast. Kami and Sarah do a full English breakfast on Christmas morning, along with all the pastries and sweet buns you can imagine. And then this afternoon we'll have dinner early. Last year Sarah even made mulled wine and cider."

"You'd think it was cold outside," Thorne said, "and here it is going to be in the forties again today. Shorts and T-shirts and mulled wine or cider to drink. Something's wrong with this picture."

"Like any Christmas you've ever celebrated has been any different," Ian scoffed. "It's miserably hot outside, but we cling to our British roots like they're all we have left."

Thorne couldn't argue with that. He hadn't had much opportunity to celebrate Christmas in the Commandos, but he remembered growing up and always having a traditional Christmas dinner with his family before going out to the beach to swim or surf.

"Okay, you've convinced me," Thorne said. "Let's get the celebration started."

They dressed quickly and headed for the canteen. Thorne hadn't asked when they usually exchanged presents on the station, but Ian hadn't mentioned it this morning, so he figured his gift could wait where it was hidden until later. He hated that he hadn't had the time or opportunity to find the perfect gift for Ian, but at least he'd selected something Ian would appreciate and use. Ian had muttered more than once recently about how ragged his hat was getting, and how the droop of the brim blocked his vision more than it blocked the sun. He'd checked the size one night while Ian was cleaning up before dinner and had offered to take the next supply run to Boorowa so he could buy a replacement. It wasn't the perfect gift, but he hoped Ian would like it.

As promised, breakfast was twice as plentiful as usual, with far more choices. Thorne wasn't even sure where to start, but Ian didn't have a problem, making a beeline for the table with the pastries on it. Thorne had figured out Ian had a sweet tooth, but today he was like a little kid on Christmas morning, an appropriate metaphor for the day.

The canteen, usually so quiet in the morning, was filled with cheerful if sleepy calls of "Happy Christmas"—and Caine's very American "Merry Christmas" in reply. They all lingered a little longer than usual over breakfast, but work eventually demanded their attention. The station didn't stop running because it was Christmas day.

Thorne expected some grumbles about that, but the special breakfast and the prospect of dinner, or simply the Christmas spirit, was enough to silence any remarks. Ian was on a crew assigned to jobs in the valley that morning, so Thorne could tag along with him instead of working with someone else. His equestrian skills were improving, but not to the point that he could ride out with the others yet. "Soon," Ian said whenever Thorne asked.

None of the jackaroos was what Thorne would call lazy, but they all threw themselves into their tasks with extra enthusiasm.

"They know the sooner everything gets done, the sooner we can stop for the day," Ian explained at one point. It made sense, and everyone's focus paid off. By noon, they'd finished their tasks and headed back to the bunkhouse or their individual houses to clean up before dinner.

"I don't have anything really nice to wear to dinner," Thorne said as they walked back to Ian's house.

"Nothing is formal on the station," Ian said. "I'll wear my nice boots instead of my grubby ones and maybe a pair of khakis instead of jeans, but that's as fancy as it gets around here."

"I can handle that," Thorne replied with a grin. "I'm used to military formal, dress uniforms and the like."

"You'd stick out like a sore thumb if you dressed up like that here," Ian said. "Carley and Linda might put on sundresses. Molly would, except I don't know if she has one that will fit over her belly. But even that is as much about temperature as being dressed up."

"Does that mean you'll wear a short-sleeved shirt?" Thorne teased.

"No, because we'll probably end up outside after dinner, and I don't want to get sunburned. Sunscreen is all well and good, but it wears off, and then I'm the color of a lobster."

Thorne wanted to cajole, for the opportunity to stare at Ian's arms in public if nothing else, but he couldn't argue with the sunburn part, and he didn't want Ian in pain or in danger of skin cancer, so he'd save his ogling for later, in private. Ian still slept in his sleeveless T-shirt at night, but that gave Thorne access to his arms, at least.

They showered and changed quickly. Ian looked good enough to eat in his khakis and a cambric shirt one step up from his usual work shirts. Thorne would enjoy peeling it off him when they were finally alone tonight. It might not go any farther than that, but he'd cherish every intimacy Ian allowed him. The thought flitted through his head that perhaps tonight he would finally learn the truth of Ian's past, but he wouldn't push. Next week, if Ian hadn't said anything, he'd ask again, but he wouldn't spoil the day by asking tonight.

They'd just got seated, their plates overflowing with food, as promised, when Neil came up to the table and slapped them both on the shoulders. "Happy Christmas," he said with his trademark grin.

"Happy Christmas," Ian replied easily. Thorne repeated his own wishes as well.

"Thank you for the bedframe you made Dani," Neil said. "She loved it. She's all ready to be a big girl now and finally agreed the baby could use her cradle."

"She's been out of that thing for eighteen months," Ian said with a shake of his head.

"I know," Neil said, "but it was still hers, even when she wasn't using it. Now she has her own special bed that's far better than the cradle because Uncle Ian made it just for her."

"I made the cradle for her too," Ian pointed out.

"We're trying not to remind her of that," Neil said. "The cradle's for babies. The new bed is just for her."

"I'm glad she likes it," Ian said.

"She does. She wanted to know when Uncle Ian and Uncle Thorne were coming over to see how it looks in her big girl room," Neil said.

Ian must have answered because Neil nodded and walked off, but Thorne didn't hear what either of them said for the rushing in his ears. Uncle Thorne… he'd given up on ever hearing that name when his brother died. Now in less than a month, he'd become honorary uncle to a domineering three-year-old who had the world wrapped around her little finger, as far as he could tell.

"Happy Christmas, mates."

Thorne startled, reaching automatically for a weapon before he settled himself and summoned a smile for Chris and Jesse who, like Neil, seemed to be making the rounds of the tables.

"Happy Christmas," Ian said. "Are you glad to have Seth home?"

"It's always good to see him," Chris said, "although I hate to see him leave when breaks are over."

"I know, but he's doing well in Sydney, right? I mean, he certainly seems happy," Ian said.

"Yes, he seems to be doing well," Chris replied. "I just wish he could get home more often."

"We're spoiled," Ian said. "Most families don't spend nearly as much time together, even if they all live in the same town."

"I know," Chris said, "but that doesn't make it easier to see him leave."

"Let him stretch his wings now and maybe someday he'll come home to roost," Ian said.

"I keep hoping," Chris said. "Also, thank you for the new table for our veranda. Now we can actually set food out if we invite people over for a beer instead of having to traipse in and out of the house."

"You're welcome," Ian said. "We expect an invitation to try it out soon."

"As soon as we can make a run into town to get stuff for a party, you and Thorne are first on the list of guests," Jesse promised.

"Did you make something for everyone on the station?" Thorne asked when Chris and Jesse headed off to get their own food.

"Not for everyone," Ian said, "but I tried to make something for the year-rounders. The seasonal jackaroos come and go, but the others, they're family."

"Yeah, I've noticed," Thorne said. "You must have spent months working on Christmas presents."

"Unless somebody needs something urgently, I tend to make things all year and give them at Christmas," Ian explained. "Macklin lets me use one of the small sheds for my finished projects so they don't clutter up my house, and everyone pretty much respects my privacy and doesn't go looking to see what I might have made for them."

"That's got to get expensive," Thorne said.

Ian shrugged. "I live on the station. I don't go into town and blow my money on booze or anything else. I buy new gear when I need it, and everything else pretty much goes into the bank and sits there. I can afford to buy the wood to make nice gifts for my friends, and if it's something for the station, like the chairs on the porch of the bunkhouse, Caine pays for the wood and for my labor, even though I keep telling him all he has to do is buy the wood."

"You can say it as often as you like," Sam said, joining them at the table. "You won't get him to listen."

"Happy Christmas, Sam," Ian said with a smile.

"Happy Christmas, and thank you for the desk. It will be nice to have a place to work without always being in Caine's space. He's out in the paddocks more than he's in the office these days, but it's still very much his office."

"You're welcome," Ian said. "I feel like that was more a 'you' gift than a 'you and Jeremy' gift. I hope Jeremy doesn't mind."

"He doesn't," Sam assured Ian. "It means I come home in the evenings instead of going back into the office to check that last thing I forgot."

Ian chuckled. "It's hard to leave work when you work where you live, isn't it?"

"As if any of us are ever completely off duty," Sam said with a laugh. "You have figured that out, haven't you, Thorne?"

"After years in the military, I wouldn't know any other way to be," Thorne admitted. "Even when we weren't on watch, it was understood we were still on duty if necessary."

"I knew there was a reason you fit right in," Sam said.

"Where's Jeremy?" Thorne asked. It was almost as odd to see Sam without Jeremy as it was to see Caine without Macklin. He occasionally saw Jeremy or Macklin without their partners, but rarely the other way around.

"He went to Taylor Peak," Sam said with a moue of displeasure on his face. "He's setting himself up for disappointment, but he won't stop trying."

"Would you, if you were in his shoes and you and Neil had a falling out?" Ian asked.

"No," Sam admitted, "but Caine took care of Neil's prejudices, so I never had to fight that battle. Sometimes I think I'll never repay everything I owe him."

"I think," Thorne said slowly, "that he doesn't keep a tally sheet. I think he gives selflessly because he knows the loyalty and love he gets in return will carry him through the rest of his life." He hadn't thought in those terms before, not exactly, but the words certainly applied to his own feelings for the station owners. They'd given him a chance because he needed one and because Neil had asked them to for Ian's benefit. They'd overlooked his temper and had let him start to put down roots. In return, he'd work to the point of exhaustion if they asked him to.

"No, he doesn't," Sam agreed. "That only makes me more aware of it. I guess it's the accountant in me. I'm going to get some food."

"You can come back and sit with us if you want, since Jeremy isn't here," Thorne offered.

"Thanks," Sam said, "but I promised Dani I'd sit with them. You'd think she'd get enough of Uncle Sam, as much time as I spend with Neil and Molly, but it's never enough as far as she's concerned."

Sam headed to join Neil and his family, and Thorne turned to Ian. Before he could figure out how to phrase his question, though, Caine walked to the front of the room and drew everyone's attention.

"Merry Christmas, everyone," he said when all the jackaroos had settled down.

"Happy Christmas!" everyone chorused back.

"Fine, happy Christmas," Caine said with a smile. "Those of you who've been around a few years know I try to take this opportunity every year to thank you all for being here, whether it's for a summer or a lifetime. For those of you who've been around before, some of this will be familiar, but it bears repeating and remembering. When Uncle Michael founded Lang Downs, he did so on a wish and a prayer, believing he could turn this valley into a prosperous sheep station while still treating the people who worked for him with basic decency and common courtesy. He didn't tolerate prejudice and he always stood up for what was right, even when it made him unpopular with his neighbors. I d-didn't get to meet him while he was alive, but I knew him through the letters we exchanged and now through the stories I've heard from all of you who did get the honor of meeting him.

"My journey to Lang Downs st-started seven years ago today, when my mother told us Uncle Michael had died. She and my father send their regrets again this year. My f-f-f-father's health d-doesn't permit them to tr-travel from Ohio to be here with us all, but they wanted me to extend their w-w-wishes for a prosperous and happy new year to all of you since they couldn't say it in person. Anyway, my journey started seven years ago today, and I hope it won't end for many, many more years. Those of you who were here then—Kami, Neil, Ian, Kyle, Patrick, Carley, and of course Macklin, among others—welcomed me despite my ignorance and taught me what I needed to know. We've followed Uncle M-Michael's tradition and opened our d-doors to new faces since then, and especially this year, so an extra welcome to the newest members of our family, Linda and Thorne. I hope your t-t-tenure on Lang Downs will be as b-b-blessed as mine has been.

"The rest of the day is yours to do with as you please. I can't do away with all work on Christmas, but I've always tried to keep it to a minimum. Enjoy your day with your friends, with your family if they're here with you, and thank you all for making Lang Downs home."

Everyone applauded as Caine sat back down next to Macklin, who promptly put his arm around Caine's shoulders, and Thorne couldn't help but notice a few people wiping their eyes surreptitiously. Only years of training at masking his emotions allowed him to keep his own feelings in check. He'd been a wanderer for so long, going where he was sent and fighting when he was told. He still wasn't sure what to do with the possibility of having a home again, but he knew one thing for certain: he wasn't giving it up without a fight. He belonged here now. Caine had said so himself. Dani called him Uncle Thorne. Jesse invited him for drinks as naturally as he'd invited Ian. Sam said he fit right in.

He turned to look at Ian, who wasn't even trying to hide how deeply Caine's speech had touched him. He smiled at Thorne and reached for his hand, there on the table, in plain sight of anyone who happened to be looking, but nobody cared. Or rather, nobody minded, because Thorne was quite sure a number of people cared that Ian and Thorne were together, and if that wasn't a reason to stay come hell or high water, Thorne didn't know what was. He had a chance at a life here, with an amazing man in a community that would accept them. He'd spent twenty years fighting for his country. He planned to spend the rest of his time fighting for this new life.

"Finish eating," Ian said softly. "I haven't given you your Christmas present yet."

TWENTY-ONE

THORNE shoveled his food as fast as he could without making himself sick. As it was, he felt bad for not taking the time to appreciate Sarah and Kami's cooking the way it deserved, but he didn't want to wait any longer to give Ian his present and to see what Ian had got—or made—for him.

"It hasn't been that long since breakfast, has it?" Caine asked. "I like to think I don't starve my jackaroos that badly."

"No, it's not that," Thorne said, wiping his mouth. "I wanted to finish dinner so I could give Ian his present."

Caine smiled. "That is important. Ian, thank you for the picture frames. I couldn't have found one the right size for that photo of Uncle Michael and Donald."

"And the hinged one is perfect for Mum's wedding photo and the one I still have of her from when I was a kid," Macklin added. "She'll fuss about me putting it out, but it's the one thing I kept when I ran away."

"I'm glad you like them," Ian said. "I love making furniture and things, but the sentimental gifts are always the best."

Macklin turned to Thorne. "We haven't run you off yet. Are you ready to sign on?"

"Caine made quite a case for staying just now," Thorne said, "but I've still got a lot to learn if I'm going to make it here year-round."

"Nothing time and experience won't fix," Macklin said. "We were all blow-ins once. We all learned. You will too."

"You've already learned a lot more than I had in a month," Caine said. "You should have seen me trying to get my feet under me. I couldn't have been any more ignorant if I'd tried. You, at least, have all the experience from your military training."

"I'm not sure how much good that does me on a sheep station," Thorne replied.

"Trust me, it's a lot more useful than ten years in a mail room was," Caine said wryly. "We won't keep you, so you can finish your dinner and open presents, but we meant the offer to sign on year-round. You don't have to decide tonight. It's open-ended."

"No," Thorne said. "I don't need to think about it. I didn't figure you'd offer so soon, but I already knew I wanted it if you did."

"We'll sign the contract in the morning, then," Caine said. "It talks about a house of your own, but I don't imagine you care that there isn't one empty at the moment."

"No, I'm perfectly happy with my current living arrangements," Thorne said, shooting Ian a heated look.

"And my track record is still perfect," Caine said with a grin. "Fifth year-rounder I've hired without having to build a new house."

"Sam and Jeremy moved into a new house," Macklin grumbled with the air of a familiar argument.

"A house we built for your mother," Caine reminded him.

"Yes, but she never lived in it."

"But we didn't build it for them. By the time they were ready to move out of the bunkhouse and in together, the house was empty. We didn't build it because they needed it."

"That's splitting hairs," Macklin protested.

Thorne chuckled as they walked off, still arguing.

"So which one of them is right?" Thorne asked Ian.

"They both are," Ian said. "They built the house for Sarah, who technically isn't a year-rounder even though she lives here permanently, but she never lived there. They'd planned to build a house for Sam and Jeremy after they finished Sarah's house, but she surprised everyone by announcing she was getting married and moving in with Kami instead of moving into her house, so Sam and Jeremy got it by default."

"And that was what? Five years ago?"

"More or less," Ian confirmed.

"And they're still arguing over it," Thorne said with a shake of his head.

Ian laughed. "That's not arguing. That's just what they do. If they ever really argue, you'll know it. It doesn't happen often, but when it does, everyone walks around on eggshells for days."

"That bad?" Thorne asked.

"Worse than your parents fighting," Ian replied.

Thorne remembered that feeling, even if he hadn't had the experience in a long time. "Then I'll be glad they don't argue for real very often." He pushed his plate back. "I don't think I can eat another bite."

"Then don't," Ian said. "We'll be eating leftovers for a week anyway."

They left their plates in the big sink and headed back to Ian's house. They hadn't gone more than a few steps when Ian threaded his fingers through Thorne's. Thorne smiled all the way home.

"I'll be right back," Thorne said when they got inside. "I have to get your present."

He went into the other room and retrieved the carefully wrapped present. When he returned to the living room, Ian was waiting for him with a small box on his lap.

"Happy Christmas," Thorne said, handing Ian the box.

"Happy Christmas to you too."

"You go first," Thorne said. He knew his gift wouldn't measure up to whatever Ian had given him, but at least it was something Ian needed.

Ian unwrapped the paper as carefully as Thorne had applied it and opened the box. His eyes lit up when he saw the new hat. "Thank you! I needed a new hat. The one I have now has had it."

"Try it on," Thorne said. "Make sure it fits. It's the same size as the one you have now, but that's about as useful as saying two pairs of shoes are the same size."

Ian fitted the hat on his head. "It's perfect. Exactly what I would have chosen for myself when I finally made it into town to buy a new one." He leaned forward and kissed Thorne gently. "Thank you."

"You're welcome," Thorne said. "I'm glad you like it."

"I do. Here, this is for you. Open it, and then I have to explain what it is."

That puzzled Thorne somewhat, but he opened the package and drew out a careful series of drawings.

"I didn't have the right wood," Ian said in a rush as Thorne studied the drawings, "and even if I did, it would take longer to make than I had before Christmas, but I couldn't give you nothing, so I thought the plans would be a start. That way too, if you don't like it, I can change it before I start building."

Thorne looked at the drawings a little more closely and the sketches suddenly resolved into something recognizable. "This is… this is for my collection."

"It's a curio cabinet," Ian agreed. "The middle and bottom sections are open so you can arrange things as you want and change it up as you get new pieces, if you get any, but the top section is custom designed for your mask. It deserves to have a place of prominence. The wood should be ready to pick up next week, and then I can get started on it. I'm sorry I didn't have it finished for Christmas."

"God, Ian, don't apologize," Thorne said. "No one has ever given me such a thoughtful gift. I can see how much time you spent on the plans alone. The cabinet itself will be magnificent."

"You really like it?" Ian asked. "I can change anything you don't like about it."

"I really like it." Thorne set the plans carefully aside and pulled Ian into his lap. He set Ian's new hat on top of the plans and then set about proving to Ian just how touched he was by the gift.

Ian's lips parted as sweetly as Thorne could have wished for as they kissed. Thorne let the moment stretch. Being with Ian had certainly taught Thorne to appreciate kissing again. He'd got jaded, seeing kisses as either a means to an end or as something too personal to be shared with a random hookup from a bar. Not with Ian, though. With Ian, kisses were an end unto themselves, and they'd spent hours in much this same position, sitting side by side or Ian sitting on Thorne's lap as they kissed. Sometimes Thorne ended up shirtless, but not always. Sometimes Ian was bold enough to caress him as they kissed, and sometimes he even allowed Thorne to touch him in return, but the thread that ran through their encounters was the delicious press of lips.

Tonight seemed to be one of the bold nights, because Ian shifted on Thorne's lap so he was straddling Thorne's legs, a much more intimate position than they usually adopted, even to sleep. Thorne closed his hands around Ian's waist to steady him, but the way Ian tensed beneath his hands changed his mind, and he moved them back to the safety of Ian's shoulders.

Ian pressed him back against the couch, and Thorne gave him the upper hand willingly. He'd already learned things progressed far more easily between them when he ceded control to Ian, and he could hardly complain when it felt so good to let Ian touch him. He sometimes felt a little selfish, but trying to reciprocate almost always resulted in Ian pulling back, so he did his best to accept it.

Ian made quick work of Thorne's buttons and stripped his shirt off. Thorne shifted as needed to facilitate his disrobing. He touched the top button of Ian's shirt and waited for permission. When Ian gave it, Thorne undid the buttons and pushed the fabric out of the way. He froze for a moment when he realized Ian had foregone his usual undershirt.

"Are you sure?"

"No," Ian admitted in a shaky voice, "but I want it. It's like there's this war going on inside me between my fear and what I want with you. I can't keep letting my fear win."

"As long as you understand you can say no or back off or whatever anytime you need to," Thorne said. "I'm not going to deny I want everything I can get with you, but I don't want to pressure you into more than you're comfortable with. There's something to be said for taking our time and enjoying each stage for what it is. I'd forgotten how good it felt to just kiss someone until you reminded me of that."

"It is good," Ian agreed, "but I want more. I'm just afraid to take it."

"What happened to you?" Thorne asked. "I know you said you'd tell me after Christmas, but I feel like I'm walking through a field of land mines, not knowing."

Ian shook his head and kissed Thorne instead of answering. He attacked all Thorne's sensitive places: the nape of his neck, the inside curve of his elbow, the spot on his side just below his ribs, whipping his passion into a frenzy. Thorne groaned into the kiss as Ian shifted in his lap, bringing their erections together. He couldn't help himself. He thrust up into the contact, needing more friction, needing to make Ian feel as good as he felt.

Ian jumped like he'd been burned, fleeing across the room in the blink of an eye, leaving Thorne on the couch panting and at the end of his rope. "Ian, please," he said. "Tell me."

"I…. I can't," Ian said, his eyes wide and wild. "You'll hate me."

"Ian," Thorne cajoled, "I couldn't ever hate you. I love you, but I need you to tell me what happened so I can stop scaring you without meaning to."

"You can't love me," Ian all but shouted. "I'm damaged. He… he broke me. He came into my room when nobody else was at home and he forced me, and when he was done, he told me I couldn't ever tell anyone because nobody would want a fucked-out whore. I couldn't stop him. I couldn't…."

Thorne tasted bile, but he forced it down. He needed to keep it together for Ian's sake. "You aren't damaged," he said, enunciating every word as clearly as he could. "Whatever he did, that's on him, not on you. You didn't ask for any of it."

"He said I did," Ian said, his voice breaking. "He said I flaunted myself. He said I made a spectacle of myself and that he was just giving me what I was asking for."

Thorne couldn't sit still and listen helplessly. He had to do something, even just pace the room. He knew he was scaring Ian, but his anger was barely caged beneath his iron will, and if he didn't find some outlet for it, he'd do something he'd regret.

"How old were you?" Thorne demanded.

Ian flinched and backed toward the kitchen.

"S-s-sixteen."

"Bloody motherfucking bastard," Thorne spat. "Who was it? I'll kill him. I'll rip his prick off and stuff it down his throat."

Ian's eyes grew wider for a moment before he bolted, leaving Thorne alone in the living room with his righteous anger. A second later, he heard the bedroom door slam and the sound of furniture being dragged across the floor.

"Fuck!" Thorne cursed. His vision narrowed with his anger and the world went blank around him.

REALITY filtered back in slowly. Thorne breathed deeply and tried to take stock of where he was and what had happened. The last thing he remembered was Ian running from him like he was the one who'd raped him, not the filthy pedophile who'd somehow got his hands on Ian. It hadn't been dark then, had it? It was dark outside now, so he'd been out of it for a while, possibly as much as an hour.

He took another deep breath and opened his eyes. He was sitting on the floor in the living room, so he'd either stayed there or had made his way back there after he was done with his rampage. A quick glance showed he was still dressed as he'd been when he blacked out, but that didn't eliminate much in the way of possibilities other than forcing his way into Ian's room and making love to him the way he deserved. Whatever he'd done, it hadn't been that, for which he could only be grateful.

He looked around the room more carefully. The papers Ian had given him with the design for the cabinet were scattered across the floor in front of the couch, but when he picked them up carefully, he could see they were undamaged, so they'd been knocked aside, not destroyed in a fit of rage. The rest of the furniture was still in its usual place as well.

He clenched his fist as he walked into the kitchen, hoping he hadn't done any damage to the beautiful cabinets Ian had made for that room. His knuckles stung, drawing his attention to the torn and bloodied skin. Fuck, he'd hit something while he was out, hard and possibly repeatedly, if the state of his hand was any indication. His knuckles were already swelling and he'd be lucky if nothing was broken. Far more importantly, though, he had no idea what he'd hit.

The kitchen was pristine, so he hadn't torn it apart in his rage, but that only added to the mystery of what he'd hit. He turned back into the living room and studied the spot where he'd been sitting. A few feet to the right, he spotted a mark on the wall. Upon closer examination, he had his answer. He'd apparently pounded his fist into the wall, because the wood paneling had a blood splatter on it now. He muffled another curse and grabbed his shirt to wipe the mark away. Fortunately the blood wiped right off the varnish, but Thorne couldn't do anything about the dent he'd left.

He sank back down to the floor and rested his head against his knees. He couldn't do this. However justifiable his anger on Ian's behalf, he'd lost control tonight to the point that he'd blacked out. He could have done anything while he was out of it like that, and the fact that the worst he'd done was try to put a hole in Ian's wall didn't change anything. Next time, he could try to put a hole in someone instead, and if it happened around someone like Laura or Dani, they might not have the strength or speed to get away from him. He was a danger to the station that had become home and to the people he loved, and that was unacceptable.

Leaving wasn't an option either, though. The people here had taken him in as one of their own. Caine and Macklin were expecting him to sign a contract in the morning. Neil's daughter called him Uncle Thorne. Chris and Jesse had promised to invite him over for a beer. He had *plans*, damn it, and he wasn't going to give those up. And then there was Ian, if Ian still wanted him after this debacle. He would understand if Ian never wanted to see him again, but if Ian would give him half a chance, Thorne would spend every waking minute winning Ian's trust again. He'd thought he'd known what love was at eighteen in an attic bedroom on a cool spring night with his best friend, but that paled in comparison to what he felt for Ian. Whatever it took, he would find a way to win Ian back, but before he could do that, he had to get help. He'd tried telling himself his issues would get better as he adjusted to civilian life again, but they weren't going away, and he feared they were getting worse. He'd talk to Caine and Macklin in the morning and then go to Wagga Wagga and check himself into the mental health unit there. He'd do it right this time and answer the questions honestly instead of playing the game and giving the "right" answers like he'd done when he'd had to see a shrink after his unit was killed. He'd get himself together, and then he'd come back and ask Ian to forgive him.

He'd find a way to make this work.

He had to, because the alternatives were unthinkable.

IAN couldn't stop shaking. He'd managed to stop himself from crawling under the bed or into the closet in his quest for safety, but he'd still ended up cowering in the corner between his bed and the wall, as far away from the door as possible. He knew Thorne wouldn't hurt him. He knew Thorne's anger was directed at Ian's foster father, but that hadn't been enough to quell his fear when Thorne started shouting.

Then the pounding had started. Ian didn't know what Thorne was hitting, but he could hear the rhythmic thuds even through the closed door. The noise had stopped now, thankfully, but Ian feared the silence nearly as much as the noise. At least if he could hear something, he would know where Thorne was and could track his progress around the house. Silence could mean anything from him leaving—*oh God, don't let him leave!*—to him lying in wait outside Ian's door, just looking for the opportunity to get in—*he wouldn't.* He *did that, not Thorne.*

When the silence continued, he made himself get up off the floor. The cedar chest he'd pushed in front of the door in his panic was right where he'd left it, a silent reproach to his lack of faith. Grimly, he made himself put it back where it belonged at the foot of his—*our, damn it, it's our bed.* He pulled on a T-shirt, took off his jeans, and climbed into bed. Even as hot as it was in the room, he shivered against the cool sheets without Thorne there to keep him warm. The other man was a regular furnace. Ian could have used the heat now. He felt like every ounce of warmth had been sucked from his body with his revelations and Thorne's subsequent explosion.

Thorne's absence nagged at him like a toothache, but he couldn't make his legs work. He wanted to go out there and tell Thorne to come to bed, but he didn't know how to face his lover—*did Thorne really tell me he loves me?*—after everything he'd revealed tonight. He couldn't bear to see the look of disgust on Thorne's face, or worse, pity. Thorne had survived far worse in his life, with his parents' deaths and everything he'd gone through in the Commandos. Compared to that, Ian's life had been a walk in the park. Sure, he'd had a few bad years, but then he'd found Lang Downs and a safe haven. Thorne hadn't known safety in twenty years.

He couldn't go out there and face Thorne, but he'd learned the first night that a closed door was all the barrier required to keep Thorne out. He couldn't go out there, but he could let Thorne know he was welcome if he came to check on his own.

His legs still trembled as he crossed the room to open the door, but he kept his feet, and once the door was open and he headed back to bed, he felt steadier. He hadn't managed to ask Thorne to come to bed, but he'd at least left the choice up to Thorne instead of barring his entrance.

Everything else would have to wait until tomorrow.

TWENTY-TWO

THORNE woke the next morning with a stiff neck and sore arse from leaning against the wall all night long. He'd slept in worse conditions, but that didn't make it any easier to haul himself off the floor. He didn't hear any sounds from Ian's room or the bathroom, but Ian had to still be in there. He couldn't have snuck out past Thorne. Even wrung out like he was, he wouldn't have slept through the front door opening and closing.

He took a couple of steps down the hall to see if he could hear anything as he got closer and caught sight of the open door. Not just ajar, but wide open in silent invitation. Thorne swallowed hard. After everything, Ian hadn't locked him out of the room last night. Not that Thorne could have faced Ian after everything he'd done, but Ian had forgiven him, it seemed. Thorne didn't know how that was possible, but the door was indisputably open. Walking as quietly as he could, he made his way into the bedroom, intending to grab a change of clothes and shower so he'd be out of the way when Ian woke.

"Missed you," Ian murmured sleepily from the bed. "Come to bed."

A choked sob rose in Thorne's throat as he crossed to the bed and took the hand Ian had stretched out to him. "Are you sure?"

"Mmhmm," Ian replied. "Cold without you."

Thorne didn't deserve the grace by which he'd earned Ian's forgiveness, but he didn't question it. He simply climbed in bed behind Ian and curved around him. Ian snuggled back against him, grabbed Thorne's hand, and pulled it over his chest with a contented sigh. That only redoubled Thorne's determination. He needed to be able to give this to Ian every night, and that meant getting help so he could make that promise and be able to keep it.

He pressed a sleepy kiss to the spot below Ian's ear and relaxed back into slumber. Ian would wake them when it was time. Until then, Thorne was content to stay right where he was.

THORNE didn't know how long they slept before Ian rolled over in his arms and kissed him. He tightened his hold and kissed Ian back, uncaring of morning breath or anything other than making sure Ian knew Thorne still loved him and always would.

When they finally broke apart to breathe, Thorne rested his forehead against Ian's. "I nearly did something unforgivable last night," he said softly, "and I'm pretty sure I left a dent in your wall." He took a deep breath and plowed on. "I meant what I said when I told you I love you. Maybe I shouldn't have said it the way I did or when I did, but I'm not sorry I said it, only that I didn't say it for the first time under better circumstances. But for me to be able to stay here and keep the promises inherent in saying that, I need help. I lost myself last night for a while. I blacked out completely and while I was out, I punched the wall enough times to leave a dent and to tear up my hand. I can't ask you to live with me like that, and I can't ask Caine and Macklin to let me stay on the station like that. There's a treatment center in Wagga Wagga. I'm going to check myself in there until I can get this under control, but I'm coming back. I swear I'm coming back."

Ian tightened his arms around him.

"I'll come back," Thorne repeated. "I hate the idea of leaving, especially now, but I won't put you in danger."

"You didn't hurt me last night," Ian said.

"No, but you weren't in the room," Thorne said. "I don't remember any of it. I don't even know if I was aware of what I was doing as I did it. I could have hurt you without meaning to. You were smart enough to get away, but what if Dani had been there, or Laura? Even if I didn't hurt them, it would scare them, and they haven't done anything to deserve that. None of you have. I thought about this a lot last night. Between the doctors on base and the ones at the mental health facility in Wagga Wagga, I'll get help. I'll get it under control, and I'll come home."

"Home?" Ian said.

"Lang Downs is home," Thorne swore. "You and Neil and Kami were all right. There's something special about this valley, and I intend to be a part of that magic for a very long time, but I'd never forgive myself if I hurt someone. Let me do this right, and when I come home, we'll set some guidelines so I don't scare you like I did last night, and we'll take care of each other and mend the ragged edges."

"As long as you come home."

"I will," Thorne said, "and I'll call you every day if they let me. If not, I'll write. I'm not leaving you. I'm just going to get help so we can be together, okay?"

"Okay," Ian said. "I guess we should get up and tell Caine and Macklin. I'm pretty sure we've missed breakfast."

"Will they still be around?" Thorne asked.

"I don't know. If they aren't, we'll find them at lunch or dinner. I know, the sooner you go, the sooner you can come back, but you can wait to leave until you've explained," Ian said.

"We'll hope they're in the office or the sheds, then," Thorne said, "because I want to come back as soon as possible. I have promises to keep."

"Me too," Ian said. "I couldn't say it last night—I was too upset—but I love you too."

The words settled like a balm into Thorne's soul, warming him and soothing past hurts and doubts. He could do anything as long as he had this to come back to—even face the demons that haunted him at night.

Demons that had been absent since he started sleeping next to Ian, he realized with a start. He hadn't had a nightmare since before the night in Wagga Wagga, when he first slept with Ian in his arms. He wasn't naïve enough to think his nightmares were a thing of the past, even with Ian, but it gave him hope. If he could find enough peace at Ian's side to sleep undisturbed through the night, maybe he could find enough peace to let go of the daytime terrors as well.

He bestowed one last kiss on Ian's smiling lips and pulled himself upright. "So where should we look for Caine and Macklin?"

"I'd try the canteen first," Ian said as he sat up on the other side of the bed. "They might still be there, or someone who is there might know where they headed. If not, we can check the sheds and the office. Do you want me to come with you when you talk to them?"

"Only if you want to," Thorne said. "I don't want to make you uncomfortable."

"It's not going to be comfortable whether I'm there or not," Ian said. "I want to support you. If I can do that best by being there with you, that's where I'll be."

"Then yes," Thorne said, "I'd like to have you there with me."

CAINE and Macklin weren't in the canteen when they finally made it there to eat, nor were they in the office when they checked in with Sam. Thorne had almost resigned himself to waiting until dinner as they went to check the sheds, but Caine and Macklin were in the machine shed with Patrick, looking at the engine of a huge contraption Thorne couldn't identify.

"Caine," Ian called, "when you're done with Patrick, Thorne and I would like a word."

"Go on," Patrick said. "I've showed you what the problem is. I'll order the part and get it fixed as soon as it comes in."

"Just me or Macklin and me both?" Caine asked when he and Macklin reached the shed door.

"Both of you, if you have time," Thorne said. "If not, just you is fine."

"We can make time," Macklin said. "Shall we go up to the house?"

They walked up the road to the big house and followed Caine and Macklin inside. "Is here okay or should I go kick Sam out of the office?" Caine asked.

"This is fine," Thorne said. He took a deep breath and tried to decide where to start. "Before I sign the contract we talked about at dinner yesterday, I need to go to Wagga Wagga again. I had a blackout last night. I lost some length of time and when I came to, I realized I'd punched Ian's wall enough times to leave a dent and to bruise my knuckles pretty bad."

He held out his hand so they could see the damage. "I want to be here. I feel like I belong here, but this isn't just a question of needing a chance to get over a rough past. This is dangerous, and I won't put Ian or anyone else at risk. There's a mental health center in Wagga Wagga. I'm going to admit myself there until I get to the point that it's safe for me to come back. I don't know how long that will take, but I hope I'll still be welcome when that time comes."

"Sit down," Macklin ordered.

Thorne took a seat on the nearest chair. Not one of Ian's, he noticed randomly, although some of the furniture in the room bore Ian's distinctive design. "Ian, ask Kami for some ice, please. Let me see your hand."

Thorne held out his hand. Macklin examined it with a frown on his face. "You did a job on it, that's for sure. We'll get some ice and make sure there aren't any splinters in the cuts, but you need to get it X-rayed when you get to Wagga Wagga. If anything is cracked or broken, you need to get it set before it gets worse."

He glanced down the hallway and then at Caine, who nodded.

"Uncle Michael never turned anyone away unless they were a threat to the station or unless they couldn't accept the people he considered family," Caine said. "We've tried to run the station as he intended, so we certainly aren't going to turn you away because you're man enough to admit you need more help than we can offer, but you have to get it under control before you return."

"I will," Thorne swore. "Believe me, the biggest reason I'm doing this is because I don't ever want to be in the position of having hurt someone I care about. I won't come back until I can do so without worrying about hurting Ian."

"Then we wish you the best of luck," Caine said, "and we expect regular updates, either directly or through Ian, so we know how you're doing. We're a family here, and we support each other in our time of need."

Ian came back into the living room with the ice pack. "Here you go, Thorne. I should have thought of this last night."

"I wasn't exactly in any state to let you help me last night," Thorne said. "And you weren't much better. I'm going to get on the road. The sooner I go, the sooner I can come back, right?"

"Right," Ian said and leaned up to kiss Thorne, heedless of their audience.

Thorne squeezed Ian's hand with his good one. "I'll call when I get there. I love you."

He walked out of the house before he could change his mind.

"I SHOULD get to work," Ian said after Thorne had left. He didn't want to. He wanted to go curl up in their bed and cling to the scent of Thorne's shampoo on his pillow, but he didn't have that luxury. He had a job to do and people depending on him.

"In a minute," Macklin said. "What happened last night, Ian?"

"Thorne told you," Ian said. "He had a flashback or something and lost control of himself."

"Did you see what he did?" Caine asked.

Ian shook his head. "I was in the bedroom. I heard noise, but I didn't see anything."

"You heard him punching the wall repeatedly and didn't go investigate?" Macklin asked. "Ian, what happened?"

Ian buried his head in his hands, trying to figure a way out of telling Caine and Macklin all the sordid details of his past, but he couldn't, and maybe he needed to tell them. Thorne had admitted to his failings. Surely Ian could do the same. "He asked about my past," he said slowly, without lifting his head, "before I came to Lang Downs. I told him… my foster father raped me. Thorne got upset, and I got scared. I hid in the bedroom like a coward while he tore his hand to shreds rather than hurt me."

Macklin muttered something under his breath, something foul, judging by the look on his face. Ian nearly flinched away from the anger, but the look on Caine's face stopped him. Macklin might be angry, but he was angry on Ian's behalf, not at Ian.

"You never said anything," Macklin said after several long moments.

"Michael knew," Ian said. "He told me I could stay, but I had to tell him the truth first. I'm not sure how he would have known if I lied, but I was too afraid of losing my job here to take the risk. I never told anyone else. I… don't like to talk about it."

"Never?" Caine repeated. "You didn't tell your social worker?"

"I was afraid to," Ian admitted. "He had me convinced no one would believe me and that if I made trouble for him, he'd do even worse than he'd already done. I counted the days until I turned eighteen and could legally leave."

"What was his name?" Macklin demanded, his voice as cold and hard as Ian had ever heard it.

"It doesn't matter now," Ian said. "He can't hurt me anymore."

"No, but if he's still taking in foster kids, he needs to be reported," Macklin insisted. "The system isn't perfect, but it needs to be reported."

"Isaac Patterson," Ian said. "In Darwin. I, um, got as far away from him as I could when I ran."

"Good," Caine said. "I'm sorry it happened, and I'm sorrier still that you've had to live with it all these years, but I'm glad you finally told someone. We're here if you need anything."

"Thanks," Ian said, "but right now I just want to get to work."

And pretend he wasn't already missing Thorne.

TWENTY-THREE

"I'M GOING to check fences," Ian told Neil when he found his friend in the paddock with a crew. "I'll take a radio."

Neil frowned. "Hold on a minute. Jesse, take this crew today. I need to talk to Ian."

Ian pursed his lips and held back a sigh. The whole point of riding out to check fences was so he didn't have to talk to anyone. He waited for Neil anyway. He'd explain and then he'd leave.

"What's going on?" Neil asked when Jesse arrived to take over the crew.

"Nothing," Ian said. "I just need some time alone, and it's been a while since anyone checked the fences in the south paddocks."

"I was planning on sending a crew next week," Neil said, "so I agree with that part, but that doesn't tell me why you're riding out by yourself to do it today."

"I told you, I need some time alone."

"Fine," Neil said. "Saddle up. I'll meet you at the gate as soon as I get my gear."

"Alone usually means without anyone else around," Ian pointed out.

"So I'll be quiet," Neil said with a shrug. "I looked at the weather this morning. Nobody's going out alone today. They're predicting bad storms with the possibility of heavy rain, lightning, and hail. If you want to ride out, that's fine, but you take me or someone else with you."

"Fine, you can come," Ian said. He chafed at the idea of having company, but he hadn't checked the weather, and if the forecast was what Neil reported, he was right not to let anyone ride out alone. Neil was usually pretty good at respecting Ian's need for silence, and if he wasn't, Ian would have plenty of time alone in his empty house and empty bed tonight.

They saddled their horses and headed out of the valley toward the south, the silence between them easy and familiar. Ian could tell Neil wanted to ask what was going on in his head, but he didn't break the silence, and for that, Ian was grateful. He still felt scraped raw inside, the stress of telling Thorne and then Caine and Macklin about his foster father leaving him hollowed out. If he said anything to Neil, he'd end up talking about Thorne, which would lead to explaining why Thorne left, which would lead to telling Neil his darkest secret, and he'd already done that twice in the past twelve hours. He'd be perfectly happy never to mention it again.

"Dani slept in her new bed last night," Neil said eventually. "And this morning, she informed us we could move the cradle to the baby's room before bedtime tonight. Little princess."

Ian laughed. "Good. I'm glad it worked, although she's going to be a handful when she's thirteen instead of three."

"Maybe I'll get lucky and there won't be any boys her age on the station and I won't have to deal with it until she's seventeen or eighteen," Neil replied.

"Maybe," Ian said, "but don't get your hopes up."

"Speaking of getting your hopes up—" Neil said.

"Don't," Ian interrupted before Neil could finish his sentence. "Whatever you were about to say, just don't."

"Did you and Thorne have a fight?" Neil asked. "I didn't see him this morning, and now you're acting like a bear with a sore head."

They'd had something, all right, but Ian wasn't sure he'd call it a fight. "I really don't want to talk about."

"Look, whatever it is, it's not as bad as it seems right now," Neil said. "I've seen you two together. I know how gone he is over you. Give it 'til evening so you can both calm back down, and I'm sure you'll figure it out."

If only it were that simple.

"That's not going to be easy when he isn't here," Ian muttered.

"What? Did you say not here? Where is he?"

"On his way to Wagga Wagga," Ian replied. "I said I didn't want to talk about this."

"Uh-huh. Why is he going to Wagga Wagga? Weren't you just there? It's not that friend of his, is it? I didn't take him for the cheating kind."

"It's not his friend, and he's not cheating," Ian said with a sigh. "He had another flashback, panic attack, blackout, something last night. He's going to get treatment. I have no idea how long he'll be gone."

"Oh."

"Yeah, oh," Ian repeated. "I told you I didn't want to talk about this."

"Look, I know you'll miss him, but it's not your fault and—"

"But it *is* my fault," Ian snapped. "I'm the reason he snapped last night, and then instead of riding it out and helping him, I ran and hid like a coward because I couldn't stand to see the look on his face after what I told him."

They reached the edge of the first paddock and rode through the gate, then closed it behind them before Neil spoke again. "I can't imagine any look on his face where you're concerned besides adoration. Maybe bewildered adoration, but he looks at you the way Macklin looks at Caine. Whatever you thought you saw on his face, it either wasn't directed at you or it wasn't what you thought it was."

"You weren't there," Ian said. "You didn't see how angry he was."

"At you?" Neil repeated.

Ian wasn't honestly sure. "Maybe not, but he was shouting, and I was upset too, and I had to get away. He punched the wall so hard he left a dent in it. His hand was so swollen this morning he couldn't make a fist."

"I think maybe you need to start at the beginning," Neil said. "What happened?"

"I told you," Ian deflected.

"You told me you were the reason he snapped. You didn't tell me why you think that," Neil insisted.

"He asked about my life before I came to Lang Downs," Ian said. "I didn't want to tell him, but he insisted. He didn't like the answer when I finally gave in."

"I don't see how finding out you were a foster child would make him angry enough to hit a wall," Neil said.

"That's because I told him the whole story," Ian said with a sigh. "The story I only ever told Michael."

Neil's eyes narrowed as he steered his horse closer to Ian's. "And that upset him enough that he lost it?"

Ian nodded.

"We're going to talk about this more," Neil said, "but we need to check out that fence first." He pointed to a section of sagging fence a hundred feet or so down the fence line.

They dismounted and checked the fence. The post and wire were still intact. The fastening had simply come loose, and a couple of knocks with a hammer set it to rights.

"I get not wanting to talk about the past," Neil said when they had mounted again and continued down the fence line. "I'm pretty sure Molly doesn't know half the things I've done that I regret, but that's mostly because it's never come up. So obviously it came up, or you wouldn't have mentioned it to Thorne if Michael's the only person you ever told."

"My foster father was abusive," Ian said. "I reacted badly to something, and Thorne asked. He deserved the truth, so I told him. He didn't take it well."

"Nobody would take well to hearing someone they loved was abused," Neil pointed out.

"It wasn't just abuse," Ian mumbled. He didn't want to do this. He didn't want to tell Neil and have Neil look at him differently. He'd already run off his lover. He didn't want to lose his best friend as well.

The lines around Neil's mouth deepened as he frowned. "Well, fuck."

A bark of bitter laughter escaped Ian's throat. "Yeah, that about sums it up."

"And you didn't say anything all these years?"

"What difference would it have made?" Ian asked. "I was here on the station alone." *Safe*. "I wasn't interested in anyone. Nobody was interested in me. He couldn't get to me here even if he'd bothered to come looking. It didn't matter."

"It matters to me," Neil said with such gravity that Ian felt tears spring to his eyes. He dashed them away. He'd done enough crying last night alone in his bed. He didn't have time for this now. "It matters because you're my friend and because nobody should have to be alone with that kind of hurt."

"I wasn't alone," Ian said. "I might not have told you, but I haven't been alone since I got here. Not in any way that matters. You know that."

"I know," Neil said, "but I think you have been alone, or you were until Thorne came. He loves you, you know."

"Yeah, he told me last night," Ian said. "I love him too, but all the love in the world can't fix what's wrong with us."

"He has PTSD or something similar, and you have an abusive past," Neil summed up, "but neither of those things are the end of the world. You said he went to Wagga Wagga to get help. You could find someone too, you know. In Cowra, even if not in Boorowa. You could go on your day off each week."

"I can barely stand to talk to you about what happened," Ian protested. "How is talking to a stranger even remotely a good idea?"

"You don't have to live and work with that stranger," Neil said. "I'm not going to treat you any differently because of what you just told me, but with a stranger, you don't ever have to wonder if the next thing you say will be the one that changes things between us. I don't know what happened last night, but if it upset you enough that you had to tell Thorne about it in order to explain how you were acting, you haven't put it behind you. And if it's going to keep getting in the way of being with Thorne, don't you owe it to yourself and to him to deal with it so it doesn't get in the way anymore?"

A crack of thunder interrupted them before Ian could reply.

"I don't like the look of those clouds," Neil said.

Ian didn't either. Lightning crackled ominously across the sky. "I don't think we're getting back to the valley before that hits."

"No," Neil agreed. "There's a drovers' hut a couple of klicks from here. I think that's our best bet."

They spurred their horses across the paddock, racing hard against the wind. The first fat drops of rain splattered across the brims of their hats, making Ian wish he'd worn his Driza-Bone, but as hot as it was, he hadn't wanted the extra layer of the thick coat. He regretted it now, as the rain increased and soaked his shirt. The horses were galloping flat-out, but they couldn't outrace the storm, and they were drenched by the time they reached the drovers' hut. They got their horses into the lean-to and wiped down, then went inside to dry out a little themselves.

"It's too hot for a fire, but we'll never dry otherwise," Neil complained. "Why did we decide to ride fences today again?"

"Because I needed to not be around people and you were too stubborn to listen to me?" Ian suggested.

"You're the one who was stubborn," Neil retorted. "I told you the weather was supposed to get bad, but you couldn't stay in the valley and repair tack or something else that would let you be alone and somewhere dry. No, you had to insist on coming out to check fences."

"I'd have finished the tack in an hour," Ian said, "and then what was I supposed to do?"

"Have a cup of tea and stay dry?" Neil said. "Get a fire going. I'll radio in to let Caine know we're safe and then see what's in the cupboards that we can heat up while we're stuck here."

Ian rolled his eyes at Neil but laid a fire in the grate as directed. They would need the heat from it to get their clothes dry and to keep from catching a chill. It might make the cabin uncomfortably warm, but it would be better than getting sick. By the time he had a merry blaze going in the fireplace, Neil had come back with a tea kettle. "Caine says to wait out the storm here."

"That's what we'd planned anyway," Ian agreed. "There wasn't any soup or anything?"

"There was, but tea first, until we see how long the storm's going to last. If it clears, we can head back to the station for lunch."

Ian hung the kettle over the flames and peeled off his soaked shirt. His undershirt wasn't in any better shape, but he left it on anyway. Neil grabbed two towels and tossed one at his head. Ian caught it and flipped

Neil off. Neil just grinned back at him. The entire exchange was so typical that Ian felt something inside him unknot. They hadn't resolved anything, but Ian had told Neil the truth and it hadn't changed them. Neil was still a smart arse, and Ian was still his foil, and they could still take the piss.

The kettle boiled, Ian made tea, and they sat drinking it in silence.

"This is probably none of my business," Neil said after a while, "but things were good between you and Thorne before he left, right? I mean, in bed. You're not worried he's going to hurt you or anything."

All sense of comfort fled.

"I'm not worried he's going to hurt me," Ian said, and he wasn't. With everything else he worried about, he didn't worry about Thorne forcing him.

Neil frowned. "That's not exactly a ringing endorsement."

Ian ran his hand through his hair and realized randomly that it was getting long again. He'd have to get Sarah or Carley to cut it again soon. Neil was waiting for an answer, though, and Ian knew he wouldn't wait for long.

"I'm not… comfortable with much," Ian admitted. "I was sixteen when I went to live with my last foster family. I didn't know any other gay kids. I spent two years in hell, and then I ran. I didn't want anything to do with sex. I came here, and it wasn't exactly on offer."

"And you didn't go looking for it, because why would you?" Neil finished. "Look, I'm not an expert on relationships and stuff, but sex is supposed to be fun and feel good and bring you closer to the person you're with. I know it wasn't that way for you—and the fucker should be shot for what he did—but I don't think no sex is the answer, especially not now that you have a great guy to have it with. Just, you know, spare me the details."

"No details," Ian promised. "That's what happened last night. Things got a little intense and I panicked. Thorne wanted to know why. It's not the first time he's asked, but it's the first time I answered him. He started cursing and shouting, at my foster father, not at me, but I was already freaked out, and I just couldn't deal with any more."

"So what did you do?" Neil asked.

"I locked myself in my room until I couldn't hear him shouting anymore, then I went to bed alone for the first time in weeks, and I hated every second of it," Ian said. "I don't think I really slept until he came in to get dressed this morning and lay down with me instead."

"You know I'd do anything for you, right?" Neil said. Ian nodded, not sure where that question was leading. "If you need to talk about this, I'll listen, details and all, but I really think what I said earlier is even more true now. You need help I don't know how to give you. You need to find someone who can help you let this go. I know it had to have been awful. I can't imagine what living like that would do to a person, but I also know it was years ago and you have a chance for something really special. I don't want you to lose that chance because you're afraid to have sex with Thorne."

"I wouldn't even know where to start looking," Ian said.

"Me either, but Doc Peters would," Neil said. "Hell, Caine might. It still amazes me the stuff he knows. The point is, we can find out, but you have to follow through. You have to believe in your relationship with Thorne enough to do what it takes to make it work."

"Then I guess we'd better call him when we get back to the valley," Ian said. "I'm scared to death, but I don't want to lose Thorne. I won't get a second chance."

TWENTY-FOUR

"FIFTEEN years. Fifteen bloody years." Macklin had a hell of a lot of sympathy for Thorne right now. The desire to put his fist into something was nearly overwhelming. The pedophile's face would be his first preference, as he was sure it would have been Thorne's, but the wall was looking like a better alternative with each passing moment.

"He didn't want anyone to know," Caine said. "You know how that feels. You didn't want to tell me about your father either."

"He knocked me around a few times," Macklin said dismissively, "but nothing like what Ian went through."

"He broke your arm because you didn't stop a goal at a game your team won," Caine retorted. "That's more than just knocking you around a few times."

"It's still not rape," Macklin said bluntly. "He's lived with that stain on his heart for years, and I didn't do anything to help."

"I think you did," Caine said. "I think you and Michael gave him a safe place to live, a place to call home where he didn't have to think about it and where he could get on with his life."

"It didn't look like he'd got on with anything when he talked to us this morning," Macklin said.

"I think that depends on what you focused on this morning," Caine insisted. "Yes, Ian is still struggling with it, but do you think Ian would even be trying to have a relationship with Thorne if they'd met fifteen years ago when he first came here?"

"No, probably not," Macklin had to admit. "He was pretty much a complete loner back then. He'd share a beer with Neil and Kyle occasionally, but he never went to town with the others, and once he got that house of his own, he guarded his privacy fiercely. I was stunned when he let Thorne start sleeping on the couch. He's never even let Neil sleep on his couch."

"Has Neil ever needed to sleep on his couch?" Caine asked with a grin.

"I don't know," Macklin said. "There was that one time when Molly was pregnant with Dani when I'm pretty sure she kicked him out of the house for a week. He stayed with Sam and Jeremy. I don't know if Ian would have refused, but I'll put money on it that Neil didn't even ask. He knew what the answer would be and he knew Sam wouldn't turn him away."

"Which all proves my point," Caine said. "He let Thorne sleep on his couch. From what I heard, he *invited* Thorne to sleep on his couch. He wants this, and he's trying to make it happen, and he couldn't have done that without the years of safety and peace here. I know you wish you'd known and that you could have helped then, or even that you could help now, but you *have* helped already, and Ian knows and appreciates that."

Macklin nodded because he knew Caine expected it, and they had work to do that wouldn't wait for him to dwell on the past and all the ways he'd failed to help Ian. Caine would say Ian was a grown man and had been since he arrived on the station and that, as such, he didn't need Macklin's protection, but Macklin had never been one to shirk his responsibilities, and all the men and women on the station were his responsibility—the year-rounders most of all.

"MUM?"

"Hello, love," Sarah said with a smile when Macklin walked into the kitchen. "I don't usually see you in the middle of the afternoon. Is everything all right?"

"Not really," Macklin admitted. "I've had better days."

"I'll make us some tea and you can tell me about it," Sarah offered. "Even if I can't help, you'll feel better for having talked about it."

Macklin nodded and waited silently while Sarah puttered around in the small kitchen of the house she and Kami shared. He steadfastly refused to think of Kami as his stepfather, but he was happy beyond words to see contentment in his mother's eyes. A few minutes later, she brought the teapot to the table and set it between them. "Now, tell me what's bothering you."

"Thorne left for Wagga Wagga this morning," Macklin began. "He's gone to get help for his flashbacks."

"That's a very brave thing for him to do," Sarah observed. "A lot of military men wouldn't be comfortable admitting they had a problem, much less doing something about it."

"That's what Caine told him," Macklin said. "And Ian too."

"Ah, yes," Sarah said. "Ian. How is he taking Thorne's departure?"

"I don't know," Macklin admitted. "You've heard enough stories to know how Michael was. He'd take in anyone who needed it. What you might not know is he made one demand in return. He wanted the truth of the past that had driven us all here. He never judged, but he had to know. I like to think it was so he could protect us. When he died, he took all our secrets to his grave with him. Caine insisted on hearing Chris and Seth's story before he took them in. Neil told us Sam's story before he came, and Jeremy told me his, but I took for granted that the established year-rounders were all adults and didn't need my protection the way Chris and Seth did."

"And Ian does?" Sarah asked.

"Not in the sense that someone is actively threatening him," Macklin replied, "but he didn't leave his troubles behind when he got here. While I was busy building on Michael's legacy and falling in love with Caine and getting more than I ever deserved in this life, Ian was suffering in silence because I didn't follow Michael's lead and insist on learning everyone's stories too."

"Macklin, love," Sarah scolded, "you're human just like the rest of us. You're going to have regrets just like the rest of us. Do you think I don't regret not finding a way to leave your father when you were younger? I still hear your arm snapping in my dreams some nights, but we survived him, and even better, we're happy now, which is a far better revenge than anything else we could have done to him. I hope he's rotting in hell, tortured by the fact that we both have husbands who love us and that his hatred and abuse didn't keep either of us from finding happiness."

Macklin was taken aback by his mother's vehemence, but he couldn't help but second her sentiment. "It would serve him right. I let you down too, though. I should have figured out a way to take you with me or, barring that, I should have found a way to come back for you after I was old enough to be free of him legally."

"Oh, my sweet boy," Sarah said, reaching across the table for Macklin's hand, "are you still beating yourself up over that all these years later? You were a child, love. I wasn't your responsibility, and even if I was, you couldn't help me when you were hurting so badly. You had to find your own feet first."

"I didn't come looking for you even then."

Sarah chuckled softly. "That's because you didn't find your feet until you met Caine," she said indulgently, "and don't give me that look. You can think whatever you want, but it's the truth. You were still just as battered on the inside at forty as you were at fourteen until he came along and taught you how to love again. I've heard stories of how you'd go to Sydney for a week every winter. A week of sex, because that's all you dared to allow yourself, even with Michael and Donald to give you a different example. Don't tell me you weren't still hurting."

"I'm not hurting now," Macklin said, "but Ian is, and I don't know how to help him."

"Maybe you can't," Sarah said. "Maybe the help he needs has to come from Thorne. He couldn't have helped you heal. You needed Caine. Thorne might be what Ian needs."

"But Thorne is going to be gone for the next several weeks," Macklin said.

"So you give him what he asks for in the meantime," Sarah said. "Whether that's time off to go to Wagga Wagga to be with Thorne or whether that's the privacy to lick his wounds."

"I will," Macklin said, "but I think there's one other thing I can give him. When Caine found you and you told me my father was dead, I knew I'd never have to worry about him hurting anyone again. I can give Ian that peace of mind."

"How?" Sarah asked.

"By making sure the authorities know what his foster father did to him," Macklin said. "It might be after the fact, but if the bastard is in jail somewhere, Ian won't have to worry about being hurt again."

"As if anyone here would let that happen," Sarah said.

"No more than they would have let Dad hurt me if he'd found me here," Macklin said, "but I didn't feel completely safe until I knew he was dead. I didn't know I was still worrying about it, but the relief when you told me was too real to deny."

MACKLIN hung up the phone with grim satisfaction. "Isaac Patterson was convicted of sexual assault of a minor ten years ago. He was sentenced to life in prison and died there a little over a year ago."

"Feel better?" Caine asked when Macklin finished.

"Yeah, as stupid as that sounds when I wasn't the one he victimized," Macklin replied.

"It's not stupid," Caine said. "He hurt your friend. It makes sense you'd be glad to see him face justice. You should tell Ian. It might help him find some closure as well."

"Come with me?" Macklin asked. "You're better at this kind of thing than I am."

"What kind of thing?" Caine teased.

"Emotions," Macklin said with a grimace. "What is it Molly says about us? We treat emotions like they're as deadly as a mulga?"

"Something like that," Caine agreed. "Fortunately for you, the partners of your stockmen seem to be more in touch with that side of themselves. Yes, I'll go with you to talk to Ian."

They found Ian in the tack room, a pile of broken reins and stirrup leathers strewn around his feet. "Awfully hot day to be doing that, isn't it?" Macklin said. "You could at least carry it outside, where there's a breeze.

"There are also people out there," Ian muttered, "and right now people are very interested in why Thorne suddenly left. Telling them it's none of their business doesn't seem to be working."

"You know they ask because they're concerned about you," Caine said. "If they didn't care about you, they'd chalk it up to him not being cut out for station life and move on."

"I know," Ian said, "but I still have to explain, and then they want to know what happened, and that brings up things I want to talk about even less than where Thorne is now."

"About that…," Macklin began.

"Relax, Ian," Caine said before Macklin could continue. Macklin saw the stricken look on Ian's face and sighed, gesturing for Caine to take over. Even when he was delivering the closest thing to good news in this kind of a situation, he still made a mess of it.

"You're not…."

"We're not anything," Caine promised when Ian didn't finish the sentence "We called DoCS in Darwin. If it had come down to actually accusing Patterson of rape, you would have had to do it, but we wanted to find out if he was still working as a foster parent so we'd know if you needed to do it."

"Is he?" Ian asked, his voice so small and broken that Macklin flashed back to his own childhood and begging his mother for an explanation of his father's abuse.

"No," Macklin said. "He was sentenced to life in prison ten years ago. He served nine years before dying in jail. Apparently some of the inmates took exception to his crimes."

"They killed him?" Ian asked.

"No, but they weren't kind to him. He died of his injuries a few days later," Macklin said. "Perforated intestine, apparently."

He hated to admit the sadistic glee he felt at the thought of Ian's abuser being forced to suffer the same kind of pain and humiliation he'd forced on Ian, but a primal part of him relished it. It didn't decrease Ian's suffering, but there was a certain poetic justice to it. He just wouldn't mention that to Caine.

Ian had no such qualms. "Good," he muttered. "Serves the bastard right to know what it feels like to be held down and forced. I hope they ripped his insides to shreds. Thank you for finding that out for me. I don't know if I would have had the courage to call on my own."

"You're welcome," Macklin said. "If you need anything else, just let us know."

"Actually," Ian said slowly, "I was thinking I might start taking my day off instead of working through it. If you can spare me, of course."

"It's your day off," Caine said. "Of course we can spare you. Was there something particular you were planning on doing with it? Not that it matters. It's your day, even if all you do with it is sleep for twenty-four hours."

"As nice as that sounds, that wasn't what I had in mind," Ian said with a lopsided smile. "Doc Peters gave me the name of someone in Cowra, someone to hopefully help me while Thorne is in Wagga Wagga getting help."

"Good," Caine said. "You should do that. If you need extra days at first, let us know. You've worked more days off than you've taken off. We'll work around your schedule."

"I have to meet her first," Ian said, "but I'll let you know."

"Just don't forget to tell us," Macklin said.

"I won't," Ian promised. "Neil's already kicked my arse once for thinking I had to do things alone. I don't need it kicked again."

"Good," Macklin said, "because I wouldn't be as nice about it as he was."

Ian smiled. "I learned my lesson, boss. If I need something, I'll be sure to tell you."

TWENTY-FIVE

THORNE had been at the Wagga Wagga Mental Health Services for three days when Walker came to visit.

"How you holding up, Lachlan?" he asked when Thorne joined him in the visitors' area of the center.

"Doing okay," Thorne said. "The doctors diagnosed me with PTSD, which shouldn't really come as a surprise after everything we've seen and done. We're trying some antianxiety meds to help with the over-the-top reactions. It's too soon to tell if it's helping, but the doctor seems to think it will. We've spent a lot of time talking, which is hard. I have to talk around a lot of stuff because it's classified, but it's not where I was or what the mission parameters were that are important."

"No, I suppose not," Walker said. "How's your boyfriend dealing with all of this?"

"I haven't talked to him since I called to let him know I made it here safely. I don't have access to my cell phone or a computer, not that Ian has an e-mail account, but I've been writing to him. The doctor said that was good for me too. I'm hoping he'll write back, but the station's so remote that they take the mail in once a week unless it's urgent. The nearest post office is in Boorowa."

"You're really serious about him, aren't you?" Walker asked.

Thorne nodded. "I love him, and if this is what it takes for me to be healthy enough to spend the rest of my life with him, then this is what I'm going to do. If it takes a week or a month, it doesn't matter."

"I hope he knows how lucky he is to get you," Walker said.

"I'm the lucky one."

Dear Ian,

God, it's strange to pick up a pen and actually write a letter by hand. I haven't written anything with a pen in years. All my reports were typed, if I was the one writing them and not giving them orally.

I made it to Wagga Wagga, but you knew that already. The center is nice, very modern, and the staff members are all friendly. I like Kevin, the therapist I'm working with. PTSD is the official diagnosis. I've started antianxiety medication that they say will help control the outbursts. I haven't had any since I got here, but it's only been a few days, and they said it'll take longer than that for the meds to kick in.

I miss you. I hated leaving you the way I did, but I couldn't put it off. It wouldn't have been any easier a day or even an hour later, and I might have talked myself out of it if I hadn't gone right away.

I hope you're doing well. It's strange not being with you after spending so much time together. I've started having nightmares again. Did you know I didn't have a single one when we slept in the same bed? I told the therapist that. He said it meant I felt safe when I was with you. I like to think you felt safe with me too. I hope I haven't ruined that with my outburst on Christmas night. I wasn't angry at you. I was angry <u>for</u> you. I realize that's not much comfort since you were the one who got to listen to me shout and hit things.

We're working on anger-management techniques. I don't think of myself as being angry most of the time, but the therapist seems to think it will help with the PTSD too. I'm willing to try anything if it gets me home to you faster.

I'll write again soon, but I want to get this out in today's mail. I'm not sure when the next trip to town will be, and I want this one at least to be waiting for you.

I love you.
Thorne

Ian finished reading the letter and set it carefully on the table in front of him. He'd called the therapist Dr. Peters had mentioned that afternoon. He'd been hoping for one in Boorowa, but it was either Cowra or Yass, and Cowra was a little closer, for a certain definition of "close." Close enough he could leave early on his day off, drive to Cowra for an appointment, and drive home that night. It would be a long day, but he could do it without having to miss work.

He could write Thorne and tell him he was doing his part to get well too, that he wanted things to work between them just as much as Thorne did, and he was doing the work to make it happen. He only wished the thought of it didn't make him sick to his stomach.

Dear Thorne,

You aren't the only one a little weirded out by the whole letter-writing thing. I thought I was done with this kind of thing when I took a job on a sheep station. No accounts to keep (for me, anyway), no more papers to write for classes, nothing. Just me and the great outdoors. And here I am writing a letter.

I'm glad you like your therapist and that you feel like it's helping. I had my first appointment with a therapist in Cowra. Not sure how I feel about talking to a woman about all of this, but it was either that or drive to Yass, which is even farther away than Cowra. I guess I'll be spending my days off in the car for the foreseeable future. She said we might get to the point where we could meet via Skype or something (I guess Sam and Caine can help me figure out how to make that work if you're not back by then) but for now, it's a long drive, a short therapy appointment, and a long drive home.

It seems you're not the only one with PTSD. Mine's maybe a little more specific than yours, related to one repeated event rather than to years in the military, but she says the symptoms are the same.

I feel like a coward doing this in a letter rather than waiting until you're home and we can talk face to face, but I'm not sure I can talk about it out loud. It's hard enough to do it with the therapist. So here goes.

I'm not sure I'll ever be comfortable with anal sex. I want to make love with you, but I don't know if that way of making love will ever be on the table. One of the exercises my therapist has me doing is visualizing different ways we could be together, different things we could do to each other, and seeing which ones I can actually imagine and which ones trigger flashbacks. I can wrap my head around almost everything but that. I can sit here and say that you would never hurt me the way he did, and I can even believe it, but there's a final step between believing it and letting it happen that I haven't been able to take. My therapist says not to force myself, that if I'm not comfortable with something, I should say so and explore other options instead, but I still feel like I'm cheating you out of something. To which she said if you made me feel that way, you weren't the right man for me.

I insisted that wasn't you, that you'd take me even if all we ever did was kiss. I need you to understand that. No matter what's screwed up in my head, it's not something you've done or added to or made worse in any way. On the contrary. Because of you, I can lie in bed and imagine touching you. I can imagine hands on my body feeling good instead of being a cause for panic.

I don't know how much of this I told you, but my mum wasn't around much when I was growing up. She was either working, when she could find a job, or out looking for a sugar daddy to pay the rent for a few weeks when she was between jobs. Even before I went into the foster system, I was pretty much on my own. The idea that someone, anyone, could touch me tenderly and with affection is one I'm still getting used to, and once you started, I couldn't get enough as long as it didn't turn overtly sexual. That's the part I'm still struggling with. Kissing like we do, holding hands, your hands on my arms or in my hair… those are things nobody has ever done to me before. We'll have to work on the part where it goes from being affectionate to being sexual. I want to get there. I will get there. I just don't know exactly where there will be.

Wow, this has got long. It's getting late and I have to get up early to drive to Cowra. I'm going to drop this in the mail on the way to my therapy session, but I'll have to wait for the supply run on Friday to see if I have a reply, and even then, it probably won't be to this letter. Any reply is better than none. I miss you.

I love you.

Ian

Thorne read Ian's letter and then read it again. He took a few deep breaths and then read it a third time, but not because he didn't remember it. He already had it imprinted on his brain. No, he read it again because until he could read it without wanting to hunt down everyone who had ever hurt Ian and slaughter them as slowly as possible, he couldn't answer him, and he wanted to answer him. He wanted to write back and tell Ian none of it mattered, that Thorne would gladly accept the sweet kisses and caresses they'd already shared and count himself lucky, but he couldn't do that until he could release some of the anger that had exploded inside him as he read Ian's fears and confessions.

He glanced at the journal his therapist had suggested he keep as a way to record his thoughts so he could examine them more clearly later, but there was too much aggression in him right now to sit and write it out. He needed to run. Fortunately the center included a small workout area with a treadmill he could use. He'd spend some time there and try writing afterward.

He was still running an hour later when Kevin joined him in the gym. "You've been here a while. The clerk was getting worried."

"I've run longer than this," Thorne said. "And harder too."

"I'm sure you have," Kevin said, "but that was in the military when your life depended on it, or could, anyway. If you're running like that here, it's because something's wrong."

"You told me exercise was a good way to deal with anger," Thorne retorted.

"I did and it is," Kevin agreed, "but if an hour on the treadmill hasn't taken care of it, then exercise isn't the answer this time." He hit the stop button. "Take a shower and meet me in my office."

"I don't want to talk about it," Thorne muttered.

"Oh, I believe that," Kevin said, "but that's all the more reason you need to. If you're not there in half an hour, I'm coming looking and we'll talk wherever I find you instead of in the privacy of my office. You're making such progress, Thorne. Don't let whatever happened today set you back."

Dear Ian,

I have so much I want to say to you and I'm not even sure where to start, so if this letter ends up feeling kind of random, that's why. First, I'm so glad you've decided to talk to someone about what happened to you. As hard as it is (and believe me, I know how hard it is), I think it will help you. I can already tell it's helping me. I have a long way to go, but I can see progress, and that's encouraging. I read your letter and wanted to go find everyone who's ever hurt you and make them suffer for what they did. I was so angry I could barely see, but instead of hitting something like I did when you first told me about it, I went to the gym here and ran on the treadmill for an hour. I probably would have run longer, but Kevin made me stop and talk to him instead.

I hurt for you when I think about what you went through, and I don't even have the words to tell you how much I respect you for not giving up and for giving me a chance. I hope it goes without saying, but I'm going to say it anyway because I need you to know it, and maybe you need to hear it.

I don't <u>expect</u> anything from you except for you to do what you're comfortable with. If that's kissing and making out on the couch, that's fine with me. If you get to the point where you want more than that someday, I won't complain, but I won't ever pressure you. I spent plenty of years relieving my tension myself. If you never get to the point of wanting to share that, I'll just keep doing it. I've gained so much by having you in my life that anything else is just icing on the cake. Nice, yes, but not necessary. The cake, the important part, that's you, sharing our days and nights, if you still want to do that after the way I acted. Sharing our lives. Sex is nice, sure, but you're what matters.

I do like the idea of you lying in bed imagining us together, though. Shall I whisper all the things you do to me in your ear when I get home? Should I tell you how good you make me feel? Would that make you bolder or just scare you off?

Fuck it all, I'm getting hard sitting here just thinking about it. This was not supposed to be a letter about sex. I'm supposed to be telling you I don't need it, but Kevin keeps insisting I have to be honest with you, so there you have it. Thinking about you turns me on, especially thinking about kissing you or touching you. The difference between me and that rat bastard is that I'm not ruled by it. It doesn't control me or make me want to control you. It makes me want to take care of you and convince you to trust me so maybe someday you'll want to experiment with me. I'm only human. I'm going to get hard when you touch me, like I did the night you told me what happened to you, but that's never going to control me. It's never going to make me do something you don't want, so you don't have to be afraid of me.

I know, I know, easy for me to say; I'm not the one who was hurt. Just know that I will never be the one to hurt you, at least not like that. I'm sure we'll say and do plenty of things to annoy each other. That's part of any relationship, but I don't ever want you to be afraid of me again. I will leave Lang Downs before I will hurt you that way.

It's been two weeks since I left. I'm having trouble believing it's been that long. I talked to Kevin today about how much longer I might need to stay. Given the distance, he'd prefer I stay until we're sure the meds are the right ones, which means staying at least another two weeks. If I lived in town and could go in for periodic checkups, it wouldn't be as much of an issue, but I'd rather do this right now and be able to come home than leave too soon and have to come back for another extended stay.

I'll write again soon. I know you won't get this any earlier because I decided to send it now instead of waiting until later in the week, but at least you'll know I answered your letter right away.

I love you.

Thorne

Ian set Thorne's letter down and stared at the bedroom wall for a minute before getting up and finding his own pen and paper. His hands shook a little as he settled at the kitchen table. More than that, though, he ached to be touched, and that was a new feeling, one only Thorne had ever inspired.

Dear Thorne,

I just got your latest batch of letters. Thank you for sending them so regularly.

I'm sitting here at the kitchen table at ten o'clock at night, when I should be in bed asleep, because I couldn't wait until after work tomorrow to answer you. I miss you, but you knew that already, although I hope you haven't got tired of hearing it.

I've started dreaming about you at night, you know. I guess all the visualization exercises are paying off, because I wake up from my dreams turned on. I used to think he'd broken me and that I'd never be able to react to anyone else's touch. Hell, I hardly react to my own hand. It's like he found some switch inside me and shut it off, but you turned it back on. I dream about you and I wake up wishing you were there because while my hand does nothing for me, your hands do. I close my eyes and imagine you're the one touching me, which helps, but it's not the same as when you were here.

Anna says that's a good sign, that my reactions are beginning to normalize where sex is concerned. I don't know if it's really where sex is concerned, but it certainly is where you're concerned. I can think of your hands on me and I can get aroused, not just my brain but my body too. I still can't get much past hands in my head, unless it's kissing. Anna gave me a list of things to try to imagine starting with kissing, which is easy because that's remembering, not imagining, and working through hand jobs and blow jobs all the way to penetrative sex. We talked about that already, and that hasn't changed, but I'm still working on the rest.

I think about you lying on the couch with your shirt off and how good you look and how much I want to touch you. I can practically feel the hair on your chest under my palms. That's how clear my memories are. And then I think about you kissing me and the way it's never just my mouth, but my cheeks and my jaw and behind my ear, and what your beard does to me, and I want to make you feel the same way. I want to kiss you and keep kissing you and maybe even kiss my way down your chest.

That's all safe, you see. He never did anything like that to me or made me do it to him. I think that's why I can think about a hand job too. He didn't touch me that way (he didn't care if I got off, thank God. I don't think I could have stood that humiliation on top of everything else) and he didn't make me touch him that way either. Yes, it's sex, but it's not tainted by being raped.

There, I said it. I called it what it was. Anna makes me practice saying it. I'm not sure if that makes it better or worse, but at least it makes it not a secret anymore, not something hidden or shameful. I didn't ask for what happened to me, and it's not my fault that I wasn't strong enough at sixteen to fight off a full-grown man.

Anyway, that's not what I wanted to write about. I wanted to tell you about my dreams and the visualizations Anna has me doing. I won't say I exactly look forward to the visualizations because she insists I not always stay with what's comfortable but that I keep considering different options, so the visualization times don't always end well. I get to the point where I try to imagine giving you a blow job and I freeze up. When I dream, though, there's no pressure to go beyond what's comfortable, and I dream, Thorne. God, how I dream! I can see your face and the way it looks when I touch you, and that just gets better the more I touch you. And then when I wake up, I keep my eyes closed and imagine it's your hand touching me, making me feel good, and it's like nothing I've ever felt before. I can only guess how much better it will be when you're really here.

I'm counting the days until it's time for the next supply run and your next batch of letters. Maybe you'll have a better idea then of when you'll be home and I can count the days until you're here again.

I love you.

Ian

TWENTY-SIX

THORNE stopped his ute when he reached the entrance to the valley. It had only been three months since he'd first laid eyes on the little piece of heaven on earth tucked into the sere tablelands, but it had already become home, a home he had sorely missed over the past five weeks. The valley was greener than when he'd first arrived, the lower temperatures and increased rain allowing it to recover from the worst of the summer heat. The paddocks weren't as dry either, although they hadn't greened up the way the valley had.

He was late for lunch and early for dinner, so he didn't expect a lot of people to be around when he arrived, but he hoped Ian would be there. They'd talked briefly the night before when Thorne called him from Walker's flat, but it had been a stilted conversation with Walker in the next room and so much they needed to say to each other without an audience.

Thorne only hoped the awkwardness of the conversation wouldn't carry over once they were together again. He'd bared so much of himself to Ian in his letters, and Ian had done the same in return, so much spoken and yet unspoken. They weren't coming back together as the same men they'd been when they parted, and while Thorne thought they were both stronger for it, they would have to find their balance again.

Sitting here at the entrance of the valley wouldn't make that any easier, so with a fortifying breath, Thorne put the ute back in gear and headed toward the station.

He parked in front of Ian's house and tossed his bag onto the veranda. He could wait to unpack until after he'd seen Ian and made sure he was still welcome either on Ian's couch or in his bed. He thought he would be, but he didn't want to assume.

He'd headed back up the road toward the canteen, hoping to find someone who could give him an idea where to find Ian, when he saw Ian walking down the road toward him.

"Hi," Ian said shyly when he neared where Thorne stood.

"Hi," Thorne replied. "I missed you."

"I missed you too," Ian said. His hands twitched at his sides like he didn't quite know what to do with them. Thorne wanted to reach out and twine his fingers through Ian's to settle them, but he'd promised to let Ian take the lead and make the first move, and he wouldn't break that promise less than a minute after he got home. "How was the drive?"

"Long," Thorne said, "but not bad. How have things been here on the station?" It wasn't what he wanted to ask, but they seemed stuck in a loop of small talk. Thorne felt his heart shrivel a little as he tried to figure out how to get past it.

"We got some rain," Ian said. "We needed it. Caine had started talking about needing to bring in hay to supplement the grass in the paddocks, but I think we'll be okay without it now."

Before Thorne could think of what to say next, Neil walked up behind Ian and bopped him on the back of the head. "Just kiss him, drongo. You've been moping around for five weeks, missing him. Whatever you're talking about, it can wait until later."

Ian ducked his head and glared at Neil, but the smile tugging at his lips spoiled it. Thorne held out his hand in offer, not quite ready to take the final step of initiating the kiss without some sign from Ian but more than happy to give Ian a sign of his welcome. That seemed to be all the invitation Ian needed, because he closed the distance between them and leaned up to kiss Thorne. Thorne bent eagerly to meet him and sighed into the kiss when their lips met. They still had to talk, they still had to work everything out, but he was home and in Ian's arms and kissing him again and nothing else mattered right now, not even Neil standing nearby.

"Get a room," someone shouted.

"Get a life," Neil shot back before Thorne could react. He lifted his head but kept Ian tucked tightly against him and watched as Neil strode down the road toward whoever had shouted at them.

"He won't have a job come morning," Ian murmured against Thorne's shoulder, "but I'd rather take this inside if it's all the same to you."

"I'll go anywhere in the world with you," Thorne replied. "Inside is easy."

He slipped his arm around Ian's waist as they walked back toward Ian's house.

"Neil already told me to take the rest of the day off when you got here," Ian said as they neared the veranda, "so I'm yours for the afternoon."

"Not just the afternoon, I hope," Thorne said.

"Not just the afternoon," Ian confirmed with a blush that turned his face nearly the color of his hair, "but tomorrow you have to share my time with the station again. I do have a job, you know, and so do you."

"I know," Thorne said, giving Ian a squeeze, "and I appreciate Neil giving us the afternoon off."

They reached the veranda and Thorne's bag.

"Why didn't you take it inside?" Ian asked. "It's just two more steps."

"Because I wanted to find you first," Thorne said, "and because I didn't want to assume."

"I appreciate that," Ian said, "but in this case, please assume. I know we've got a lot to talk about and I know I have a long way to go—and maybe I'll never get all the way there, although Anna says I'm making good progress—but I missed you while you were gone, a constant ache like a missing limb. I'm sure we'll argue and fight and have missteps and everything else, but there's only one place I want you to sleep at night, and that's in our bed, next to me. If you have to spend a night in one of the drovers' huts, I'll live with that because I'm sure there will be nights I'm stuck out there too, but I don't ever want you to doubt your welcome."

Thorne grabbed his bag as they crossed the veranda and then promptly dropped it again when they made it inside because he couldn't let a declaration like that go without kissing Ian as thoroughly as he knew how.

Ian returned the kiss eagerly, drawing Thorne deeper into the house without pulling back. For a moment, Thorne thought Ian was leading them toward the bedroom and was going to slow things down, but then he detoured toward the couch. Thorne had no problem following him there, especially not after Ian's later letters. Thorne didn't want to rush into anything, but he'd follow Ian's lead wherever that took them.

He'd lost track of how many times he'd jerked off thinking about Ian's letters and about Ian lying in bed dreaming of him. He'd like nothing more than to make those dreams a reality right now, but that would be up to Ian.

IAN broke the kiss, his body tingling with need. He'd been so afraid the passion from his dreams wouldn't carry over to reality when Thorne returned. He needn't have worried. Thorne still tasted of peppermint, far more delicious in reality than it had been in his dreams. His beard still rasped against Ian's lips, an extra layer of stimulation, as if he needed more. His chest was still solid and strong beneath Ian's hands, and best of all, Ian's body reacted to it, filling him with desire and need.

He tugged at the hem of Thorne's shirt, eager now to get his hands on his lover's body again. Thorne moved easily with him, allowing Ian to strip him to the waist. A wave of shyness hit him for a moment, but he focused on Thorne's face and on the need and desire he saw that echoed his own. Thorne wanted this as badly as Ian did, whatever "this" turned out to be.

He ran his hands up Thorne's chest from his waist to his shoulders, relishing the feel of thick, dark hair beneath his palms and the occasional patch of rough skin from a scar. Thorne arched into the caress, making Ian smile. He took his time, reacquainting himself with Thorne's body, finding all his sensitive spots and lavishing attention on them, and when that was no longer enough, he nudged Thorne to lie back against the arm of the couch as they had done so many times already. When Ian moved to continue their lovemaking—for he was ready for this to be more than just making out—he didn't roll off to the side as he had always done before.

Instead he straddled Thorne as he had done that fateful night that had resulted in so many changes. He hissed when the position brought their erections together through their clothes, but he didn't panic this time. Thorne wouldn't hurt him. The bulge in his trousers was no threat to him, just another way he could make Thorne feel good. He rocked against Thorne hesitantly, gratified beyond words when Thorne's gaze went dark with need and he spread his legs and encouraged Ian to settle between them.

He rocked again with a little more determination as he lowered his head to taste the skin of Thorne's collarbone.

"F-fuck," Thorne gasped. "Who are you and what have you done with my Ian?"

Ian grinned up at him. "I told you what I'd been dreaming about, or did you not believe me?"

"I believed you, but I didn't expect you to be quite so…."

"Eager?" Ian suggested, rubbing against Thorne again. "Well, I am. Is that going to be a problem?"

"Jesus, fuck, no problem," Thorne cursed. "*No* problem. Just, God, don't stop."

Ian grinned and kept rocking and licking and loving the way Thorne squirmed and writhed and bucked beneath him. He felt like he was flying on the huge rush of adrenaline from having this magnificent man spread out for his enjoyment. He rutted against the vee of Thorne's legs, the friction far more potent than the touch of his own hand had been. He panted hard, little puffs of breath against Thorne's chest as he struggled for control. He didn't want this to be over yet. He wanted the sense of freedom to continue. He didn't have to think like this; he could turn off his mind and let his body take over.

Beneath him Thorne stiffened suddenly and then went lax, and Ian flushed hot, realizing what must have happened. He buried his face against Thorne's neck and let himself go, giving in to the flood of sensation.

Only then did Thorne put his arms around his shoulders, lightly enough he could get away if he wanted to… but he didn't want to. No, he never wanted to move from where they were right at that moment. Besides, he was quite sure his legs wouldn't support his weight, so they were stuck there.

He breathed in the scent of Thorne's skin, overlaid with the scent of sex between them, and thought he'd never smelled anything so wonderful in his life. It was a smell he'd always been keen to wash away before, but now, with Thorne warm and pliant beneath him, it represented safety, not shame or fear or pain.

"Love you," Thorne murmured into Ian's hair.

"Love you too," Ian replied and pressed a kiss to Thorne's neck. He took a few more deep breaths and lifted his head. "I didn't think I could feel this way."

"Loving someone or having sex with someone?" Thorne asked.

"Either," Ian said. "They tend to go together, and sex wasn't an option before."

"Speaking of sex," Thorne said, shifting on the couch a little, "we're going to be very uncomfortable here in a few minutes if we don't get out of these sticky pants. You wrecked me, you know that."

"I kind of guessed it, yeah," Ian said, flushing a bit.

Thorne sat up and juggled their arms and legs until Ian was sitting on his lap. "Want to join me in the shower?"

Ian froze.

"Just to rinse off," Thorne assured him.

Ian swallowed hard and focused on how good it had felt to rub off against Thorne and then to remember all the things he'd dreamed about while they were apart. "And if I want to do more than rinse off?"

"Baby, you can do anything you want to me anytime you want."

Ian grinned, grabbed Thorne's hand, and pulled him toward the bathroom.

THORNE braced himself for the teasing he was sure he and Ian would receive as they walked into the canteen for breakfast the next morning. They hadn't made it to dinner last night, and he figured that would earn them at least a few off-color comments. They'd be mostly off base, since other than a few tentative caresses in the shower—he was already completely addicted to the touch of Ian's hands and only hoped Ian was starting to feel the same about him—he and Ian had spent the evening talking, not fucking, but nobody else would know that. They'd see a couple separated for weeks and imagine how they would spend their reunion.

To his surprise, although everyone looked up and smiled or waved when they came in, no one catcalled or reacted to their presence in any way out of the ordinary.

"Is Neil watching out for us again?" Thorne murmured as he joined Ian in the line for breakfast.

"Probably," Ian replied, "but I'm not going to complain. He's been really protective of my feelings since you left. I, um, I told him everything. He was a little annoyed at me for not telling him sooner."

Thorne smoothed a hand over Ian's side. "You weren't ready to talk about it before now."

"And he gets that," Ian said. "He just feels the need to make sure nobody else makes it worse now that he knows."

"Does that include me?" Thorne asked.

"If he thought you were making it worse, maybe," Ian replied, "but he knows you're the one making it better. I'm pretty sure you're now included under his protective umbrella too. If there's one thing Neil is good at, it's defending the people he calls his own."

Thorne squeezed Ian's hip and let go to grab his tray. He could live with being one of the people Neil called his own. It meant he'd been accepted here in a real and tangible way. They made their way over to a couple of empty seats, and Thorne couldn't help but smile as Chris and Jesse scooted over to make room for them.

"Welcome home," Chris said. "Are you glad to be back?"

"Very glad," Thorne said. "I missed everyone."

"Uh-huh," Jesse said. "You mean you missed Ian."

"I did miss Ian," Thorne said, because he could hardly deny that he'd missed his lover, "but I missed the rest of you as well. Lang Downs has become home."

"It does that, doesn't it?" Jesse agreed. "I'll get Titan saddled up for you. I imagine you'll want to ride out with Ian today."

"I have to talk to Caine and Macklin first," Thorne said. "I have a contract to sign."

Ian smiled at him, the light in his eyes nearly blinding in its intensity. "We'll be out as soon as that's done," he told Jesse. "It shouldn't take us long."

The rest of breakfast passed in the same vein, the other year-rounders welcoming Thorne home and offering any assistance he needed in settling in. By the time they finished eating, Thorne felt completely overwhelmed. Ian smiled at him as they walked toward the station house.

"Doing okay?"

"I'm fine," Thorne said. "Just a little surprised at how much everyone seemed to miss me. I mean, I knew you did, but there's no reason for everyone else to have noticed, much less cared."

"There's every reason for them to have noticed," Ian disagreed. "We're a family, remember?"

"You keep telling me that," Thorne said, "but it's been so long since I've had anyone but Walker…."

"And now you have more people than you know what to do with," Ian said. "I remember how overwhelming it was when I first got here. Some of the faces have changed in that time. Michael is gone and some of the older year-rounders from the first few years have retired and chosen to go elsewhere, but the feeling hasn't changed in fifteen years. You just have to trust us."

"Welcome back, Thorne," Caine said when he opened the door to the station house. "Are you ready to sign that contract now?"

"I am," Thorne said. "I shouldn't need to go back to Wagga Wagga for any extended period of time now, but I will need to log in to the station's Internet on my days off. My therapist wants to continue our sessions via Skype."

"That's easy enough to arrange," Caine said. "Get the password from Sam. We only have it protected because of the station accounts on the computer."

"You'll have to teach me how to use that," Ian said. "It would be easier than driving to Cowra once a week, since I'm not exactly done either."

"We'll get you sorted," Caine promised, the Australian idiom in Caine's Yank accent making Thorne smile.

Amusement aside, Thorne finally believed it. He'd arrived at Lang Downs three months earlier a broken man. He didn't claim to be healed yet—he wasn't sure such a thing existed with all the black marks on his soul—but he was better than he'd been in years. Best of all, he had Ian now, and he'd do whatever it took to protect that. Caine set the contract in front of him. Thorne skimmed through it and picked up a pen.

This was a contract he'd willingly spend the rest of his life honoring.

ARIEL TACHNA lives outside of Houston with her husband, her daughter and son, and their cat. Before moving there, she traveled all over the world, having fallen in love with both France, where she found her husband, and India, where she dreams of retiring someday. She's bilingual with snippets of four other languages to her credit and is as in love with languages as she is with writing.

Visit Ariel's website at http://www.arieltachna.com/ and her blog at http://arieltachna.livejournal.com/.

ARIEL TACHNA

Inherit
theSky

http://www.dreamspinnerpress.com

Lang Downs Book 2

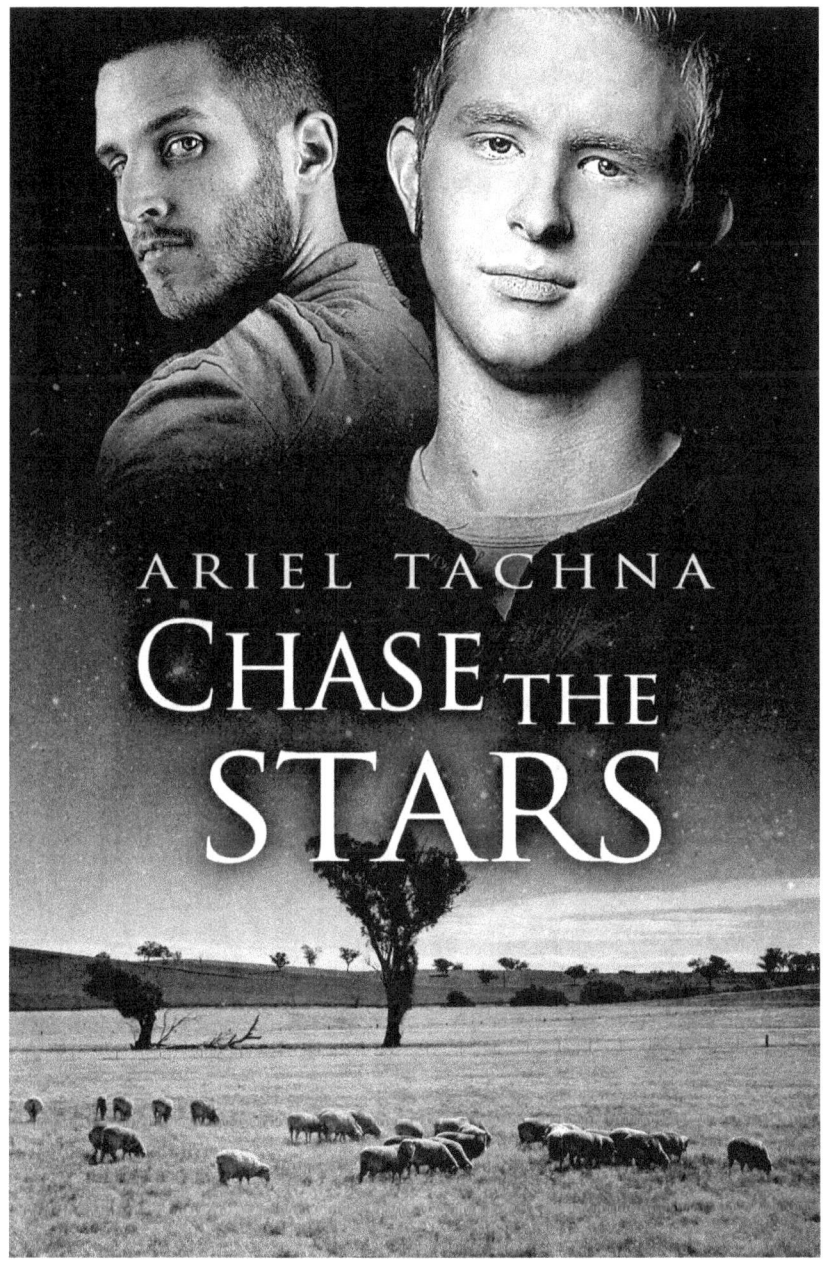

ARIEL TACHNA

CHASE THE
STARS

http://www.dreamspinnerpress.com

Lang Downs Book 3

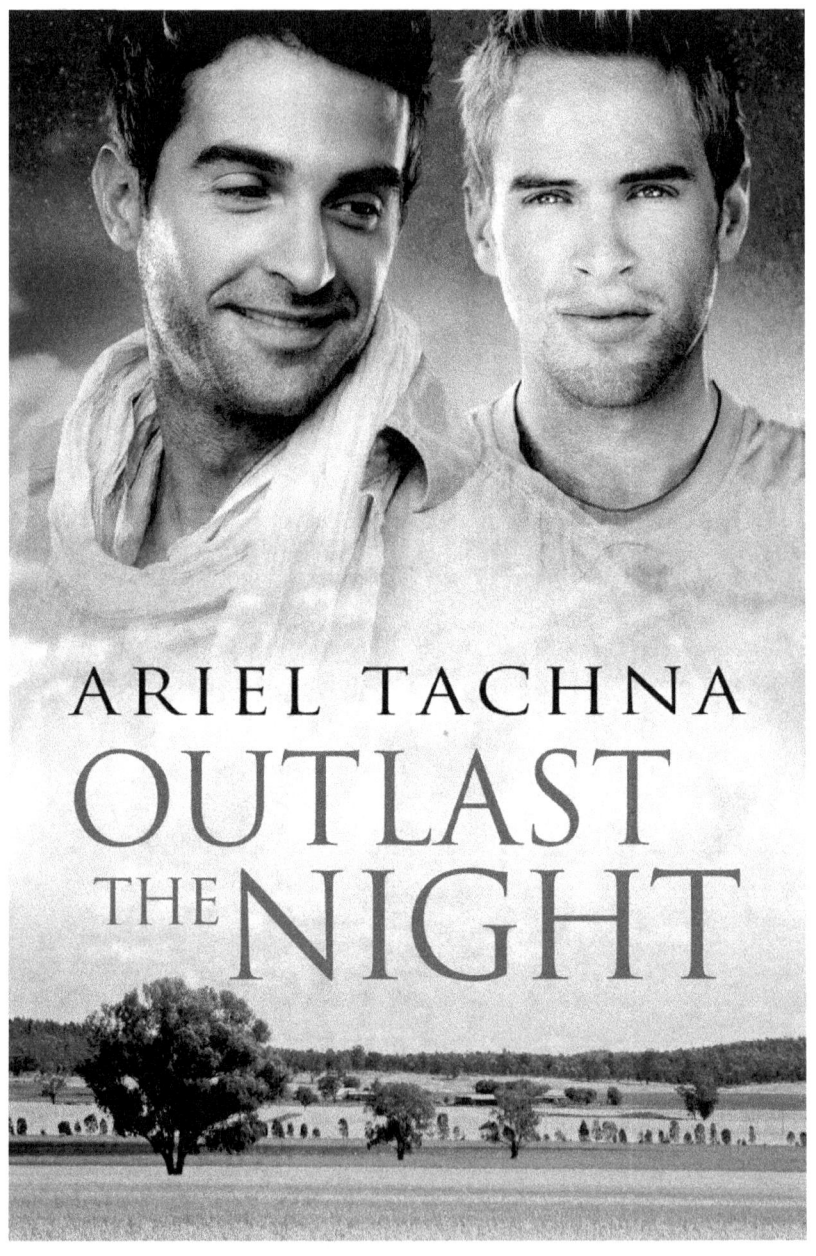

ARIEL TACHNA

OUTLAST
THE NIGHT

http://www.dreamspinnerpress.com

Contemporary Romance by ARIEL TACHNA

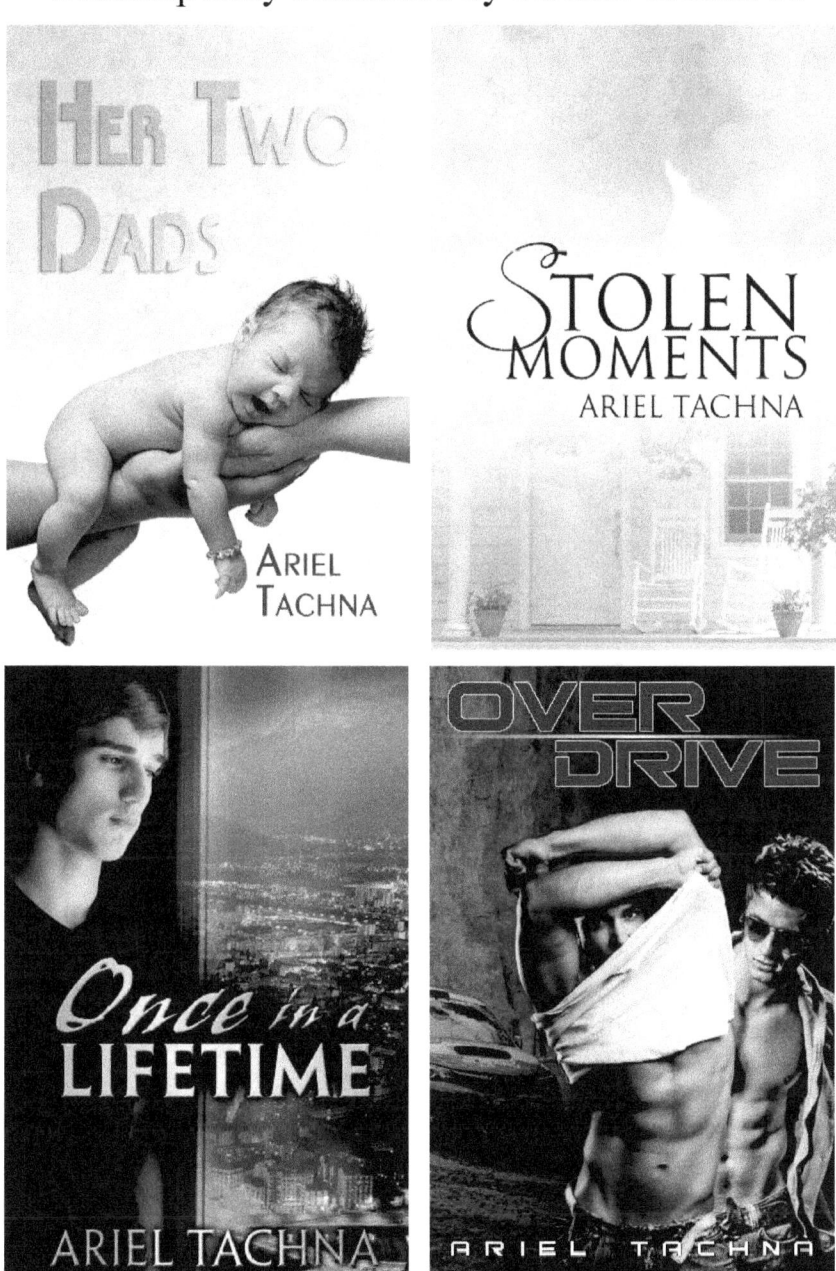

Also by ARIEL TACHNA

http://www.dreamspinnerpress.com

Also by ARIEL TACHNA

http://www.dreamspinnerpress.com

In Italian by ARIEL TACHNA

I SUOI DUE
PADRI

ARIEL
TACHNA

http://www.dreamspinnerpress.com

Romance in Australia from DREAMSPINNER PRESS

www.ingramcontent.com/pod-product-compliance
Lightning Source LLC
Chambersburg PA
CBHW051635260626
47170CB00004B/1184